CAL SMYTH

THE FINAL MILE

First Published in 2013
By Iponymous publishing Limited
Iponymous Swansea United Kingdom SA6 6BP

Design: www.GMID.co.uk

A CIP record for this book
Is available from the British Library

(EBook) ISBN 978-1-908773-55-5
(Physical Book) ISBN 978-1-908773-56-2

www.iponymous.com

1

The explosion ripped through the armed vehicle, vibrated along the ground and threw Ryan backwards off his feet. Heavy in his bomb disposal suit, it felt like he was in slow motion as he forced himself back up.

He'd spotted the wires in the road and had immediately called for the vehicles to halt while he checked them out, but something had already set off the first bomb.

He turned away from the shards of metal and body parts. If anybody was still alive, it was up to the other guys to save them. His job was to disarm the gravel-covered bomb in front of the remaining vehicle.

Inside the vehicle was the fuckwit of a general who had made them take this route. The men had warned him that it was insurgent territory and hadn't been properly cleared. The idiot had ignored them. But there was no time to think about that. What Ryan had to focus on was de-wiring the explosive.

The vehicle couldn't go backwards because it was

blocked by the blown up vehicle. For all of them, the only way out was forwards. That couldn't happen unless Ryan disarmed the bomb. And until then, they were sitting ducks for any snipers. Ryan knew the rest of the unit were covering his back as best they could but they could only do it for so long.

He stepped cautiously to the bomb poking out of the loose ground and examined the wiring. He had to get this right. Sweat dripped into his eyes.

Ryan blinked away the memory of his time in Kuwait. He had to focus. The footfalls were echoing his own, right behind him, breath on the back of his neck.

He forced his tired legs to move faster as he heard the footfalls close in behind him. Sweat glistened in the greying stubble of his closely cropped hair, drips stinging his eyes and making him squint in the sunlight. He could hear his breathing getting deeper and evened it out while pumping his legs and arms, ignoring the ache in his thigh muscles. He didn't take in the crowd to the side, but he heard the cries go up.

Ryan pushed through the pain, put in a final surge and tore through the tape at the finishing line.

Bent over as he regained his breath, Ryan was joined by Evan. The two men breathed heavily in tandem as they stood in similar positions. Evan looked across at his old school friend:

'One day I'll catch you.'

Ryan met Evan's eyes and gave a weary nod:

'Maybe next time.'

Back in senior school the two of them had been

cross-country champions several years in a row, always finishing in the same positions in the Swansea interschool races – Ryan first, Evan second.

Their competitiveness hadn't ruined their friendship, but later they'd gone their separate ways – or Ryan had, into the armed forces for ten years while Evan worked his way up to DCI in the local police force. Ryan had been back in Swansea for twenty years now. They never met socially, though they always said they would. But they always met up once a year at the race.

It wasn't that Ryan had to beat Evan, just that if he was going to run in a race then he was in it to win it. He was in great shape for his fifty years, partly down to his genetic make-up and partly due to learnt behaviour – habits that were entrenched even before he joined the army. Not just his daily run, but his morning routine for the last thirty four years of pull-ups, sit-ups and press-ups.

Six foot two and wiry, Ryan's arms dangled when he strode places, his limber fingers ideal for playing guitar, though he'd never picked one up. His handsome face never betrayed much emotion, but his startling blue eyes were always alert - Ryan was never able to switch off. When he laughed or was pained, the lines around his eyes would crease up; that was the giveaway.

Right now, his eyes squinted from the glare of the mid-morning sun and took in his wife. She smiled at him across a table outside Verdi's, the seafront café. Sandra was looking at him with her calm expression, but she had a slight frown and she was smiling out of the side of her mouth, something she always did when she felt nervous. She was talking to a guy with designer sunglasses, pushed up in his precisely parted hair, the man with an untouched coffee in front of him. Swansea was such a small city, thought Ryan as he recognised the man. It was Huw, his bank manager.

Sandra said something to Huw before walking over to Ryan and Evan, a bottle of water in each hand, one for each man. She was wearing a skirt today, a black one that ended a few inches above her knees, and a pale white sleeveless blouse. Ryan liked the skirt a lot and he liked how she moved in it.

Sandra smiled as she reached the two men, shook her head as she coolly appraised the state of both Ryan and Evan:

'It's supposed to be a run for charity, not a race to the death.'

Ryan shrugged as he took a bottle of water, nimbly unscrewing the cap. He gulped the water down, his Adam's apple bobbing as the water gushed down his throat. Evan smiled as he took his bottle:

'Maybe you can tell your husband to be charitable and let me win one year.'

Ryan stopped drinking. He'd always been able to focus completely on the task in hand, but he'd let his mind wander back to memories of Kuwait and had nearly let Evan in this time.

Sandra turned to Ryan and kissed him on the lips. As ever, she looked fantastic and much younger than forty nine. She wasn't a fitness fanatic, but she looked after herself – zumba on Tuesday nights, swimming Thursday mornings. Monthly hair and beauty treatments, a holiday somewhere hot at least once a year.

She didn't hide her age through any artificial means, apart from dying her hair and using moisturisers, but which woman didn't? Ryan was staring at Sandra's profile: head slightly lowered, her dark hair falling past her shoulder, bare in the sleeveless blouse with a bra strap exposed. No doubt the bra was some kind of fashionable brand. Ryan wouldn't know what as he left that kind of thing to her. He'd once bought her underwear from La Senza as an anniversary gift, but only after she'd told him where to go and what to get. He'd been so flustered in the shop, he never did it again. The whole chain had since closed down anyway.

Ryan didn't tell her how good she looked, but was pretty sure she knew it by the way he looked at her. Just as he was certain she'd liked it that he'd won the race even if she didn't say so. Thirty four years together and they still fancied the pants off each other. Sex had always been great between them, first as excited teenagers, then in heightened reunions after his stints in Kuwait, secretive once Gerard came along, and openly joyful now that their son was away at University.

Gerard ambled over just at that moment, shoulder-length hair bobbing in time with the satchel slung over his shoulder, Gerard's arms flung out in his usual gregarious manner:

'Hey, I missed you two finish?'

Evan smiled:

'You missed your dad beating me another year. I would have thought an aspiring journo like you would be there to get the winner's first thoughts.'

'You two coming first and second is old news.'

Gerard looked over toward the Cancer Trust stall:

'I was over there talking to the people who set up this run, about the work they do.'

That was his son, thought Ryan. He'd talk to anyone, unlike himself. Ryan guessed journalism was the right career for Gerard, but who knew if there was any work out there.

The Evening Post guys came over to take a photo, Ryan holding up a cheque for the amount raised in the Run for Cancer. Coincidentally his parents had both died of the disease a year before in quick succession, but he'd done the run for the last twenty years without having any personal reason.

The Trust couldn't do much for his parents as it all happened so quickly. It was no surprise when his dad – always a heavy smoker - got cancer. It must have been all the passive smoking in the small terraced house that did for his mum.

While Gerard talked to the journalist from the Post, Ryan followed Sandra and Evan who had gravitated toward the café. Both had stopped at Huw's table and were talking with the bank manager.

Huw was in his Sunday casuals, a polo t-shirt tucked into his jeans. He wasn't overweight, but his rugby playing days were long gone and Ryan knew it wasn't muscle that made Huw's clothes too tight.

Huw made as if to shake hands with Ryan but thought better of it, presumably not wanting to get sweaty:

'If I were allowed to bet on the run instead of sponsoring it, I'd have placed my money on you, boy.'

Ryan looked at Huw blankly, thinking they were both fifty years old and Huw still used the term 'boy', only out of the office of course. Huw was a chameleon and Ryan knew he altered his speech depending on the setting and who he was speaking to.

Huw glanced at the ensemble, his eyes lingering a little too long on Sandra's cleavage:

'Successful businessman, beautiful younger wife…'

Sandra rolled her eyes. Huw knew full well she was only a year younger, but he was unabashed as he gestured over toward Gerard:

'…Son at university, you deserve a medal Ryan – though you've probably already got one of those too. Bloody pin up boy for the city you are.'

Huw glanced at Evan:

'No offence to our most prominent policeman.'

Evan exchanged glances with Ryan, who simply shrugged. You had to be careful with Huw as, behind the smarmy charm, his words were always barbed, Huw having a knack for getting under people's skin. Huw smiled as he stood and tossed a ten pound note onto the table, making sure both Ryan and Evan got a good long look at his bulging wallet.

'I'm off. Good to see you all.'

Ryan saw that Huw's latte was untouched. It was Sandra's favourite type of coffee but too milky for Ryan so he could understand Huw not drinking it. But then why buy it? It was Huw's ten pound note that Sandra noticed:

'That's a tip and a half.'

Huw shrugged and tossed another ten pound note onto the table:

'They need all the money they can get at present.'

He winked at Sandra:

'I don't like to tell tales out of school but on the Q.T. they might not be around much longer, times are tough and the bank may have to foreclose.'

Huw smiled gratingly:

'You never heard it from me.'

It was typical Huw, thought Ryan, always playing the big man. Ryan meant to keep silent but couldn't help comment:

'So who did we hear it from then?'

Huw opened his mouth to answer, but was confused, not getting that Ryan was making fun of his patter. He turned to go, then stopped and looked back at Ryan as if he'd just remembered:

'I'll see you on Tuesday, yeah?'

Ryan's face hardened as Huw smiled and sauntered off, not waiting for an answer. Sandra frowned at Ryan:

'You're seeing him Tuesday?'

Ryan waved a dismissive hand.

'Annual meeting with the bank.'

'Everything okay?'

'It's nothing to worry about. I just don't like talking shop on my day off.'

Evan snorted:

'Huw never tires of talking about money. Did you see him flash the cash, like we're supposed to be impressed? The guy was an arsehole at school and he hasn't changed much since.'

Sandra smiled thinly.

'Makes the world go around.'

Sidling up to the group, Gerard joined in:

'That's what people want us to think, but it doesn't have to be that way…'

Sandra interrupted her son:

'Do you think there's some kind of magic fairy that funds you to live in London?'

Ryan chided his wife:

'Give him a break Sandra, he's going to become a famous journalist, make loads of cash and look after us in our old age.'

'I'll say it again, because you two never seem to listen to a word I say, but with his grades he should be in medical school.'

Evan smiled:

'I'll leave you to it. I've got to pick up Julie from that Sofa Store, the one having a closing down sale.'

Sandra shook her head:

'There won't be many shops left open soon.'

She looked pointedly at Ryan, who shifted his gaze to stare out across the Bay. Evan grabbed a handshake with Ryan, looking for eye contact as he said:

'Don't forget that drink we're going to have.'

Ryan nodded, his eyes darting away once again to the yachts gliding on the horizon. Evan jogged off, leaving Ryan with his wife and son. Sandra linked arms with both Ryan and Gerard, propelling them along the promenade. The three of them headed towards Mumbles, rivulets of seawater lit up on the vast sand beach. As Gerard got back into his anti-capitalist diatribe, Ryan exhaled in happiness. Strolling along Swansea Bay on a sunny Sunday morning with his family, you couldn't beat it. He couldn't let his worries ruin this time. There were plenty of things to worry about, the Tuesday bank meeting being one. But Ryan was determined not to deal with them until Monday.

2

To celebrate their son being down for the weekend, they went out for Sunday lunch at The King Arthur hotel. Nearby, high on the plain, with a view of the whole peninsula, was Arthur's rock. The legend was that Arthur had been irritated by a stone in his shoe so had thrown it as far as he could – the stone coming all the way over from England and landing in the Gower, where it turned into a rock.

Ryan had loved the story as a kid and it was one of the places he used to take Gerard. In his youth, Ryan had gone for bracing runs across the windswept downs, but what with work and commitments he restricted his runs to the Bay area now.

In the hotel dining area, all wooden beams and stone hearth, Gerard was speaking excitedly as he ate:

'…so I'll be going on the demo next weekend.'

Sandra looked concerned:

'You sure that's a good idea?'

'We have to do something, mum. This is my

generation's future. The government's bailing out banks and giving them tax breaks while cutting benefits and public sector pay. It's a systematic pillaging of the poor by the wealthy.'

'There's not many jobs out there, you don't want to ruin your chances by getting a criminal record.'

'That's exactly why I should go on the demo - to make things better.'

Sandra looked over at Ryan:

'Can you say something?'

Ryan looked up from his Sunday roast:

'What can I say – that people should stop moaning and get a job?'

Gerard retorted:

'They would if there were any.'

Ryan shrugged to his wife:

'See, nothing I say is going to make a difference.'

Ryan cut into his roast beef. Sandra sighed and took a sip of her Chardonnay.

Later, Ryan drove his son to the train station, seated high in the Morgan's Security Systems van. They didn't say much. What was he going to say, that by the time he was Gerard's age he was enlisted, spent the next ten years in training, culminating in the Gulf War – the first one. It wasn't as if Gerard was going to listen to any of it.

Ryan's dad had been a big union man, always banging on about workers' rights and injustice. But in the end all the strikes he'd gone on had cost him jobs. And his oration had gone in one ear and out the other. What Ryan had taken on board was the practical skills he'd passed on. An electrician, Ryan's dad had wired up a lot of the post-war buildings in Swansea, including the hospital where Ryan had been born. To this day he remembered his dad showing him how to take apart a plug and put it back together.

So all he could do was show Gerard by example. Work hard and treat people right.

When Gerard was a kid, Ryan had been a great dad – always ready to climb rocks at Caswell bay, cycle to Mumbles pier, go on runs in Clyne Wood. But once Gerard had become a young adult they grew apart. There hadn't been teenage tantrums, well not many, it was just that Gerard had developed his own distinct persona - socially adept yet social rebel – and Ryan just wasn't party to either of those particular modes.

With Gerard getting on the train to Paddington, Ryan gave his son a fatherly pat on the shoulder. He wanted to tell Gerard he loved him, but somehow he could never naturally say it, so settled for his usual inept parting words:

'Keep out of trouble, okay.'

After dropping Gerard off, Ryan drove back to their Mumbles home. Not one of the old stone houses in the twisty back streets, but a new build on the coastal road. It had a loft conversion, side garage extension and glass conservatory at the back - all tastefully done, not ostentatiously displaying wealth but costly nonetheless. They still had five years left on the mortgage, plus payments on the loan for the conservatory, which brought him back to Huw and the meeting next week. There were things he couldn't postpone for ever.

Ryan parked the Mercedes-Benz van in the drive, Sandra's silver Mercedes already in the garage. The other work van was also parked outside, advertising Morgan's Security Systems to any passing drivers. They'd never been burgled themselves, but still had the latest security system fitted. Sandra had insisted and Ryan reasoned that he should probably set an example by installing one of his own products, although there was no real need as there wasn't much crime in this salubrious part of Swansea. Out of habit, on entering the house Ryan checked that the system was fully functioning.

Sandra was finishing her Sunday evening chores, making sure they were both ready for the working week. She hung up her suit and his shirt. Standing on tip toe she reached up and took his face in her hands and kissed him on the mouth. Feeling emotional, Ryan held onto her to make it last a little longer. She gently pulled away from him and held out her hand.

'Why don't we go to bed?'

Ryan had too much on his mind to sleep, but he was pretty sure that wasn't what she meant, so he let her lead the way.

Afterwards, having showered and slipped back between the sheets, Sandra intertwined her fingers with Ryan's.

She loved his hands. Those long nimble fingers always sent a shiver through her whenever they stroked her. She sometimes thought of those same fingers dismantling bombs or installing security devices. But it was what he did with them on her that she really cared about. His whole body had always been hard and solid. He never showered her with romantic words, but she knew that his eyes never strayed and when they made love, she could feel the emotion all coiled up. It was like an electrical surge when he came inside her.

When they'd been based in Sandhurst, she was the dutiful army wife and had played the part to perfection. It was a position better thought of than the housewives of her parents' generation but not as coveted as the WAGS of future generations. She'd kept herself fit in the army gym and had taken a course in hotel management, which she effortlessly sailed through.

She'd never once had an affair, although there had been plenty of opportunities, especially while Ryan did his stints away in Kuwait. He was away for months and she'd been tempted to have a fling, but always managed to make her excuses and leave before anything happened. And in the hotels she managed, she had more than her share of proposals. Sandra found it flattering as it kept her feeling young and wanted.

It drove her nuts sometimes how Ryan said so little. Most of the time that was okay, she could do the talking at social events for both of them. She was good at that. She even bought all his clothes for him. If she didn't, he'd walk around naked like some caveman.

He was your strong, silent, stoic type, but then that's what partly attracted her. Right now however, she needed him to open up, and decided on the direct approach:

'It's not the annual meeting at the bank.'

Ryan cringed inside. He had hoped she'd forgotten:

'I just need to have a talk with him, that's all.'

'You seemed pretty annoyed by it.'

'It's a man thing, the way he looks at you. I ought to break his jaw for him.'

It was a pleasant thought, but Sandra dismissed his answer:

'He's looked at me that way for over thirty years and it's never bothered you much before.'

A smile cracked across Ryan's face. It was true, it didn't occur to him to be jealous. Sandra wasn't interested in Huw. No matter how much the guy pined after Sandra, she only ever had eyes for Ryan. Right now, she was looking him straight in the eyes, not convinced by his attempts at distraction.

'So?'

'It's just a hiccup.'

'That's not what Huw said.'

Ryan's face turned to granite. Huw could look at Sandra with all the desire he wanted because he'd never have her. But going behind Ryan's back to tell tales was uncalled for, although it was typical Huw behaviour and he shouldn't have been surprised.

'What else did he say?'

'I asked because I was concerned.'

Ryan's jaw clenched tight. He was doing his best to

keep hold of his temper. Sandra held his hand.

'Talk to me.'

'You want a cold drink?'

'Not right now, thanks.'

Ryan made to get out of bed.

'Ryan…'

Sandra's fingers continued to move on his. Ryan exhaled:

'It looks like the financial situation is tougher than I first thought.'

'What does your accountant say?'

'That I should lay off staff, cut overheads, cut just about every bloody thing.'

'And?'

'Sandra, those guys have worked there a long time.'

'What, you'd put them before us?'

'A few salaries less isn't going to make much of a difference in the grand scheme of things.'

Ryan sighed:

'I'm running just to stand still at the moment. Things are tough out there.'

'So in fact it's a much bigger financial situation than you've been letting on?'

Ryan opened his mouth to speak, and then thought better of it. He hated getting into a conflict with Sandra. It was rare that it happened, but when it did he was always confused by her illogical logic, and he'd never come out the right side of any previous arguments. He kept his mouth shut. It had always served him well in the past. But she wasn't letting his silence stop her:

'I love you, and unlike some people in this room I have no problem with showing my emotion.'

Ryan looked around, wide eyed, as if searching for the person she was referring to. Sandra smiled at his attempt to be funny, but it was a nervous smile that twitched at the side of her mouth. She wasn't to be distracted:

'If you don't start sorting stuff out, we might lose what we've built together. This is serious. Huw said…'

Ryan couldn't help parroting her:

'Huw said…'

His anger got the better of him:

'That prick should keep out of our business.'

'This is his business, he's the bank manager for Christ's sake.'

Ryan didn't respond. There hadn't been a question, so as far as he could see there was no reason for him to give an answer. Sandra removed her hand from his:

'It's no good shutting up shop. That's not going to solve anything. And you can't bury your head in the sand over this, it's not going to go away. You've got to get a handle on it. Jesus, Ryan, you're ex army, come up with a plan of attack.'

Ryan nodded. She had him there, he did need a plan. For the past few weeks he'd been putting off the inevitable and it had felt as if he'd been floundering. Sandra hadn't finished:

'You don't even show your own son how proud you are of him.'

Ryan was thrown by that. Where the hell did that come from? He hated it when she threw in something from far off left field. How could she say that? Maybe he didn't express it, but he loved his son. Besides, it wasn't as if Gerard displayed any admiration for him. He hadn't even bothered to watch the race. Ryan bit back this childish thought and instead he made a valiant attempt to counter Sandra's argument:

'You wanted me to be angry with him earlier.'

'It's the same bloody thing!'

In exasperation, Sandra turned off the bedside lamp and turned her back on Ryan.

He lay motionless until his eyes grew accustomed to the dark. It was no use trying to make up. He was no good at light remarks and it was better to just let her ease out of her anger. But Sandra was not far off the mark. The problems at work were far bigger than he'd let on. He was going to have to take measures, starting tomorrow.

Ryan glanced over and checked that Sandra's breathing was even. Satisfied she was asleep, he silently crept out of bed. He padded downstairs, took out the tool box and felt for the Phillips.

Sat on the living room floor in the dark, he unscrewed the TV plug, and laid the screws and fuse on the carpet. By touch, he put the plug back together. Then disassembled and began to put it back together again. It was a habit, from when he was a kid, and something he had always done when he had a problem to chew over and needed to get rid of a little stress. Although it wasn't a little stress he was wrestling with this time, it was a lot.

3

Without looking, Ryan keyed in the numbers to unset the alarm and strode into the offices of Morgan's Security Systems. Always in before his staff, this morning he was especially early, awake and up after a restless night brooding over which employee he should make redundant.

The age old dictum was last in first out, that's what his dad would have said. And in this case, that meant Johnny the twenty-one-year-old ex-trainee. He'd only been with the company three years, and just the last two years on a full time contract. So he was last in by a mile. He also had no family to support.

All the others – Stu and Owen, Tim and Dave – had wives and kids that relied on their income. They were all in their late thirties, so it would be hard for them to suddenly change job.

That wasn't quite everyone. There was also Paul. A miserable bastard whose wife had left him years ago, Paul was forty nine going on sixty. A hard drinker, as soon as work finished on a Friday night he bolted for the nearest pub, starting in on a session that no doubt carried on throughout Saturday with Sunday as a recovery day. Although saying that, he sometimes stank of booze on Monday morning. But he was always there on the dot, never late, rolling his cigarette. Paul had been with the firm since day one, Ryan taking him straight on the day after he registered the business with Companies' House. Ryan wasn't sure how Paul did it – habit, natural talent – but Paul had never messed a job up and whatever new device came in he could work out the wiring blindfolded, although with modern remote technology less of this was required.

Ryan mulled it over. Paul was the longest serving employee and therefore the highest paid. If Ryan laid him off he'd save more than any other redundancy. Paul, just like Johnny, had no-one to support, no family, no kids, no-one apart from his friend Jack Daniels.

And unlike Johnny, Paul had no future to lose. Johnny had been brought up in the Townhill council estate, in a non-working one-parent family of four. Johnny had studied electronics at college and had done a traineeship with Ryan – one of the last places that still did it probably. Immaculate in his work, Johnny excelled at everything. Extremely grateful to Ryan for giving him an opportunity, he even spent his spare time checking out the latest wireless security devices. It would be a shame to lose Johnny, he was conscientious and Ryan often thought about him taking over the management somewhere downstream, allowing Ryan to take more of a back seat. Ryan guessed there wouldn't be too many other opportunities for Johnny, not with the way the economy was tanking.

Ryan cracked his jaw to loosen the granite in his rock heavy head. His jaw always seemed to lock up in times of stress. It was a character trait he wasn't happy with as it gave away what he was feeling.

The door opened and the guys shuffled in to get their Monday morning schedules. Johnny was as eager as ever. Paul was his usual seemingly disinterested self, a roll-up between his stained fingers. Stu and Owen jostled each other bantering back and forth in a good natured, it's Monday but it'll be Friday soon, kind of way. Tim and Dave entered last, probably having dropped off the kids to school, and judging by the scowls no doubt argued with their wives over something or other.

Dave was English, married to a Welsh woman, but Ryan didn't hold that against him. He'd overheard more and more casual racism towards the English as times got harder, with some pressing for an independent Wales. From what Ryan had read, Wales actually received more money from England than vice versa in terms of tax at least, and there was a higher rate of Welsh unemployment so it would probably be worse off going it alone. He kept an eye on the news, but politics had never really interested him much. He wasn't bothered which bunch of monkeys had their hands on the levers of power, they were all as bad as each other, career politicians who had never done an honest day's labour in their lives.

Ryan's dad had been a staunch Labour supporter. Ryan hadn't voted for years, but when he was a young man, he'd voted Conservative. He'd done it because he liked the idea of setting up your own business, as promoted by Thatcher. The woman had destroyed the miners though and after that Ryan had never voted again. It caused too much conflict, both internally and with his dad. Thatcher dying was news Ryan couldn't miss as it was everywhere. Ryan's dad would probably be rejoicing in heaven or wherever he was. Although he would also no doubt be seething that Thatcher's funeral was paid for by the taxpayer. It did seem hypocritical to Ryan. The woman had privatised everything, derided social help and promoted individualism. So how come her funeral was paid for by the rest of society?

Ryan was Welsh without doubt, but had no antipathy towards the English. Ryan had of course been nicknamed Taff when he first joined the forces, but it had soon got changed. When he de-wired explosives he didn't panic but kept at it until he succeeded, in a zone of his own. Ryan was the only cadet in class to take it to the wire, always managing to defuse the practice bombs, sometimes just seconds before detonation. His instructors were impressed and he always passed first in class. Another cadet, a fellow Welshman from Cardiff, had once grudgingly said, 'You go right to the edge of the fucking cliff you do, you Jack bastard.' After that, Cliff had stuck.

With thoughts of who to make redundant, Ryan

couldn't quite meet everyone's eyes but forced himself to look up from the clipboard as he dished out the day's orders:

'Paul and Johnny, you've got the hospital.'

Johnny glanced eagerly towards the storeroom:

'Are we putting in the new TVLs?'

Ryan nodded and carried on:

'Tim, Dave, the hotel job hasn't come through yet so you can help with the hospital. You can share out the CCTV to install – Paul's got the blueprint.'

Tim and Dave nodded in agreement, but exchanged a cautious glance, both aware that Ryan had been relying on that job to keep things ticking over. Paul snorted as he thumbed at Johnny:

'What, it's not enough babysitting this one, now I've got these two slackers to look after as well.'

Tim and Dave simultaneously fixed him with a stare and Paul blew them both a kiss.

Ryan ignored the antics, turned to Owen and Stu:

'You two still need a day on the footballer's place?'

Owen smiled:

'Stu would love a day on the guy's WAG. She's as fit a butcher's dog...'

Stu retorted:

'And you wouldn't? Your tongue's been hanging out the side of your mouth the past few days, you pussy hound.'

'I'm a married man.'

'And I'm not?'

'I'm happily married. Unlike you, you doss cunt...'

Ryan interrupted the banter:

'Call me when you're done and I'll tell you where you are tomorrow.'

Ryan couldn't bring himself to tell them that unless a new job came instantly in, it would be the hospital, again. He really hoped he could string that job out until something came in, or he was in trouble. The footballer's seafront apartment was one of the few private jobs they'd got in the last year.

As the men tooled up, Kristine put her head around the door. Secretary, HR and PR all rolled into one, not to mention reception and office manager, she was integral to Morgan's Security and Ryan hadn't even considered her for redundancy. The place would grind to a halt without her. Right now she was giving him an urgent look:

'You need to come now, they are clamping our vans.'

Kristine was already on her way back out. Ryan was right behind her, the rest of the men immediately on his tail. Ryan saw that three Morgan's Security vans were parked illegally on yellow lines, the last one clamped and the parking enforcement officers moving onto the second.

Their normal parking area in the alley at the back of Morgan's had been out of bounds for several months. An old stone wall had fallen from a back garden into the alley. The wall was both on private property and public land, the owners of the house and garden arguing with the council about who should pay. Until that was resolved, the alley had been deemed unsafe and cordoned off, the fallen wall still left scattered across the alley.

It was a pain for Ryan and his workforce because it meant they had to find parking each morning and carry equipment to wherever their vans were. Ryan had applied to the council for temporary parking permits on Walter Road but had been refused. So each morning, they had to try and grab one of the one hour parking bays. Starting work before the solicitors and accountants whose offices lined the road, it was never normally a problem. That morning however, a removals truck had taken up all four parking spaces. Ryan had left his van several streets away. He'd assumed the others would do the same. There was no point in castigating them as that wouldn't solve anything. And he could see why they'd done it – five minutes in and out at that time in the morning, what was the likelihood of getting clamped?

If Kristine's charm didn't work with the parking enforcement officers, Ryan knew he'd have difficulty. She was pretty persuasive verbally and her looks didn't hurt. She was never rude but her Latvian bluntness cut through a lot of bullshit. Combined with her striking features and sudden smile, Kristine's approach was pretty disarming.

In her first week at Morgan's, she'd shown that not only could she ably cope with reception work, but secretarial stuff too. Until then, Ryan had employed two women. On top of that, Kristine came up with several ideas for promoting Morgan's. Previously, Ryan had paid freelance marketing people. Kristine had instantly merged three jobs into one. What had clinched it was the way she'd dealt with the guys.

Tim and Dave had been doing their usual Welsh-English riff, Tim singing 'always shit on the English side of the bridge' because Wales had just thrashed England in the six nations. Dave had tried to maintain one up:

'We've still won more grand slams.'

Tim had scoffed:

'What, going back to when it was just the home nations?'

'All counts.'

'In that case, we've won more titles.'

'Er, no, twenty six each.'

'Er, plus twelve shared titles to your ten.'

'Shared fucking titles don't count.'

Kristine had looked up from her desk, where she was trying to work:

'Guys, everybody knows Latvia has best rugby team.'

Tim and Dave had both turned to look at her with disbelief, but Ryan burst out laughing. The guys were flummoxed by her deadpan humour, but she'd shut them up.

Right now, Kristine was working on one of the parking officers, the guy standing nervously as she spoke to him. The other guy though just carried on clamping the second van. Ryan bit down on his temper. It was tough, but he told himself to be nice:

'Hey guys, there a need for this? It was literally just a few minutes, we can move them right now.'

Stu and Owen were already moving towards their

van, as were Tim and Dave. The guy clamping them raised his head:

'We've already taken photos. You move the vans, we'll clamp them when we next see them.'

Stu, Owen, Tim and Dave all looked to Ryan. He patted his hand in the air for them to wait, a rictus grin on his face, and turned back to the clampers:

'We just want to go about our jobs.'

'And we're just doing ours.'

Paul weighed in:

'What kind of job is that – one for wankers, you go around fucking clamping, you fucking Muppets. You can see the parking bay's taken up by the truck. Take off the fucking clamp you cunts.'

The clamper moved on to the third van, talking over his shoulder all the while:

'Any threatening behaviour will be reported to the police.'

Ryan held up a calming hand. He certainly didn't feel calm, but everyone was looking to him to sort the situation out:

'There's no threatening behaviour, officer, warden, or whatever your title is. We just need our vans.'

'Go to the council and pay the fine and you'll have the clamps taken off.'

The other parking officer tentatively handed Ryan a clamping notice. Ryan stared at it. He had enough to think about without this. His thoughts were interrupted by a familiar voice:

'Oh dear, what's going on here?'

Ryan turned to see Huw leaning out of his silver

Mercedes, the car pulled over to the side of the road, Huw in his pinstriped shirt and tie, a smug grin plastered to his fat face. Ryan frowned. He was sure he'd glimpsed Huw's Mercedes earlier on his way into the office. He knew the car because it was identical to Sandra's.

Huw bunched his fist up and rubbed at his eyes, pretending to wipe away tears:

'How sad. You just can't catch a break with those parking wardens. Not a good way to start the day. I do hope it gets better for you.'

Huw seemed to have actual tears, but not from sadness, unable to stop his smile. He tooted the horn on his car in two short peeps and pulled back into the traffic.

Ryan watched Huw drive off, Huw waving as he passed the removals truck. There was nothing strange about Huw driving past. He did so every day as his bank was just a few streets away. What was wrong was that Ryan was now absolutely sure he had seen Huw earlier. Was Huw so mean-minded as to see the vans parked on yellow lines and go to the trouble of phoning up the clamping company? Ryan dismissed the thought. What he had to do now was solve the situation.

He was annoyed at the guys parking on yellow lines and even more at the council for blocking access to the alley and refusing them parking permits. But he knew there would be no point arguing with the council. The only thing was to pay for the clamps to be taken off and get on with the working day. Fuck, it wasn't as if he didn't have enough on his plate.

It wasn't worth getting his van. It was quicker to walk to the council offices than drive through the one way streets and numerous traffic lights. Leaving Kristine to stop the guys from killing the clampers, Ryan jogged to the council headquarters.

Ryan's ambition of getting things done as soon as possible was instantly thwarted upon entering the offices. The customer service desks weren't officially open for another thirty minutes and the waiting area was already full. Ryan ripped a ticket from the machine and snatched a look at the number. There were twenty seven people in front of him.

4

The two clampers had retreated into their Swan Parking Enforcement van, one of them filling in forms while the other kept glancing out at Morgan's Security Systems. Kristine had herded the men back to the entrance, but hadn't managed to get them inside. The seven of them leant against the shop front, waiting for Ryan to return and the vans to be unclamped.

Paul approached the parking enforcement van. He rolled a cigarette, looking all the time at the two men inside, then he sparked up and puffed away. After a little while, he tapped on the window, smiling encouragingly. The officer cautiously wound down the passenger side window on the van. Paul heaved and spat a big tobacco stained spittle in the man's face, which hung between his nose and mouth. There was a little ripple of applause from his workmates.

Owen laughed and got out his mobile to make a call. Stu immediately got on his back:

'Calling the missus?'

Owen ignored Stu, who pretended he was his workmate:

'"Honey, someone's clamped my van."'

Walking out of earshot, Owen shot up his middle finger.

In fact he was calling his wife to apologise, not directly say sorry, but see how she was. They were under a lot of strain at the moment and seemed to argue every morning. Their youngest, Rhys, had severe autism and it was taking its toll. Owen loved the boy and wanted him at home, but this meant a private care worker was required. Rhys was a big lad and, when he lost the plot, Sarah simply wasn't able to physically deal with him.

There was a place near Neath Rhys could go to, a live-in centre with fully trained staff. They'd visited and been impressed, but it was also costly.

As the woman at the centre had explained, government subsidies had been cut and donations to the centre had dried up. It didn't want to charge people so much, but there was no choice. Meanwhile, thought Owen, the government was bailing out banks left, right and centre. There was no money to help a few autistic kids, but there was enough to keep rich bankers going.

Not to mention the millions that went towards Thatcher's funeral, all of it taxpayers' money. Fucking ironic if you asked him. The bitch had fucked the working class over, especially the Welsh, and now they all had to pay for her body to be taken through the streets of London.

If Owen didn't work, they'd be eligible for benefits and Rhys could get in free. It made Owen wonder if it was worth working.

It wasn't just about deciding what to do with Rhys, but that they didn't have the money for either choice. In the past, Owen could do overtime, but that had long since dried up. He wasn't a mug, he knew Ryan was struggling, he just hoped that things would work themselves out. Sarah had worked weekends as a cashier in Tesco but her hours had been cut. Owen had hoped she could take on the secretary role at Morgan's but Ryan had brought in Kristine. Owen knew Kristine did a great job and didn't want to feel bitter about it, but he couldn't help thinking an Eastern European immigrant had taken a job that should have been his wife's.

The country was going to the dogs. There wasn't enough work as there was, so why were immigrants allowed to pour in? He'd always voted Labour, but at the last local elections he'd gone for UKIP. Someone had to stand up for the rights of British workers.

Sarah didn't answer, so Owen left a message on voicemail telling her he would call again later, and re-joined the others.

Kristine was waiting for Ryan to call. Outwardly calm, she didn't like the morning starting like this. It felt like a bad omen. She was the only one who knew Ryan had meetings with the accountant and bank this week, and that Ryan was going to have to make some difficult decisions about who he had to let go. It was possibly going to be Johnny, who she was only half listening to at that very moment. He was going on about the latest cameras – VTVs or something.

She knew Johnny fancied her, but he was too young for her. Besides, he wasn't her type. He was nice enough, but didn't have strength of character. Not that she would have a relationship with any of Morgan's employees. She loved the job and didn't want to jeopardise it in any way.

In Latvia, work had been scarce. Coming over to Swansea in her early twenties, she'd done cleaning and bar work until she got the job with Ryan. He'd immediately entrusted her with responsibility, respected her and never once come onto her.

This had set the tone for the other guys. She accepted all their banter, but no innuendoes were ever made towards her. Men were attracted to her, she knew that, so she could pick and choose. If she had to choose from Morgan's, it would always be Ryan. Her boss was different from his employees.

Although Kristine was nearer in age to Johnny, she was closer in maturity to Ryan, or at least she hoped so, if he would only see it. That's why she couldn't understand his fidelity. Kristine could match Ryan's wife for maturity and outmatch the old witch in every other way.

Kristine had met Sandra at a works Christmas meal and had sensed her surprise straight away. It was blatantly apparent Ryan hadn't fully described Kristine to his wife. That told her Ryan liked her more than he let on, otherwise he would have been straight with Sandra. And when Kristine gave him a Christmas kiss at the end of the night, she felt how flustered he was, not to mention noticing Sandra's jealous glare.

Sandra looked good for her age, Kristine would give her that. But her age was exactly the issue. Kristine was twenty one years younger. Her breasts were firm, her stomach was flat and she didn't have to pluck grey pubic hairs. It was no competition as to who had the better body and Ryan deserved to sample hers.

In the New Year, she told Ryan directly when they were alone in the office. She'd missed him during the holidays. She didn't want to ruin his marriage, but she liked him, a lot. Ryan had made as if it was one of her jokes, laughed that he was too old for her. She knew that he knew she wasn't joking, but she didn't pursue it. She didn't chase men. She found it puzzling that Ryan chose to be faithful with his wife, but it was his loss.

There was a guy at the gym that was about Ryan's age. He was always starting conversations with her, always asking if she wanted a coffee one time or another, maybe. She knew what he really wanted and politely refused.

What Kristine did when she needed a man was go to Wind Street on a Friday night. She'd been wide-eyed when she'd first gone there. The women were half naked, no matter what the weather was like, and most of them inebriated. The men were the same. Initially appalled, she'd learnt to utilise the hedonistic street. Kristine would just have one drink, find a good-looking guy who'd had a couple but not too many. She'd take him home, ride him senseless, get what she wanted and then toss him out, bewildered, in the morning.

She never let a man stay more than a night. She'd worked hard for her independence, for her small studio flat in the marina. She wasn't going to give it up.

The thing Johnny liked about Kristine was how she listened. Of course there were her eyes too, and her breasts. But those weren't things that he could mention, so he stuck to TVL's, hoping that somehow she would see what he was really doing was declaring his love for her, surely she could see that.

He was just getting onto the best thing about TVL's being the image they captured when he saw his two housemates stumble along the pavement towards him. His face had turned red before they even spoke. He knew they were going to embarrass him, just knew it, the drunken pricks. The only reason they could be up so early was because they had to sign on.

One of his housemates, Frank, shouted as if he was across the road rather than only a metre away:

'Johnnny-boy, how's it hanging like!'

The other housemate, Dan, joined in:

'Johnny, Johnny, Johnny! Get your tits out...'

Johnny grimly nodded in acknowledgement. Frank grinned as he looked Kristine over:

'She your girlfriend mate, you stuffing that you dark horse?'

Kristine raised her eyebrows in disbelief. Johnny spluttered:

'She's my workmate.'

'And? I'd give her one.'

Kristine gave Frank a disdainful look:

'In your dreams.'

All the Morgan's guys laughed. Frank didn't have enough wit about him to offer a comeback. Kristine eyed the can of Carling in Frank's hand, moved her eyes downwards and looked unimpressed at his groin:

'You couldn't even get it up.'

Frank didn't have an answer to Kristine's putdowns. To keep his pride intact, he focused his attention on Johnny:

'We're on our way to pick up the weekly allowance - a few bevies tonight, you up for it?'

Johnny shook his head. He could hardly get his words out, he was that embarrassed:

'Na, I got work tomorrow.'

Dan raised his eyebrows at Frank and smirked:

'You catch a load of that… Oooh, he's got work tomorrow.'

Frank puckered his mouth in a mock kiss:

'With his workmates. Ahhh… bless, he'll be taking it in the arse next, just you wait…'

Johnny's two housemates laughed as they stumbled away.

Kristine shook her head. They reminded her of the drunken England fans that had descended on Riga for a football match years ago. She was just a teenager at the time and had been appalled at the fans' behaviour, grown men pissing in the street and starting fights. Now, she'd grown used to this peculiarly British behaviour. She could see Johnny was embarrassed but couldn't help teasing him:

'Nice friends.'

Johnny went on the defensive:

'They're my housemates, not my friends.

Paul spat in disgust:

'Fucking wasters. That's the fucking young generation of today – living off government benefits. I've never once signed on in my life, I'd rather cut my wrists.'

Owen muttered to the others:

'Never had a drop to drink either.'

The other guys sniggered, and Paul fixed him with a glare.

'What's that?'

Owen spoke louder:

'I said they won't have money to spend on drink soon – what with the new government rules. Take what job you're given or have your benefits cut.'

Paul stubbed out his roll up:

'Too fucking right you ask me.'

Ryan sat, his fingers drumming a marching tune on his knees, his eyes boring into the numbers, glacially encroaching and ticking forward on the electronic board. He willed them to change, praying for them to speed up, but in vain. After forty five minutes, his number was finally next. By sheer control he had managed to remain in his seat, but he was a whisker away from venting his frustration and pulling one of the smug council clerks over the counter and beating him to death.

He'd phoned Kristine to tell her the situation and explain he was in limbo. The crew were all waiting for the vans to be unclamped to start the day's jobs. If Ryan had been thinking clearly, he could have left his van keys with Stu and Owen, who could have at least gone on to the footballer's place and finished up there.

The digits on the board changed, mind numbingly slowly. Taking a deep breath, Ryan rose and went to the desk. Looking at his computer rather than at Ryan, a distracted council office clerk in a dishevelled shirt asked how he could help. Holding his credit card out to pay, Ryan explained the situation.

The office clerk offered an apologetic smile, though it wasn't that apologetic, more of a smirk really. This was obviously going to make his day and provide him with his lunchtime story about the 'shit I have to deal with'.

'I'm afraid our system is down at the moment and we can't accept card payments right now.'

Ryan stared at the clerk, who smiled uneasily. Ryan quickly ran over in his mind the situation and best course of action. To remove the clamps was a hundred pounds per van. He didn't have three hundred pounds on him so would have to go back into town to the nearest cash point. Determined to find a solution, Ryan offered one:

'If I go and get cash, will you make a priority for me so that I don't have to wait again?'

The office clerk screwed up his face. He hadn't had so much fun for a good few shifts, wait until Mandy in recall got a load of this, she'd spit her tuna melt all over the cafe and probably piss her panties laughing. Conscious that he needed to keep a straight face, the clerk smiled inwardly as he trotted out his facetious response:

'Afraid it doesn't matter even if you bring cash because I couldn't get on the system to print out a receipt and show that you've paid.'

'You can just write me out a receipt.'

'I'm not authorised to do that.'

'Fine, I don't need a receipt.'

'Yes, but we need evidence that you've paid.'

Exasperated, Ryan pointed to the CCTV camera in the ceiling:

'It will be on camera. The council can see me hand over the cash.'

'That's not what the cameras are there for.'

Ryan clamped his jaw shut. He knew that wasn't what the cameras were for, installing CCTV was how he made his living. He was simply searching for a solution to the problem, desperately trying to make the office clerk see reason. Ryan damped down the urge to reach across the desk and bounce the clerk's head off of his computer. He unclamped his mouth:

'Three of my vans have been clamped. I need those vans so I can get today's jobs done. I am ready to pay the fine so that the vans can be unclamped but your system is down. So how about you take my credit card details, make a call so that the clamps are removed and take my payment once the system is back up.'

The office clerk grimaced:

'Unfortunately it isn't the council who operates the clamping but a private company and the company will only remove the clamps once a payment has been made on the system.'

The office clerk typed impotently on the computer keyboard. He shook his head and shrugged, his voice lethargic:

'No, computer still not working.'

The clerk bit his lip to stop himself from laughing, proud of his own riff on 'computer says no'. He didn't think the man in front of him would get the Little Britain link.

Ryan eyed the clerk suspiciously. Before, he'd thought the guy was incompetent. Now he thought the clerk was nuts. Ryan rubbed the stubble on the back of his head, agitated at the stupidity of the situation. The council clerk fidgeted with the computer mouse. Abruptly, Ryan stood and strode out of the council offices, too full of fury to say anything else to the clerk. He was wasting his time and needed to come up with another plan.

5

Ryan didn't get to see his accountant until mid-afternoon, Kristine rearranging the appointment for him. He spent his morning ferrying the men to their jobs in the one van. Meanwhile Kristine persistently contacted the council until she was told their system was back up and running. Ryan was finally able to pay the fine and have the van clamps removed. With the vans delivered to the guys, Ryan walked across Walter Road to the accountant.

Ryan had been unable to decide between Paul and Johnny as to who should be made redundant, so he'd consulted Kristine. He'd put it to her that he was thinking of letting Johnny go out of respect for Paul's longevity. Kristine had said 'yes, and we can pay him in whiskey and cigarettes instead of money.' Her sarcasm showed who she thought should go, so now Ryan was thinking Paul. He was unsure how it would make much of a difference anyway. If he had less workers, then there was less work he could take on.

Ryan had set up the company in ninety two. He'd left the army once Sandra was pregnant, decided to use his skills with electronics and set himself up in business. Other ex-soldiers often turned to security work, mostly as bodyguards, but with his skills in bomb disposal he'd turned to security systems - everything from your standard burglar alarm to state of the art CCTV with police link-up.

At the height of an economic boom, Morgan's had done well and was quickly in profit. People were getting rich, so it seemed, and wanted to protect their properties. Swansea wasn't the richest city in the UK but "keeping up with the Jones's" was no doubt coined by the Welsh. People wanted to show they had as much wealth as their neighbour so Ryan fitted alarms in marina apartments and country houses in the Gower. And businesses sprouted up in several out of town developments, all requiring CCTV with police link ups.

For the initial set up, the bank had loaned Ryan money without hesitation. He'd had the chance to pay it off, but instead, on advice from his accountant and bank, had expanded, upping the loan. By the end of the nineties it seemed like a wise move. But a decade later, Ryan had downsized to his original one office and still owed the loan. He hadn't been extravagant, but his staff were well paid and they used top of the range equipment. His house had had a lot of work done to it and holidays were never cheap, whether it was a Nile cruise or an African safari. Sandra expected the best and he never wanted to disappoint her. They worked hard and deserved a little luxury now and again. And recently, there were Gerard's University fees. It all mounted up. Lately, it wasn't just that there wasn't enough money to pay off the loan, there wasn't even enough to pay the monthly instalments. He was only just about managing to settle the wage bill.

Ryan believed in the system, although 'believe' was the wrong word, it was more a case of adhering to the ethos. There was opportunity for everyone in a free market. Work hard and you'd get a reward. Whenever he'd looked around, it seemed to be true. Until now. He'd worked hard. He was a fair boss and had never cheated the system. So what had gone wrong?

Ryan was in a foul mood as he entered the accountant's offices, the windows shaking as the door shut behind him. Ryan had never met an accountant that he liked, but Brian was the least unlikable. Brian was in the same cramped office, with single-glazed windows, after forty years, Brian seeming to advertise his accountancy by showing he didn't spend money on anything unnecessary. He didn't seem to spend money on anything at all. Ryan was pretty sure the threadbare suit he was presently wearing was the same suit he had worn when Ryan first retained him, back in the early 90s. Ryan liked the idea that his was a local business, not a national corporation. Sandra was always telling him to change to one of the big accountancy firms, but Ryan wasn't sure how he'd take to some young guy in pinstripes advising him about creative accounting and the best ways of avoiding paying any tax.

Brian was a weasely little man who looked like he didn't do much exercise. He adjusted the glasses on his nose:

'Mr Morgan how are you this morning?'

Twenty years and he still referred to Ryan by his surname, but it was better than pretending to be best buddies. Ryan decided to dispense with the formalities:

'I'm letting an employee go as you suggested.'

Brian's eyebrows moved up and down over his glasses:

'Good, good, but that was two months ago.'

Ryan shrugged:

'I needed time to think who to lay off.'

Brian frowned some more, pressed his hands together, his fingertips pointed upwards:

'I'm afraid it's staff plural, not singular.'

Ryan's jaw throbbed. The day just kept getting worse. Though at least it meant he didn't have to choose between Paul and Johnny. Brian tapped his fingertips against his lips:

'And even that may not be enough. In the short term it will look to the bank like you are cutting costs, but in the long term if you have less employees, there will be less work you can take on.'

Ryan's jaw muscles clenched tight. That was exactly what he had said when Brian initially suggested the lay-offs.

'I'm meeting the bank tomorrow. Should I cancel?'

'No need to be dramatic, Mr Morgan. The cuts may well appease them. If you leave me details of the redundancies to be made, I'll have the spread sheets ready by this afternoon.'

Ryan drove to the hospital, to see how the guys were getting on. With less and less private houses, he'd come to rely on businesses and corporations. The hospital didn't have enough money to make sure there were no waiting lists, Sandra's mother had been waiting over eighteen months for her hip operation, but it was able to spend money on new security systems. In this day and age, what with injury lawyers and no-win no-fee sharks, it had to cover itself, and check no-one was stealing any babies or assaulting staff. The hospital had recently been modernised and as soon as the builders had moved out Ryan had moved in to fit the new systems.

It was a big job to get but he'd only got it by offering an extremely low price. He was hardly making a profit. The other option was for one of the big guns like ADT to get the job. When you were getting fleeced by a hospital, you knew you were in trouble. That and waiting for the next job to come through word of mouth via your wife.

Ryan found Paul and Johnny outside the maternity ward, Johnny holding the camera in place while Paul wired it up. Ryan nodded:

'Everything okay?'

With a screwdriver in his mouth, Paul growled around it:

'I have to answer that?'

Ryan nodded in satisfaction, turned to leave then paused:

'When you two get back, stop in the office for a few minutes okay?'

Jesus, he was getting as bad as Huw. He'd tried to make it casual, but he was no good at that shit. Paul just scowled at him and seemed to know something was up.

Five o'clock back in the office, Ryan sat behind his desk, letting his mind wander around the issue, deciding to tell it straight. He didn't know any other way to do it. Paul suddenly appeared and stood in his customary position by the doorway, working on a roll-up. Johnny came out of the storeroom, having made sure any unused equipment was safely packed away. Ryan swallowed, looked them both in the eye, his throat dry:

'I'm going to cut to it. With the economy the way it is, I have to make redundancies…'

Paul cut him off:

'You're fucking firing me?'

In the army, no-one would have sworn directly at their commanding officer. But they weren't in the army so Ryan didn't mention that:

'Look Paul, I weighed it up. You both have less people who depend on you. Try and see things from my perspective.'

'So what, we're worthless in our own right?'

Ryan wasn't going to answer that. Paul pointed his

roll-up at him:

'You've never fucking liked me, I know that. But I was here from the start, I helped you get off the fucking ground.'

Ryan stood up, making sure Paul felt his height and wouldn't do something stupid.

'You're right. I've never thought much of your drinking. But I've always admired your work and that's why you've stayed on so long. You'll both get a month's pay.'

Paul just sneered:

'Good luck with the hospital.'

He slammed out of the doorway. Ryan turned to Johnny, who stood there silently. He looked devastated, his eyes welling up. Ryan put an arm around his shoulder:

'You'll get a good reference.'

Ryan mulled silently over dinner, not having much of an appetite. Sandra smiled sympathetically:

'You did what you had to.'

'I hope it was worth it.'

'Of course it is – we are.'

'I'm just not sure it's going to make any difference to the bank.'

'Did the accountant say that?'

'In words – and numbers.'

He knew what she was going to say, she'd told him again and again over the years to change accountant. But Ryan didn't blame Brian. He'd come to see that Brian was there to decipher numbers, not come up with ideas on how to change them.

Wasn't it enough that he had to ask her about the hotel contract? He'd got down on his knees and begged his wife to help land him a contract to keep the company afloat, trying to make a big joke out of it. Sandra had enquired with the Village Inn chain for him. They hadn't decided who to give the contract to yet. Ryan was trying hard not to show his desperation, but was sweating buckets in the hope of landing the hotel job. Fuck, he was starting to hide things from his wife. Starting to? He should have told her months ago. He was about to own up to the dire straits the company was in when she said:

'Do you want me to speak to him?'

'The accountant?'

'Huw.'

Ryan glanced at his wife before quickly turning to stare at the untouched food in front of him, before she could see what was in his eyes, his hands gripping the cutlery, knuckles turning white. A bank meeting was a bank meeting. It was a dent to his male pride that she was even suggesting she should do his job. But what could she do that he couldn't? For the first time in thirty years of marriage, Ryan felt a sickening unease.

In the morning, Paul turned up as Ryan knew he would. But Johnny didn't. Ryan didn't have time to sort it out, leaving Kristine to try and contact him. With the five other guys all onto the hospital, Ryan strode to the nearby bank.

Ryan had never liked Huw, but as with the accountant, he'd wanted to keep it local and Huw was originally the manager at South Wales Bank. In the late nineties, it had merged with the bigger South West National which was England-based with branches throughout the UK. Huw had managed to stay manager and Ryan hadn't bothered changing banks.

Huw rose from behind his desk, shirt sleeve riding up his wrist. Strange, thought Ryan, no matter what the man wore, it was always slightly too tight. It wasn't that Ryan cared how people looked, just that they should look after themselves. With Huw in bank manager mode, there were no familial greetings or enquiries after Sandra, which suited Ryan. Taking a seat, Ryan handed over the accountant's spread sheets:

'We're making staff cuts, that should be enough to make sure the next loan instalment gets paid on time.'

Huw sat back down, gave the spread sheet a cursory glance:

'The bank has a system. When an instalment isn't delivered on time, it's instantly flagged up on the computer – you'd understand that, like a sensor on one of your security devices.'

Ryan squinted as he said:

'Thanks for the metaphor.'

'Just trying to make things clear.'

'It was a one off, it won't happen again.'

'But how can the bank be sure?'

'I already told you, we're cutting staff.'

'So who will do the work when it comes in?'

'I'll do it unpaid – I've been starting to already.'

'But if you're not paying yourself, how will you have money of your own?'

Ryan clenched the muscles in his jaw. Huw was as bad as Sandra with his warped logic. Huw gave Ryan a serious look:

'It's important you understand the gravity of the situation. And you have to understand that it is out of my hands – bank's directives and all that, my hands are tied.'

Anger was starting to build up inside Ryan. He took a couple of deep breaths to try and calm himself. The last thing he wanted was Huw's helping hand as some kind of favour. Huw couldn't keep the smirk off his face as he shrugged:

'It's not personal.'

Ryan knew that the opposite was true, that Huw was enjoying his predicament. Ryan took another deep breath. He had to focus and lose the anger. The quick-fire calculation he'd made of how far it was across the desk for his hand to reach Huw's neck was just a distraction.

Huw slid a document across the desk to Ryan:

'This is the standard letter that is being sent to you. I'm letting you see it first, to give you a bit of extra time.'

Ryan froze as his eyes caught the heading:

'Proposal of Liquidation.'

6

Ryan tried to digest the proposal of liquidation, reading that, as Morgan's creditor, the bank was suggesting liquidation on the grounds of inability to maintain present and future loan payments. He had one week from the date of the letter to oppose the order, providing evidence as to why it shouldn't occur.

Ryan had come to the bank expecting an informal meeting about how he could manage his company's finances and Huw had socked him unexpectedly with this. Ryan kept his eyes on the paper, not wanting Huw to see his shock. It was hard to take in, so he focused on a minor detail:

'It's dated yesterday.'

'It went out in the afternoon post.'

Kristine was probably right now dealing with the post. So what was the extra time Huw was talking about? In fact, by being in the meeting, Ryan was receiving the news later than he would have if he'd been sitting in the office. Huw seemed to read Ryan's thoughts:

'Oh dear, I guess that means you aren't getting any advance warning after all.'

Ryan slowly raised his eyes to meet Huw's. The man was supposed to be his bank manager but at this precise moment he was taking the piss. Huw pretended to be concerned:

'If you are going to cry, I can call in the secretary to bring some tissues.'

Huw was keeping a straight face, but his mouth was twitching as he tried to suppress a smile. It reminded Ryan of Sandra when she smiled nervously. Ryan knew that Huw was mean spirited, but to hand over a letter of liquidation then take the piss was too much. Leaving the letter on the desk, Ryan stood and made to leave. Huw followed suit, unable to resist a parting dig:

'Guess you won't be taking Sandra on holiday this year.'

Ryan paused with his hand on the door handle. He knew he should just go, but his pause allowed Huw to continue:

'You know, Sandra was supposed to go camping with me that summer.'

Ryan frowned. What was Huw talking about? He waited and sure enough Huw explained:

'You had to get the school sports achievement award, didn't you? The rugby team won that year, but your solo run was apparently more important than our team effort.'

Ryan recalled the award. It was given to him in the

final assembly of his school life. He wasn't sure what the connection was between that and Sandra not camping with Huw. But he was pretty sure Huw was going to tell him.

'I was so angry I punched the wall and broke my wrist. While I spent the summer with my hand in plaster, off Sandra went with you. She was going to go with me - we had planned it months in advance. Bet you didn't know that did you?'

Ryan didn't know that, but he didn't say so. He knew what Huw was talking about now. That camping trip was when Ryan and Sandra had first got together. But it was thirty four years ago. Ryan was hardly going to question his wife about it. Did Huw really hold a grudge from then?

The answer became more than evident as Huw carried on, his face puce with indignation:

'The first year when you were both still around was hard because I had to see you together. But then you went to the army and Sandra dutifully went along with you. That made it a bit easier. If I saw headlines about soldiers killed in Iraq, I hoped it was you so that she could come back alone.'

'False hope I'm afraid, I was in Kuwait not Iraq.'

Ryan looked at Huw with bewilderment. Was this guy serious? Yes, he clearly was:

'Wherever you were, you had to come back and rub it in. It wasn't enough that I had to see you two play happy families, no, you wanted me to loan you money for your new business.'

'Not you personally, I was just offering my custom

to a local bank.'

'Really? That's why you came to me for the mortgage as well. I'd always imagined Sandra and me ending up in Mumbles. Instead I was giving you money to set up home with her there. I guess it all seemed funny to you.'

Ryan involuntarily let out a small laugh. Unless he could prevent it, his company was about to be liquidated, which would mean not only dire straits for his own family but also his employees. And all Huw was concerned about was a series of perceived injustices to his dignity over the last thirty odd years. Ryan hadn't even known that Sandra and Huw had once shared a teenage kiss, so it didn't even make sense that he would have deliberately rubbed it in. Ryan wasn't going to explain that though:

'Huw, I never even thought about how it seemed to you.'

'Well, we'll see who has the last laugh. Good luck with the liquidation.'

Ryan internally shook himself. What was he doing getting into a stupid pissing competition with Huw? He didn't have time for this. Not bothering to respond to Huw's last remark, Ryan left the office. Behind him, Ryan heard Huw speak to his secretary:

'Send in the next appointment when they arrive.'

It was amazing, thought Ryan, how quickly Huw transformed. A few minutes earlier, the guy had been acting like a mix between school bully and baby whose rattle had been thrown out of the pram. Yet straight away he was back to his bank manager mode.

There was something wrong with the man, but Ryan didn't have to time to think about it. He had more pressing issues, like stopping his company from being closed the fuck down.

Kristine looked up as soon as Ryan strode in. He saw from her eyes that she knew:

'You read the letter?'

She nodded sadly:

'It is not fair. When bank is in debt for billions, government bails them out, in fact we do, the taxpayers. And now, when we owe just few thousand, they try to close us.'

Ryan frowned. He'd been so wrapped up in keeping his own business afloat, he hadn't been paying attention to which banks were receiving government bail outs. He knew about RBS, but he'd missed the news about South West.

'Is that true?'

'Of course, it was in news.'

Ryan cursed internally. He felt like going back to Huw and telling him where to stuff the letter of liquidation, say that when the bank paid back its debts, Ryan would pay back his. He fumed at the bank's hypocrisy. But what could he do about it, write a letter to the government? Morgan's would be liquidated before he got a reply. He shrugged:

'Not much we can do about it.'

'We could hold bank manager hostage. If bank doesn't wipe off loan, we kill him.'

Ryan couldn't help but smile at Kristine's dark

humour.

'And even if it doesn't, kill him anyway.'

'But maybe then we have to go to prison.'

Ryan nodded, getting serious. He was furious at the bank for its double standards and he appreciated Kristine's humour but they needed to be practical as to how they found a solution:

'Another plan might be better. We need to draw up a list of every possible building that might need security – for the next week, we'll be salespeople.'

Kristine nodded solemnly:

'I'm on it. About Johnny, there is no answer from him. You want his address?'

Ryan took it. He had a lot to do, but he felt a duty to Johnny so went to check on him.

Johnny lived in a house-share just around the corner on Hanover Street, known for housing students, the jobless and prostitutes. Ryan banged on the door of the terraced house, rubbish bags torn by seagulls on the pavement outside. There was no answer so he banged harder.

Johnny blinked in the daylight as he slowly opened the door. Ryan took in his dishevelled state, vest and pants on his wiry frame:

'Get showered, I want you in work.'

'No point anymore.'

'This isn't the end Johnny. You're one of the best I've ever had. You'll get the best reference I can write and you'll get a job with one of the big companies.'

'They're not going to take me on, there's no jobs out there.'

Ryan wanted to shake him, but on seeing Johnny stumble against the doorframe, saw there was no point. He was probably still inebriated.

'Sleep it off today. But I want to see you in tomorrow - do not give up.'

The rest of the week was non-stop, Ryan and Kristine working late every day as they pitched to every company they thought might need security cameras or shops that required alarms. In the previous months, Kristine had already done every kind of advertising possible – flyers through letterboxes, ads in The Evening Post, even turning her personal Facebook page into a plea for jobs. It had all been more of a money loss than gain. Ryan wasn't good as a salesman. Kristine had a much better manner, but still only got a few maybes.

There just wasn't the demand. Half the out of town stores had closed down, the city centre was half dead and most people didn't have any spare money to buy food and essentials let alone to fit house alarms.

Ryan hardly saw Sandra. The night after the bank meeting she'd come in late, tipsy after too many white wines, the Mercedes left at her work. With no choice but to ask, Ryan did:

'Any news on the contract?'

'They're going with ADT.'

'Fuck.'

Ryan never swore. Sandra raised her eyebrows as she leaned unsteadily against the kitchen counter, the kitchen one of Sandra's grand designs – several thousand pounds worth. Ryan was waiting for her to ask about the bank meeting, but she just turned to refill her glass of wine. It was strange that she didn't ask about the bank meeting, so he asked:

'You been out with Huw?'

Sandra turned and faced him:

'I was out with the girls from work – I thought as my husband's about to lose everything we have, I might as well get smashed. That okay with you?'

'So he told you.'

'I met him for lunch.'

Ryan stared at her. She curled her top lip upwards, suddenly sober:

'You weren't going to tell me, were you?'

It was a statement, not a question so Ryan didn't answer it. Instead, he had his own questions:

'Just lunch was it? Or did you go up to one of the hotel rooms afterwards? Was that how you got the bastard to tell you everything?'

It was the first time in their marriage Ryan had ever made such a jealous insinuation. He already hated himself for it, but she was riling him:

'I don't need to fuck Huw to get him to speak.'

'No, he's so obsessed with you, you just have to flutter your eyelashes.'

'At least he does speak to me, which is more than you do.'

With every jibe from Sandra, Ryan felt himself getting lower:

'I'm pretty sure it's against bank procedure to be giving out confidential information. A word in the right place could get him sacked.'

Not only was it something he would never actually do, it was a pathetic thing to say and he knew it. Sandra simply placed her wine glass on the surface. She faced him coldly:

'You should be more concerned with your being out of work rather than him being sacked.'

Sandra moved past him and went to bed, leaving Ryan alone in the kitchen.

7

With just Kristine in the loop, she told Ryan how the guys were apprehensive after Paul told them all he'd been given notice. They weren't mad at Ryan, more relieved it wasn't them and worried for their own futures.

Only Ryan and Kristine knew how worried the guys should be. Their late nights didn't achieve much, apart from drawing them closer. Spring was warming up and Kristine was wearing less, her bare arms often coming into contact with Ryan's. He felt her warmth, but didn't let it distract him from the task in hand. One night, he realised they neither of them had eaten for hours so offered to take her for dinner. Strangely, she bridled at it, saying she didn't need a man to pay for her. He held up his hands in peace, said she wasn't being paid for all the overtime and he was just trying to make it up. She accepted and suggested they went to La Fina on the Kingsway.

La Fina was a Spanish restaurant, the manager,

chefs and waiters all having come from Spain in the last year or so. Kristine liked it because they were immigrants like her, trying to set up a life in the UK. Plus, the tapas was fantastic.

As Kristine told Ryan about the restaurant, the world-wide economic crisis finally started to dawn on him. Eastern Europeans like Kristine had been coming over to the UK for a few years. Now that Spain had no work, people were coming from there too. But Britain was on the verge itself, Ryan's own business about to go bust, so where would he go?

On the way to the restaurant, they passed South West National. The shutters were down for the night but the cash machine was lit up. Ryan couldn't help feeling bitter. Despite owing billions to the taxpayer, the bank would carry on functioning. Morgan's was about to be foreclosed for owing the very same bank a few thousand. Ryan felt an urge to find a rock and smash the cash machine but he knew that would achieve nothing.

Ryan saw that Kristine was also scowling at the bank. He had an idea:

'Can you drive fast?'

'If I need to, sure.'

'Okay, I have a new plan. Tomorrow, I go in and rob the bank. You have the getaway car ready and we get out of here.'

'Sounds like good plan. Where to, America?'

'Sure, why not.'

Kristine frowned:

'But maybe they will chase us and we will crash.

I'm too young to die.'

'Okay, we'll have to think of another plan.'

With their mood lightened, Ryan and Kristine walked on through the empty city centre streets. Only a Big Issue seller was still standing on a corner, which gave Kristine an idea:

'I know, we can do busking. Can you play any instrument?'

'Er, no.'

'Never mind, you can clap your hands while I dance.'

Ryan smiled at the image. They were being silly, but if they didn't laugh, they'd cry. They were exhausted from their constant long days and knew it had all been futile. In the next week, Ryan would no longer run Morgan's and Kristine wouldn't have a job there. In their near delirious state, all they could do was keep coming up with ridiculous plans to get money.

When they reached La Fina, they were both in stitches. The laughter froze on Ryan's face as he went to open the restaurant door. Holding it open from inside was Huw. And coming out of the door was Sandra.

The four of them took each other in. Sandra was the first to react, glaring at Ryan:

'So this is how you spend your evenings? While your company's about to go bust, you go out to restaurants with women half your age. What is this, some sort of midlife crisis?'

Behind Sandra, Huw shook his head and silently tutted, barely able to suppress a smile. Ryan was taken aback by Sandra's venom, doubly embarrassing as it was in public. He tried to calm the situation:

'Sandra, we've been working non-stop. We haven't eaten all day, so we're just getting some food. And it's woman single, not women plural.'

Ryan's attempt at humour didn't go down well, Sandra not appeased:

'Well I'm glad you've got enough money to take 'woman single' out.'

Kristine reacted, pointing to Huw who was standing amused behind Sandra as she said:

'And what are you doing here, with this man instead of your husband?'

Sandra turned on Kristine:

'Not that it's any of your business, but I've been getting financial advice on how it might be possible to save my husband's business.'

Behind her, Huw piped up:

'That's right.'

Kristine ignored him:

'I am about to lose my job, so I think it is my business. And I still stick by Ryan, not shout at him in street.'

Sandra's face tightened in rage, but she didn't have a response to Kristine. Instead she turned back to Ryan:

'Are you just going to stand there?'

'No Sandra, I'm going to eat, with Kristine. We've had a long day and we're hungry. You two are welcome to join us, but I guess you've already eaten while you were getting financial advice.'

Sandra let Ryan's reply sink in before putting in her parting words:

'I'll be staying at the hotel tonight.'

She turned to Huw:

'Could you give me a lift?'

Huw nodded vigorously:

'Of course, Sandra, I'd be delighted.'

Sandra turned abruptly on her heel and walked off. Huw made to follow her, pausing by Ryan to speak in a lowered voice:

'Looks like you fucked up there, old pal.'

Huw looked over at Kristine:

'Maybe the meal will buy you a fuck – she looks cheap enough.'

'Go and trot after Sandra, you lapdog.'

Huw wanted to retort but couldn't think of anything to say. Sandra was waiting by his car for him, so he slid the sneer off his face and replaced it with a smile as he trotted to her. Kristine stepped to Ryan's side:

'What did he say?'

'Nothing worth repeating.'

'We don't have to eat if you want to go after your wife.'

'Come on, I'm hungry.'

During the meal, Kristine tried to lighten the mood by making more jokes about how they could make money and escape, suggesting they steal a yacht and sail off to another country, but Ryan remained morose.

After the meal, Ryan walked Kristine to her marina

flat. She could see that he wasn't going to be swayed out of his dark mood, so gave him a peck on the cheek and went in. Ryan looked across the marina at the Village Inn hotel where Sandra had said she was staying. He was tempted to go over, try and make things up. But he knew it would look like he was checking up on her. And if she wasn't there, then where did that leave him?

Sandra had gone on the attack straight away so Ryan hadn't had a chance to question what she was doing with Huw. He couldn't help the jealous twinge, but he was hardly going to lower himself to show it. Besides, Kristine had said what needed to be said.

Kristine was right. It would be nice just to get in a yacht and sail away from all the problems. Unfortunately that wasn't possible. So he walked along the beach all the way to Mumbles, home to bed where he lay alone.

With nothing concrete coming in by Friday, Ryan gave up trying to sell security systems and went to help out at the hospital. Despite Ryan's wake up call, Johnny hadn't made it in for the rest of the week.

Alongside Paul, who gave him the silent treatment, Ryan helped fit the last camera into place. With all the guys having been on the same job, it had been done well ahead of schedule.

Ryan went to check with the hospital security guy in his monitor room. On one screen, he saw an exhausted but beaming mother wheeled out of the maternity ward, cradling her newborn. On another screen a wizened old man, whose hospital pyjamas were too loose on his bones, was wheeled past the reception. The place where Ryan had taken his first breath and his parents their last, a place his dad had wired up for electric and now Ryan had wired for security. It seemed a fitting last job.

They all gathered in the small office as Ryan had requested, Paul leaning against the doorway, Johnny absent, the other four murmuring nervously. Ryan stood in front of his desk and told them it was their last day of work. They all had a month's notice, fully paid.

For a second there was complete silence. Owen was the first to speak up:

'I've got two fucking kids.'

Stu joined in:

'Just like that? How long have you known?'

Ryan didn't defend himself, thinking it best that they vent their anger. Tearful, Kristine tried to explain:

'We've done everything we could. We could maybe take on another job or two, but it wouldn't be enough for everyone and the bank would close us before we even finished.'

Anger turned to desperation as Dave came up with an idea:

'We could all take it in turns…'

'It wouldn't make a difference to them.'

Ryan wanted to hold up the liquidation letter, say these are the bastards whose fault it is, but he was to blame as much as anyone else.

Owen kicked over a chair:

'It's alright for you and Sandra in your big fancy Mumbles home, how are we going to pay the mortgage now?'

Bowing his head in acknowledgement of Owen's situation, Ryan stayed calm. He wasn't frightened of the men, but didn't want to listen to them anymore. Owen though was ready to lose it, coming right up to Ryan. Spittle flew out of Owen's mouth as he spoke rapidly:

'You know my wife doesn't work, you know looking after Rhys is a full time job. My whole bloody income goes on his care and medication. You know that.'

Seeing Owen's hands come up, Ryan braced himself. He could have prevented it, but instead let Owen shove him roughly in the chest. With everyone in the office tense, Ryan raised his eyes to Owen's:

'Don't do it.'

Owen was younger and full of fury, but he was no fighter. His face, throat and balls were all vulnerable to attack. It would only take one hit from Ryan to take him down. But the man had already lost his livelihood, he didn't need to be humiliated as well. So instead Ryan readied his body to take more blows. Owen was unable to contain his rage, his face turning puce and tears seeping out as he reacted:

'Don't do it? Don't fucking do it? That's all you can fucking say?'

Not knowing how to express his anger, Owen grabbed Ryan by the shirt as he shoved forward. The desk shifted. Kristine urged them to stop. No-one heard her, but the scuffle had already halted, Ryan and Owen bent awkwardly over the desk. Owen let go of Ryan's shirt and kicked at the desk:

'Fuck.'

Owen breathed heavily, coughing back sobs, feeling stupid and impotent. Ryan straightened up, his breathing even as he tried to blank out any emotion. Strangely, it was Paul who realised what he'd done for them:

'He's done us a favour. If he carries on, when the bank comes in, employees' wages will be well down the list. By the time loans are recovered and liquidators fees paid, there might not be anything left. Paying us now, we're getting a month's wages upfront before the bank gets a penny.'

The others were still too stunned to thank Ryan. Instead, they silently traipsed out, ignoring Paul's suggestion of a final drink. Paul and Ryan nodded to each other in acknowledgement. Paul put the roll-up in his mouth and exited the premises.

With only Kristine and Ryan left, she exhaled:

'You did what you could.'

Ryan nodded, but didn't respond, still restraining himself. Kristine stepped close to him:

'Ryan?'

Ryan focused on her. She looked him in the eyes:

'It is good you didn't hit him.'

Kristine put her hand on Ryan's heart. She was shaking more than him, but she could feel the tension inside Ryan.

Ryan took her by the shoulders. And held her close,

her head against his chest, her hair getting stuck in his stubble. He kissed the top of her head. They relaxed their embrace. Kristine stood on her toes, took Ryan's face in her hands and kissed him on the lips. She smiled:

'Call me.'

Biting her lip so that she wouldn't cry, Kristine turned and fled the office.

Ryan felt an urge to run after her. His business had just collapsed and Kristine had just lost her job. Unlike his wife, she didn't blame him, but was offering herself, a woman over twenty years younger. But he also knew that it wasn't any kind of solution. For an hour or so maybe, but not long term. And he still loved Sandra.

Ryan shifted the desk back to its original position. He sat behind it, palms calmly on the wooden surface. If he had a gun in his hand, he wasn't sure what he'd do with it. Back in the day, he'd had his service revolver. He no longer had that, but when the liquidators came, he'd be ready for them.

8

In fact, the liquidation occurred without much conflict. The agency people brought in by the bank were mildly surprised by Ryan's stance, being used to company owners either reacting in fury as they were forced to close or acting resigned as they called in the closure themselves. Ryan was neither resigned nor angry. He was a proud guy, the agency people thought, and then thought no more of it.

Apart from owing the bank, Morgan's Security had been well run. There were no hidden tax evasions to check on and hardly any assets to strip. Ryan ordered in equipment as it was needed so there were just a couple of CCTV cameras remaining in the storeroom. That only left the vans to be sold and the office to be cleared, Ryan watching as the guys from the liquidation agency drove the vans away. His hand clutched the one item he'd kept as a keepsake, a miniature CCTV camera.

With the staff already paid, the agency just had

to make sure they got their own fees and the bank got what it was owed. As Morgan's no longer had an operating account, Ryan was responsible for this personally – unless he wanted to fight it with a long drawn out and costly court case. With his jaw clenched tight in silent anger, Ryan emptied his personal account. Not wanting to face Huw, he did it online rather than in person.

Ryan knew he couldn't postpone the next meeting indefinitely. And when the letter arrived at the house, he took it stoically, having expected as much. Yes, he thought it was downright unjust that South West could owe so much and that not be a problem, while the very same bank first took his business and then tried to take his house. But he didn't know how to rally against that. It was enough work simply trying to survive.

Ryan didn't need to go to the accountant to know what the letter meant. With no income and his personal account debited, how was he going to pay the remaining mortgage instalments?

Thankfully it was a weekday and Sandra was at work, so he had some slight breathing space before having to discuss it with her. The mortgage was solely in his name as he'd bought the house on coming out of the army, Ryan the only one with money while Sandra was pregnant with Gerard. Once she set herself up as a hotel manager, she paid for her own personal items, such as the car – starting off with a Fiesta before graduating upwards to an Audi and now the Mercedes. She also paid for anything she wanted done to the house, like the designer kitchen Ryan was now standing in, his t-shirt stuck to his lean body with the sweat from his morning workout.

With no work to go to, he'd done more than his usual amount of lifts and sit-ups. He relaxed his breathing and phoned the bank. After arranging a meeting for the next day with Huw, Ryan headed to the bathroom, another of Sandra's outlays.

As the shower powered down on his head, he thought it was great to have such conveniences but knew he could live without if he had to. He doubted Sandra could though. He had a couple of plans in mind of how to keep the house. And if he couldn't he had a fall-back plan. They wouldn't be homeless.

Huw seemed even smugger than last time. He was hardly able to keep the smirk off his face:

'You have to understand I take no pleasure in this – it's nothing personal.'

'So you keep saying.'

Huw glanced at Ryan to see if his words carried any menace, but Ryan's face betrayed no feelings. Ryan waited, giving Huw time to think about what he might say next. Huw was obviously expecting Ryan to beg for help, come crawling, but Ryan wasn't following Huw's script and didn't feel like helping him out. Huw continued:

'The bank has no option but to confirm mortgage payments can be made…'

'I understand. The bank wants its money back. Bit ironic seeing as the bank owes the taxpayer billions but there we are.'

'Well, you would have to take that up with the government.'

Huw attempted a pleasant smile that fell sideways off his face. He couldn't work out why Ryan was so calm in the face of losing everything. He'd had fun that very morning talking to himself in the mirror as he shaved, imagining all sorts of scenarios taking place. Huw's favourite was Ryan breaking down and crying, Huw patting Ryan gently on the shoulder as he delivered the perfect put down, something like: 'You sit at the table with the big boys, you got to expect to roll with the punches. Leave it with your old friend Huw, I'll see about getting you a little part-time security job with one of the supermarkets, I've got my contacts…' This certainly wasn't unfolding as he'd expected.

Ryan looked quizzically across at Huw, trying to work something out:

'What I don't understand is why you've got such a hard on for me.'

Huw balked at Ryan's words. Ryan went on:

'Although I guess it's Sandra who you've always had a hard on for. Is this really all because of some teenage wet dream that never came true for you?'

Huw reddened, wishing he had never told Ryan about Sandra not camping with him as a teenager. He almost blurted out that they'd kissed once, as adults not children, but realised it would sound pathetic. Ryan didn't stop:

'Every time you wank at night, have you imagined

Sandra with you? Thirty four years, that's a lot of wanking.'

Huw just sat there in impotent fury, not having any rebuttal as it was all true.

Ryan hadn't planned to let out this bitter stream of vindictiveness, but he couldn't stop himself:

'If it's still bothering you that Sandra went with me instead of you as a teenager, why don't we fight it out?'

Huw gulped, seeing Ryan was serious. Ryan gestured out of the door:

'Come on, I'll let you get a couple of good punches in, help you get it out of your system. Then I'm going to knock seven shades of shit out of you and help straighten you out, fix that faulty wiring you've got in your head.'

Huw cleared his throat, his voice cracking:

'You need help, you're crazy.'

'Huw, there's only one person in this room who needs professional help and I'm looking at him.'

Huw pointed a shaking finger at Ryan. He wasn't prepared to fight Ryan, but it was his office and he couldn't let Ryan forget that, Huw's voice rising into a shout:

'YOU do not tell ME I need help!'

Ryan raised his eyebrows. So this was Huw when he was flustered. The door opened and Huw's secretary popped her head around. She smiled apologetically:

'Just checking everything's okay?'

Huw's crazed face instantly morphed back into his placid bank manager appearance, his hand going to his throat:

'All fine Karen, just a little throat problem.'

Huw's secretary nodded slowly and eyed Ryan suspiciously. He was sitting calmly and didn't seem to be posing any threat to Huw but she was sure she'd heard Huw shouting. She backed out of the room.

Ryan looked over at Huw. Now he was sure the man was nuts. He'd always known that Huw could be chameleon-like, but to alter his face and mood so quickly was fucked up. The problem was, he was still Ryan's bank manager. Ryan acted concerned:

'Your throat okay now?'

Huw ignored Ryan's jibe, cleared his throat and desperately tried to reclaim the conversation:

'Fighting me isn't going to solve this situation you've got yourself in. I really think we should get back to the business in hand, rather than waste time brawling like two infants.'

Ryan couldn't help but smile at that. Huw looked fit to burst a gasket. He certainly was no longer his usual smarmy self, although he was attempting to get back on track:

'I'm asking what you plan to do. How do you plan to proceed with your mortgage payments?'

Ryan slid a letter across the desk:

'That's legal confirmation that I'm entitled to half my parents' house as soon as I sell it.'

Huw nodded again, hardly glancing at the letter:

'That's definitely a step in the right direction.'

To Ryan, Huw didn't seem surprised by the letter, when it wasn't something he should know about. The only people who knew were the solicitor and Sandra. The first wouldn't be legally allowed to divulge the information. The latter he didn't want to think about.

'It will of course take time to sell.'

'With no work, I've got time to do it up.'

'And you're entitled to half?'

'My sister gets the other half.'

'Has she agreed to the sale?'

Ryan was no good at lying and turned to stare out the window, wishing he was anywhere else but where he was sat at that moment.

'I'll sell it.'

'Have you had it valued?'

'I've booked the valuation for tomorrow, but going prices for similar properties are seventy to eighty thousand.'

Huw gently pushed the letter aside:

'Let's put this to the side for the moment.'

Ryan guessed it was another of Huw's obvious metaphors. Huw was oblivious:

'If you sell the house, it may be worth, let's say, seventy five thousand, half of which is thirty five thousand.'

Huw typed unnecessarily on a calculator before grudgingly accepting:

'It would be enough to pay off the mortgage.'

Ryan just looked at Huw. Did he think he hadn't worked that out already? But Huw had a different question:

'The question is, how long will it take? In today's market, it could be over a year before the house is sold

– and during that time you have mortgage payments to meet each month.'

'As you know, my wife works.'

'And as I'm sure you know, she's not the mortgage payer.'

Ryan stared at Huw, who didn't want to let it go:

'In fact, you need to think how this could affect her. I don't know what legal documents you have drawn up, but as your spouse she could be liable for your debts.'

Ryan slammed a hand on the desk and Huw almost jumped out of his seat. Ryan stared across the desk at Huw:

'I'm touched by your concern, I truly am, but do not tell me how to look after my wife.'

Huw's eyes darted nervously between the door, telephone and ceiling. Ryan was well aware there was a camera up there as he'd bloody installed the thing. Huw tried, unsuccessfully, to regain his composure:

'If you want, I can call security and have you removed.'

Ryan took a deep breath:

'Just tell me what the bank requires.'

'If your wife…'

'You know her name.'

'If Sandra is going to take on the payments, you need to bring in legal proof of this. And once your parents' property is sold, evidence of this will also be required.'

'How long have I got?'

'That would be until the next payment is due,

which is…'

'Two weeks.'

Ryan stood. Huw got in a parting shot:

'You know, if you'd had your house in order, you wouldn't be in this mess.'

9

By the time Sandra got home, Ryan had already eaten. He poured her a glass of white and sat across from her with a shot of whiskey. It was usually just his annual drink at New Year, but he felt deserving of a stiffener. He felt more nervous than when he'd asked her to marry him. They'd lived together for so long and now it seemed as if they were slightly estranged. Neither of them had mentioned the night at the restaurant with Huw and Kristine. It was just left simmering in the background, with all the other unsaid things.

After a quick whiskey hit, Ryan put the situation to her, as soon as his parents' house was sold the mortgage would be completely paid off. Sandra took little sips of wine as she listened and waited for him to finish.

'Provided you can get your sister to agree.'

Ryan nodded.

'I'll make her come around to it.'

Sandra looked thoughtful. She knew he could

do anything once he was focused on it. He hadn't pursued his sister about it before because it hadn't been necessary. She swilled her glass:

'The problem is how long is it going to take?'

There was a silence. Ryan looked directly at his wife and gave her a tired smile:

'That's where you could come in – if you want to.'

She looked into her glass. If she looked anywhere else her emotions might get the better of her. She bit down on her bottom lip and felt an urge to toss the wine glass at the wall. It looked like they were about to lose the house they'd lived in for thirty years. But it wasn't just the material side of things – it had been their base from which they'd achieved so much as a family. Thinking about losing their home made her want to cry.

And if she looked at Ryan, she'd want to slap him. She knew it wasn't all his fault, he worked harder than anyone she knew. But he should have told her earlier – maybe together they could have saved his company.

Sure, he was talking now. It was a bit late though. And yes, she'd been seeing Huw, not seeing in a romantic way but twice now without Ryan knowing. That didn't include dinner in La Fina when Ryan had waltzed in with Miss Latvia on his arm. She wasn't going to let him forget that.

Sandra told herself that the meetings with Huw were to see how she could save her home and marriage, but she knew it was a dangerous game. Huw never failed to flatter her and she knew he still carried a torch for her, even after all these years.

Sandra did also see Huw every Christmas as his bank's Christmas party was held in her hotel. Thirty odd years and he never stopped telling her how she'd be better off with him instead of Ryan. At the Christmas bank bashes, Huw was always with his colleagues so she was never alone with him. One year though, just the two of them had somehow ended up by the side of the pool. Sandra had joined in the festivities and had drunk more than her fair share of bubbly. Huw had looked at her with drunken devotion:

'Just imagine, we could have our own hotel pool in Spain.'

Sandra had played along:

'Yea, and how would that happen?'

'Easy. The bank could arrange a business loan, you know I can get that sorted. And of course I have my own savings we can add. We set up the hotel out there, you design the place how you like and I come out to help you run it when it's ready.'

Sandra had closed her eyes, imagining the hotel of her dreams, seeing herself and the hotel guests by the palm-dotted pool, basking in the sun. With her eyes still shut, Huw had leaned in even closer. She opened her eyes to find him ready with the old mistletoe trick. She let him have his kiss, but when his hands started to cop a feel, she drew the line and pushed him away.

They'd never mentioned the kiss or the dream hotel again. She'd dismissed it as his drunken fantasy. Spain's economy was more kaput than the UK's now so it would never happen anyway. And she'd certainly never told Ryan about that night. He'd probably have gone and killed Huw.

Ryan was patient, waiting and wondering if Sandra was going to go for it, and help them out of the hole. But guessing that she wasn't sure about being responsible for the mortgage, Ryan offered the alternative:

'Or, we can always move into my parents' place.'

That got a reaction. Sandra burst out laughing, almost snorting wine through her nose. Ryan's face turned to granite.

Sandra asked:

'Come on, you don't think it's funny?'

She saw he didn't, so she made herself clear:

'I'm not moving in there!'

Ryan shrugged.

'It's just if it comes to it – I can do it up.'

Sandra got serious:

'Ryan, I'm forty nine and you're fifty. We have a nice life because we've worked bloody hard. I'm not about to move into my dead parents in law's dilapidated house like some teenage squatter.'

He watched her. She took a gulp of wine before going on, more evenly:

'I can't take on the payments. I went to a solicitor after work and he strongly advised me not to. This way at least one of us is safe from bankruptcy. No job is safe these days – what if I lost mine?'

'You went to a solicitor?'

Sandra rolled her eyes.

'Before you say why didn't you tell me, ask yourself why you didn't tell me anything for the last few months – and I'm not just talking about the company going down the drain.'

Ryan's jaw throbbed. He was never clever when it came to Sandra's arguments:

'What do you mean?'

'I mean all those late nights with Miss Latvia.'

'What are you talking about?'

'With your secretary, the girl who you strangely forgot to tell me you'd employed until I met her at the Christmas bash.'

'Do you tell me about every person who works at the hotel?'

'Bit different isn't it as your secretary is twenty years younger and I don't take mine out for dinner.'

'It was work related. She was working overtime for free so I just wanted to repay her.'

'Really, just like that Christmas kiss right in front of me was work related too.'

Ryan took a moment to reflect. He was genuinely perplexed. Yes, he admired Kristine and they'd had that emotional kiss goodbye, but nothing had ever happened between them. Why was he forced to defend himself about taking Kristine for a meal when Sandra had been in the same restaurant with Huw? He didn't get a chance to pose the question as Sandra gulped down the last of her wine:

'You better find your sister quickly.'

Sandra got up and left Ryan alone. He let her go. He might not be clever in the midst of a row but he could work things out afterwards, like how if Sandra had been to a solicitor, she'd already known about his meeting with Huw. And the innuendo about him and Kristine having an affair was a distraction. He was no psychologist or even a betting man, but he'd place money that Sandra had said it because she was feeling guilty herself.

The last time Ryan saw his sister was at their mum's funeral, so soon after their dad's, meaning those two meetings were the sum total in the last thirty years. Having fallen out with their parents as a teenager because they didn't sanction a move to Art College in London, she'd run away. As far as Ryan knew, she never did make it to Art College but had spent her entire life as a reclusive alcoholic.

At the first funeral she'd turned up a mess, but seemed to be in recovery by the second funeral, promising to keep in touch, which of course hadn't happened.

The will had stipulated that the house would be split between them, which was fine with Ryan. At the time he was even prepared for Alice to have it all. But she'd slipped back to London before he could arrange a trip to the solicitor, and hadn't been bothered to answer any of his calls about resolving the situation. Since then he'd been so busy trying to keep his business afloat he hadn't had time to do anything about the house one way or another.

Assuming that, as usual, she wouldn't answer the phone, Ryan was surprised when she did.

'Has someone else died?'

'No, but I want to sell the house.'

'Ooo, housey house.'

'Are you drunk?'

'Just on life and how shit it is.'

Ryan sighed. As someone who'd never worked and lived her whole life on various benefits, it was a bit rich. But at least she wasn't slurring her words, too much.

'Not sure I want to sell it.'

He couldn't believe she wanted to keep it because of the fond memories.

'You'll get half the money. It should sell for about seventy five thousand. Minus the costs incurred, thirty thousand each could be very useful.'

He felt stupid talking to her as if she was stupid, which she wasn't.

'I thought you were going to let me have it all.'

'Something's come up.'

'What, Sandra need a new kitchen?'

'If I don't get the money we won't even be able to use the kitchen we have.'

'So let me understand, my big bro the businessman, the war hero, the dutiful husband and father, phones me when he suddenly needs my signature – is that right?'

Ryan looked out of the window without responding and wondered why his sister existed. It was an awful thought he knew, but as far as he could see she contributed nothing to society. Her voice continued to drone out of the phone:

'Well let me tell you, I'm not going to sell. Maybe you don't follow the news that affects us poor folk, but the government's made cuts. Next year's benefits won't cover London costs, so maybe I'll need that house to live in.'

Ryan tried to rub away the headache that was starting to form and take up residence. Would it be possible to show that his sister was incapacitated and therefore not legally responsible to participate in the division of the will?

'Okay Alice, I'll speak to you another time.'

'I haven't finished...'

He put the phone down.

Leaving his sister to deal with another day, Ryan went to check out his parents' old home to see what work needed doing. He hadn't been there for several months. A two up, two down terrace, the house was in the Townhill council estate but had great views over Swansea Bay.

The estate was originally conceived as a socialist venture – post war homes for the working class, Ryan's dad proud to inhabit one of the houses. Ryan had enjoyed playing in the streets as a kid, but the inability to escape the community had always irritated his sister. A few of his dad's ilk still existed, but now the estate was a haven for the local unemployed and government-supported addicts as well as housing Eastern European immigrant workers and Middle-East asylum seekers. It wasn't a healthy mix.

Ryan shoved open the old wooden door, his dad never having bothered to upgrade to PVC. With all the facilities cut off there were no bills, but Pizza Hut didn't know no-one was at home anymore. The place was dank and dark. With no electrics, he opened up the net curtains, once white but now yellowed from all the years of his dad's smoking. What he saw was that the place needed serious work before anyone even thought of buying it. A lot was in boxes, Ryan having started a clear out after his mum's funeral, but he'd never got around to finishing, getting waylaid with all the pressures of work. It wasn't just the clutter, the walls were peeling from damp and there was a leak somewhere as the carpet was wet along one wall.

He'd often offered to help renovate when his parents were alive, but his dad wouldn't hear of it. He calculated what needed doing now – boxes into storage or to the tip, leak fixed, carpets and wallpaper replaced. He could get that done within two weeks. But the house going on the market and being sold was out of his hands. Even if it sold straight away, it would never be done before the next mortgage instalment. He had all the time in the world, but the bank didn't.

10

Ryan didn't need a reminder but the bank sent one anyway. He'd been getting his parents' house ready and hadn't even thought about trying his sister again. Feeling despondent, he was surprised when Sandra spoke softly from the doorway:

'I've had an idea. There's the annual reunion next week.'

She held up the letter addressed to Ryan. It wasn't secret, he'd left it open on the kitchen shelf. But he wasn't sure he liked where she was going with it:

'You saved lives. There are people who owe you.'

Ryan didn't want to listen. Even if he went to the reunion, which he'd hardly done since he left the forces, it wasn't meant for calling in favours, didn't she understand that?

'I can't do what you're going to ask me.'

'Why not?'

Ryan wanted to ask: why couldn't she just take over the mortgage temporarily, trust him that he'd get his parents' house sold? Sandra wasn't going to wait for Ryan to reply:

'I thought army guys stick together, bail each other out in times of need.'

In a war situation yes, but not financially, thought Ryan. Even if he asked for help, who would he turn to? He'd never been that big on camaraderie, and had long ago lost touch with all his old comrades. And none of the men would be in a position to help anyway. Of those who'd stayed in, most had got fucked up in Gulf War Two, either physically or mentally, most of the lads were on disability benefit of some kind or other. Others like himself, who had long been out of the forces, worked to survive, same as any other civilian, so how exactly would they have any spare money floating about? Sandra just didn't get it.

There was only one person who would be financially stable – Ryan's former Lieutenant General, a guy every soldier despised. Edward Cameron should never have become Lieutenant General but had been given the position by his father, who had connections in the army, royalty and government.

Lieutenant General Edward Cameron had been good at telling people what to do, Ryan would give him that. The man seemed to think it was his right to give orders to others. But Cameron had been useless in every other aspect. And that was being generous. With his pig-headed bluster, Cameron had been determined to show Ryan's unit who was the boss. Soldiers had been killed because of Cameron's actions.

Ryan always tried to forget what had happened, but he had never forgiven Cameron. To top it all, the hypocrite had ended up rewarded for services to his country.

As so often, it was as if Sandra had read his mind, pointing to the General's name on the letter:

'Look, Ed's CEO of South West National now.'

Ryan squirmed. He hated it when she referred to the Lieutenant General by his abbreviated Christian name. She'd always been enthralled by his supercilious flirting, 'call me Ed, old girl, Ryan's a very lucky egg, what...' He had hated the way she hung on the old coward's every word. The last time they'd met up was fifteen years ago and Sandra was still calling him Ed as if they were close acquaintances.

Ryan hadn't known that Edward Cameron was CEO of the same bank that had just put him into liquidation. Now that he did, he couldn't stop the surge of anger that flowed through him. The same bastard who had ordered Ryan's unit into a death-trap was also head of the bank that had fucked him over.

Ryan knew that Cameron had gone on to have some sort of liaison role between the British Army and MoD. Every few years, Cameron's name cropped up on the news, never in a good way. A few years after Gulf War Two, it was alleged that Cameron had been involved in the sale of weapons to Iraq. He'd denied it and had somehow got it hushed up.

It was at that point that Ryan stopped going to the reunions. Whether Cameron was guilty or not, the hypocrisy made him sick. British soldiers had died at the hands of weapons sold to Iraqis by British manufacturers.

Cameron's name had also come up in connection with government money meant for the army vanishing and something else about fake bomb detection equipment being bought by the army. Ryan had tuned out as he simply didn't want to know. All the bad press obviously hadn't harmed Cameron if he was now CEO of South West National.

Ryan knew what Sandra wanted him to do, but he couldn't do it.

'You want me to ask for financial help from a man who betrayed his country?'

'What are you talking about, he served with you.'

'And then sold weapons to Iraq.'

'Oh, that was never proven.'

'What about his stupidity getting people killed in Kuwait? That can be proven because I was there. He'd be dead himself if it wasn't for me.'

'Exactly. He owes you.'

Ryan waved a dismissive hand:

'I haven't been to a reunion for fifteen years.'

'That won't matter. Come on, we'll go together, make an occasion of it.'

Sandra smiled at Ryan. He looked at his wife sadly. If he said no, he knew how she'd react. But if he agreed, he wouldn't feel great – about himself or her for making him do it. It was lose, lose, whichever way you looked at it.

Ryan felt awkward in his dress uniform. It had been

kept in a vacuum-sealed bag but he'd changed shape over the years, the uniform too tight in some places, too loose in others. He was also apprehensive about seeing ex comrades after so long. But he needn't have been. A stocky guy in uniform was coming straight over to Ryan and Sandra:

'Cliff, you Jack bastard!'

Ryan grabbed a handshake with Jack Jones. Jack was the Cardiff cadet who had given Ryan his nickname of 'Cliff.' Ryan hadn't been called that name for fifteen years. Jack looked appraisingly at Sandra:

'And who's this? You traded in your wife for a younger model?'

Jack winked at Sandra. Sandra smiled as she rolled her eyes. Jack hadn't changed. But she was all for Ryan getting his spirits up with some banter:

'I'll leave you boys to it for a minute while I get some drinks.'

Sandra wanted to encourage Ryan to get talking with Ed, and if that meant a bit of Dutch courage was needed, she'd provide it. As she went over to the drinks table, she spotted Ed at the other end of the room, two other men laughing at something he said. She was tempted to use her skills on Ed, but knew she had to let Ryan try his way. She appreciated the effort Ryan was making and didn't want to completely undermine him.

Ryan watched Sandra, saw her spot Lieutenant General Edward Cameron and felt a stab of unease. Jack slapped Ryan on the shoulder, getting his attention.

'Seriously Cliff, Sandra looks great. Amazing, you've been together since you were kids, haven't you?'

Ryan nodded. He wasn't going to say that for the first time in their marriage, they were at a crisis. He turned the focus on Jack:

'What about you, still married?'

'Twice divorced, two kids with each. Love them all to bits, the kids that is. Just wish they weren't so bloody expensive to maintain. I pay what I can, but I just can't keep up with the payments. Got both my exes hounding me daily. The first one is taking me to court next month, which is a bit bloody ironic because I work there as a security guard.'

'What happened to your security firm?'

'Went tits up. How's your business?'

In the face of Jack's ebullience, Ryan couldn't but help open up:

'Got liquidated a few weeks ago.'

'Fuck man, welcome to the party.'

Jack nodded over to where Lieutenant General Edward Cameron stood with his guffawing companions:

'Meanwhile General Fuckwit's just given himself a million pounds bonus as CEO of South West. Nice life for some.'

This was news to Ryan:

'A million pounds?'

'Don't you watch the news?'

'Jack, I've been so busy trying to save my business I've hardly had time to piss.'

'Well, the bastard's up to his old tricks. What I

don't get is his bank was only just bailed out by the Government. You know how much for? Thirty four billion. So as taxpayers, we've just paid for his bonus.'

Ryan felt the anger mount. He knew about the government bail out because Kristine had told him, but hadn't wanted to think about it because he simply couldn't see what he could do about it. He was just left in impotent rage. His business had been liquidated by Cameron's bank, which was itself in debt. Instead of being punished like Ryan, Cameron had rewarded himself with a million pounds bonus. Ryan shook his head in disbelief:

'How does he get away with it?'

'Like everything else he's got away with – friends in high places. First time he fucked up was when he bought all those fake bomb detection kits for the army. Turned out years later, they were golf ball detectors. Cameron claimed his innocence, but it was his Oxford chum who sold the stuff to him. I mean, fuck, think of all the times you checked for bombs and it was all clear. How do you know if you were using fake equipment or you just got lucky?'

Ryan started to breathe hard as he thought about one particular incident. Did that explain things? Jack was going on:

'And what about the missing millions from the government that was never explained? A hundred million that went towards advanced, high-tech military hardware. In the accounts of the next year, only half of that money could be accounted for. The other half had simply disappeared. Who was in charge of it at the time? Lieutenant General Edward Cameron.

'But the worst of it was his involvement in selling weapons to the Iraqis. The second time we went over, we were being killed by weapons he'd fucking sold them.'

Ryan couldn't grasp what he was hearing:

'How come he hasn't been done for it?'

'He comes from privilege doesn't he? Every time, he's had some friend in Government to back him up. See that guy with him now, that's Sir Howard Pilkington, he's not even army so what the fuck's he doing here? They turn up at each others' events to make themselves look important: got his knighthood for services to industry, whatever the fuck that means. What I think it means is he made a shitload of money while he was in the MoD, co-incidentally attending the same meetings as our beloved General during the arms to Iraq scandal. Sure, he was forced to resign at the time, but it hardly damaged his career. Now, he's CEO of Southern Gas and Electric.

'When they were accused of profiteering, they both used the same excuse, claiming it was all down to their friend Henry Foxton. But why was Foxton at their MoD meetings in the first place? And why did they both receive a donation of a half a million pounds from Foxton? It's all bullshit.'

Jack tried to calm himself down:

'I know, I shouldn't let it bother me, got enough of my own shit to deal with. But I'm not making this stuff up.'

Ryan tried to contain his own fury as he listened to Jack. He had known in general about Cameron's profiteering, but not in detail. It made him sick. Even sicker that Sandra was making him ask Cameron for help.

The only thing convincing Ryan to go through with it was that Cameron owed people. He owed Ryan for saving his life, he owed the dead soldiers he had got killed and he owed the whole nation's population for ripping the country off. The least Cameron could do was help out a former soldier.

Ryan hated the idea of asking anyone for help, especially a man like Edward Cameron, a man Ryan despised. But if there was anyone in this life who owed Ryan, it was the Lieutenant General.

Sandra came over with a whiskey in one hand, water in the other. Feeling thirsty, Ryan reached for the glass of water and downed it in a few gulps. Sandra nudged him to go over and talk to the Lieutenant General. Did she even realise how much this was gnawing away at his pride? He damped down the thought, he was doing this for the family. It was time to man up. He took the whiskey from Sandra, swigged a hit and gave her back the glass. Leaving Sandra in Jack's company, Ryan strode over to where Lieutenant General Edward Cameron was holding court with Sir Howard Pilkington.

Lieutenant General Edward Cameron didn't look too healthy. You expected a man with his name and reputation to look different – a man who sat at the top tables. He'd let himself go since the army, and he was already running to fat back then. He made a person look at him when he walked in, it was the sense of entitlement, the breeding, but once the person had looked, Cameron wasn't that different than anybody else. Most of the small coterie around him were trying to act natural and somebody would laugh every once in a while at some unpleasant remark or other.

Cameron glanced at Ryan and gave a hearty hand shake:

'Ah, here's a hero from years past.'

Cameron was clearly having trouble remembering Ryan's name, though he tried his luck as he explained to Sir Howard Pilkington:

'Nicknamed The Edge because he always went right up to it.'

Ryan corrected him:

'Cliff.'

'Sorry?'

'My nickname was Cliff, not The Edge.'

'Oh, yes, quite so.'

Cameron peered narrowly at Ryan. He didn't like to be contradicted. Ryan stood awkwardly, not knowing how to proceed. With a condescending smile, Sir Howard Pilkington broke the silence:

'Yes, I think I can recall your deeds. Saved a few lives I believe, well done, bloody good effort.'

Sir Howard turned to Cameron:

'Didn't he even save your bacon one time?'

Edward Cameron offered a nervous laugh:

'I wouldn't say saved my life, but yes, he got me out of a tricky situation or two, certainly earned his medal. It's the chaps who died that I feel for. I would have sacrificed my life for theirs, but it was a very difficult decision to choose which vehicle to go to first.'

Ryan stared at Cameron. Had the guy completely forgotten how things had happened? Or had he just got used to the lie he'd told so many times? It was only one person's fault that the other vehicle got blown up – Lieutenant General Edward Cameron. It was his sole decision for the unit to go in and the other vehicle had got hit before Ryan could get anywhere near it.

The men had warned Cameron that they were driving into an ambush in insurgent territory, but he'd dismissed it as nonsense and questioned their bravery.

Ryan could sense Jack and some of the other men looking over, waiting to see how he would react to Cameron's comments. It made Ryan think back to the incident he always tried not to think about…

At the cross section of streets, one armoured vehicle was already up in flames, bits of body parts strewn across the shredded metal. The other armoured vehicle, containing Cameron, was stuck in front of the blown up one. It couldn't move forward because Ryan had detected a bomb wired up in the dust.

In his bomb disposal gear, Ryan focused solely on disconnecting the right wires. All around him soldiers were firing at insurgent snipers that kept popping up through windows. Bullets shattered glass and pinged off metal. Men shouted. It was chaos.

As Ryan worked on the wiring, he heard a dull

thud by his feet. He glanced down and saw the lifeless body of another soldier, blood seeping out of a neck shot. Ryan had to ignore it. He took a breath and disconnected the final wire. With no explosion, the tank rumbled on as fast as it could, the surviving unit using it as cover until they made it to safety. They'd lost four men.

Cameron had never taken responsibility for their deaths. Back in the UK, he'd made a point of making the surviving members publicly known as heroes. He thought it was this that had bought the soldier's silence, but he was wrong. It was simply because you didn't go against one of your own, and like it or not that included Lieutenant General Edward Cameron.

Ryan came out of his reverie. Cameron was waiting impatiently:

'So what can I do for you?'

'I wanted to talk with you for a minute, alone if possible.'

Cameron shrugged:

'Bad form old boy, it's a party, spit out what you want to say.'

'Well, it's about my business.'

'What business?'

'Morgan's Security Systems, your bank just foreclosed on us.'

Cameron's face reddened, always a clear giveaway that his temper was about to get the better of him:

'Say what you want then move on and mingle.'

'Well, we were talking – me and my wife. You know who I mean, Sandra. We thought you might be able to help?'

'You came here to tell me that?'

'Well we were talking about it…'

Ryan looked around the assembled gathering but no-one would hold his gaze, eyes shifting uncomfortably to the floor. Ryan struggled on:

'…and I thought, why don't I see you about it?'

'You want me to pay you some money, make good your foreclosure? You want me to write you a cheque right now, is that it?'

'No, if you'd just take the time to listen a minute.'

'Look Ryan, times are tough, we're all in it together. God knows I'm struggling too. But it's a pretty bad show to rock up here and buttonhole me for money to save your struggling little business. I run a tight ship at South West and if one of my managers has pulled the rug on you, well you must have had it coming.'

Sir Howard Pilkington shook his head in disbelief:

'Good God man, have you no self-respect?'

Ryan couldn't do this. He glanced at Sandra who was now by his side, his humiliation complete. She nodded encouragement. Ryan swallowed, his pride sinking to his stomach as he asked:

'I'm not asking for money. I'm just asking if your bank needs any security system work?'

Cameron laughed nervously. Gesturing at all the other soldiers in the room, he spoke loudly enough for them all to hear:

'I really do feel terribly sorry for your situation old chap, but it seems to me it's of your own making. I can hardly go around giving jobs to every soldier that was once under my command and has fallen on hard times. We are all of us struggling to make ends meet.'

'All of us? Strange, because I heard you just gave yourself a million pounds bonus.'

Sir Howard once again butted in:

'How dare you be so insolent to your superiors!'

Ryan ignored Sir Howard Pilkington and stared into the bloodshot eyes of Lieutenant General Edward Cameron. What did Cameron want, for Ryan to get down on his knees and beg? The man thought he was so high and mighty but he wasn't even a man. He was spineless and hypocritical, a coward and a crook. It should be the other way around, Cameron begging, for his life. Ryan envisaged making it happen.

As if reading his thoughts, Cameron piped up, playing to the crowd:

'Look, it's a reunion and Ryan's obviously had a little too much to drink, no hard feelings.'

Cameron dug a business card out of his wallet and leant in conspiratorially towards Ryan:

'I can't promise anything, but if you email me a CV, I'll see what I can do about some security guard work.'

Ryan took the card. He was unable to look Sandra in the eyes, but he looked at Cameron:

'Guess it's just Oxford pals who help each other out.'

As Ryan led Sandra away, Sir Howard spoke loud enough for him to hear:

'The man's a bloody disgrace Ed, you ought to bar the bugger from attending any further reunions.'

Lieutenant General Edward Cameron nodded absently. Watching Ryan leave, he wondered if he had just made a big mistake.

Ryan and Sandra drove from the Sandhurst army base to their Swansea home without saying a word. Sandra nearly opened her mouth, but seeing how Ryan's face had hardened into an unbreakable concrete mask, she thought better of it and refrained. Instead, she concentrated on the road, at the wheel as Ryan wasn't insured to drive the Mercedes. It wasn't Ryan's fault that Ed hadn't offered anything. Maybe, in retrospect, it would have been better if she had got Ed alone, flirted a little, then laid it all out. What it meant now she didn't want to think about, but she knew she would, she had to go to her fall back plan. What choice did she have?

Staring out of the side window, Ryan didn't know who to be livid with. He was furious at himself for even attempting the humiliating request to Cameron, but just as angry at Cameron for being a pompous prick, not to mention at Sandra for pushing him to do it in the first place.

The rest of the week was spent in similar silence. Ryan was used to his own, but not to Sandra's. When the repossession order came through, Sandra spoke up:

'I'll leave it to you to tell Gerard.'

He made the call, thinking Gerard shouldn't mind about the house as he was always banging on about how money wasn't important. His son was in fact very taken aback by the news, making Ryan feel guilty for his dismissive thoughts. Doubly so when Gerard grew concerned for his parents, Gerard ready to come and help with the move to Townhill. Ryan insisted he didn't need to, that he should concentrate on his final exams. After the call, Ryan told Sandra:

'He's fine with it.'

Sandra just scowled at him. Ryan could see that she blamed him. He realised that they'd never really had any difficulties in their marriage to test them before now. It must have been hard for her when he was in Kuwait, waiting to see if he would come back alive, but they were short stints and they were both young.

This was the first time they'd ever been under any real pressure. He knew he could remain calm and not panic. She wasn't dealing with it so well. He thought speaking would only lead to arguments so he reasoned that all he could do was to be rock solid. This might be enough to get her back on side, maybe she'd see sense and finally agree to take on the mortgage, and give him a chance to get back on his feet.

With no other options, he'd got his parents' house quickly habitable. The task to focus on now was packing and moving. He'd never been much of a hoarder and found he just had a set of everything he needed – a garage full of tools that were easily packed, exercise equipment likewise. His clothes divided into work gear and casual wear, all bought by Sandra.

Sandra packed all her personal items – clothes, jewellery, cosmetics etc. For kitchen utensils and the like, she hired in help.

On the day of the move, Ryan had his boxes ready for the self-drive van he'd hired. Sandra had left early without leaving a message. He packed his stuff and waited, not knowing what of hers she wanted where. Her mobile went to voicemail and she didn't respond to his texts so he dropped his load off first, then drove back to Mumbles.

The driveway was blocked by a huge removal truck that he hadn't ordered.

11

Harris & Sons was blazed across the removal van's side. Ryan had seen the name before. It was the same removal company that had been parked outside Morgan's when they'd all been clamped. He guessed removals did well in a recession. It was a bit of a coincidence though.

Two beefed-up guys were bringing out a sofa, a designer one that Sandra had ordered. The two young guys looked like brothers and both looked like they played rugby, one with an out of joint nose and the other with cauliflower ears. Ryan presumed they were the sons in the company's name. They glanced his way as they tossed the sofa into the van.

Ryan moved towards the house. It felt like he was going in slow motion, knowing that he was about to find out something bad. He found Sandra in the living room, giving instructions to a guy Ryan's age, presumably the father in Harris & Sons.

Ryan realised he had briefly spoken with the man

the morning they'd got clamped, asking how long the van would be in the parking bay. The man's face had been half hidden with a newspaper as he gruffly answered 'all morning'. Ryan waited while Sandra finished off:

'That's it thanks, Jim. The rest is to go to the other address.'

The name Jim Harris set off a childhood memory for Ryan. There had been a Jim Harris in school, Huw's best friend in fact. The man turned. Ryan recognised him now. It was definitely the same Jim Harris. He'd always been an ugly bastard. Jim chewed gum as he eyed Ryan, a snide smile at the corner of his mouth as he moved past Ryan.

It came back to Ryan. Huw and Jim had been part of the same gang. They were the fatties while Ryan and Evan were the skinnies, one lot into rugby while the other pair was into running. Jim had been a real bully at school, Huw's henchman when they went around collecting money from other kids. Huw and Jim had tried it on with Ryan and Evan, but they had always made sure they didn't get isolated and didn't take shit. That shit was so long ago that Ryan had forgotten all about it.

Ryan watched through the window as the Harris & Sons removal van drove out of the drive. He was sure now that the whole clamping event had been a set up by Huw. It was simply too much of a coincidence that Huw's best mate from school had been there at the same time. It was vindictive, but there was nothing he could do about it now.

Ryan brought his attention back to Sandra. She didn't look at him as she busied herself with a check list. Ryan made the first move:

'You found a storage place then?'

Sandra quickly looked his way and attempted a smile:

'Sorry, I should have told you.'

She looked quickly away.

If Ryan hadn't already deduced something was wrong with the situation, he was sure aware of it now. She'd hardly spoken with him for the last two weeks and now her first sentence was an apology.

Ryan scanned the living room. All the furniture was gone, just several boxes containing Sandra's personal items left against one wall. And if she was using Harris & Sons rather than Ryan's self-drive, the 'other address' wasn't his parents' place.

Even though she didn't need to, Sandra checked the contents of the boxes. Upright and motionless, Ryan could see she was nervous, but he could wait. Sure enough, Sandra's patience snapped first:

'Aren't you going to say something?'

'I understand.'

His calm manner unnerved her further:

'What do you understand?'

'Why you're moving in with Huw.'

Sandra's lips trembled:

'This isn't easy Ryan.'

Ryan shrugged:

'Sure it is. You want a certain lifestyle. I can't provide it anymore and he can.'

Sandra flared, her hand shooting up to slap Ryan, leaving a red hand mark imprinted on the side of his face.

'You bastard.'

Ryan stood impassively, infuriating Sandra even further:

'Can't you even be mad at me?'

With his eyes as hard as the rest of his face, Ryan wondered what she wanted – that he'd reacted quicker and snapped back her arm before her hand had reached his face? And he genuinely did understand, it wasn't just a comment to get to her. In a way, he had played the game. For many years he had won, but now he had lost. He'd always played fairly, never looked down on anyone or taken part in big dick swinging competitions with other males. But he'd always striven to win and to be successful at whatever task he took on. Sandra had loved those qualities in him. Now, he had lost his business and their home. So it followed, she would go too.

Sandra tried to look into Ryan's deadened eyes. Didn't he understand that she still loved him? Couldn't he grab her - argue, make up, make love – then somehow assure her that they could carry on life together? Maybe they could live in the hotel while he got his parents' house sold, start over again. In fact, why hadn't she thought of that before? She'd been too busy being furious with him and letting Huw flatter her. And with that thought, she knew no words would make things better. Ryan would never forgive her. She stood up on her toes, kissed Ryan on the cheek where her handprint was still visible and abruptly rushed out of the house, tears streaming down her cheeks.

Ryan didn't hear the door shut or Sandra's car engine start up. It was the click of the electric timer on the washing machine that broke his trance. Looking around at the empty room, he saw the house for what it was – a construction of floors, walls and ceilings. A place to shelter, nothing more.

Strangely, looking down at Sandra's boxes, he remembered the nomads he'd encountered in Kuwait. It had been an almost surreal meeting as the small army unit trekked past the nomads on their camels, heading in the opposite direction. No words had been spoken, just brief eye contact as both groups passed each other on the windswept plain.

Ryan imagined they shared a silent bond, both nomads and soldiers able to travel and live with just the bare necessities. The other guys in his unit made jokes about the 'camel jockeys' but Ryan was in awe. No, the nomads weren't equal, they were superior. They didn't need tracking devices to make sure they were going the right way or long range walkie-talkies to keep in contact with command. They had all the command of the land they needed.

Ryan snapped out of his reverie. With his belongings already transported, he might as well move on to his new place of shelter.

In the living room of his parent's old house, Ryan found himself standing in a similar position to the one he'd been in at his now ex house. The floor was carpeted instead of laminated, the front windows flat rather than bay – though they offered a better view of the sea far below. Why had his parents always lived with net curtains closed?

His newly placed boxes were against one wall and his parents' against another. He'd quickly fitted a new carpet and re-papered the walls but hadn't had time to sort out which of his parents' stuff was to be dumped and which to be given to charity.

He decided this would be his next task. He had to have a task or he would be lost. He didn't want to think long term yet. He had no job and, apart from a thousand-odd pounds in cash, no money, not to last him for long without work anyway. But there was no way he could go on benefits, there was a part of him that wouldn't sanction it and fought against asking for that kind of help. He felt as if he was running on auto pilot and tried to get his mind in order as to what he needed to accomplish in order to survive.

He didn't need to pay rent but bills would soon come in for the gas and electricity he'd re-connected. As soon as the energy company found out he was bankrupt, the utilities would be cut. But that was okay, summer was coming with longer days so he wouldn't need lights and he could cook on a fire in the back garden if necessary. And meanwhile he could turn the garden into a vegetable patch.

Knowing he would survive, Ryan turned his attention to the boxes. Unpacking the first one, he found his dad's old videos, not newly bought films but taped from TV. A box for the tip, thought Ryan, then stopped – suddenly remembering his dad trying to get him as a teenager to watch the old black and white films with him. Back then, Ryan hadn't been interested, preferring to be outside.

Ryan took out some of the videos and read the faded hand-written titles. 'On Dangerous Ground' – was that where Ryan was? Not compared to his stints in Kuwait. 'The Set Up' – just how Sandra and Huw had stitched him up, though he was as much to blame for letting it happen. 'Odds Against Tomorrow' – who knew what they were?

On the side of the video box, Ryan's dad had meticulously listed director and cast – Robert Ryan in every film. This was his dad's favourite actor, Ryan's name coming from him rather than because it was typically Welsh.

Ryan had always tuned out when his dad had started going on about politics but he remembered what he said about his namesake. Apparently he'd spent his early life as a rancher then in the military before becoming an actor, turning pacifist and standing up to the Un-American committee in the fifties that hounded Communist sympathisers. Yet he always played tough, often dislikeable characters. Ryan's dad had admired the man and marvelled at how he could play characters he in fact despised.

Ryan hadn't sat and watched a film for years. Sandra was the film buff in the family, sitting with a glass of wine as she played a DVD on the plasma screen. Ryan slid the clunky video cassette out of its flimsy cardboard sleeve and inserted it into the video player. Would the machine still work?

He turned on the huge old telly and almost smiled as the picture slowly flickered into life, glowing on the curved screen. It might be old, but his dad had made sure any electrical appliance in the house was long lasting. Ready to watch, Ryan glanced at the sunlight coming through the windows and closed the curtains. Now he understood his parents – they'd liked watching films in the dark.

He sank into the old sofa and watched the first film – 'The Set Up'. Robert Ryan played an ageing boxer supposed to take a fall, his wife leaving because she couldn't stand seeing him get beat to a pulp anymore. Out of pride, the guy managed to win the fight, but then struggled to get to his wife before the betting syndicate got to him.

When the credits came up, Ryan was the nearest he'd ever been to tears. The character was a hero and didn't deserve his fall. And his wife loved him, she just couldn't bear to watch. To avoid thinking about Sandra, Ryan put on the next film – 'On Dangerous Ground'.

This time the actor played a ruthless cop, brutalised by all the violence he witnessed in the city. Sent out to the wilderness to track a killer, he met a blind woman full of love and peace – the cop having to choose between his ferocious pursuit and redemption. After, Ryan just sat there. The film was maybe fifty years old, but the themes were just as relevant today. Could you combat violence and corruption though peace?

Ryan stood up, opened the curtains and blinked. It

was late in the day but still daylight. Time for his daily run. Ryan was determined to carry on his routine despite all the upsets of the past few weeks.

Ryan usually went for a run when Sandra was at home so he would normally leave his keys inside. Now, he was on his own. His shorts didn't have pockets and he wasn't going to run with the keys in his hand, so he left them under a stone in the back garden – just like when he was a kid, innocent days before homes were fitted out with security systems. Not Ryan's parents' house of course, as his dad had always declined the offer of a free alarm. Ryan did his stretches, shook his long limbs loose and set off.

As he jogged at a steady pace through Townhill, Ryan took in his surroundings. Each street had at least one house with windows all smashed or boarded up, either way an empty dwelling. People who had lost their jobs? Or had their benefits cut more like. Why didn't people try harder, find work of some kind? If they did, maybe the country wouldn't be in the mess it was.

And thinking of mess, most of the lived in houses were completely unkempt – paint flaking off the outside walls, broken toys left in the front garden, rubbish bags ripped and overflowing on the pavement outside. Though this impoverished dereliction didn't stop the houses from having Sky TV dishes attached. In the doorway of one house Ryan passed, a young mum who could have been at work shouted at a small girl who should have been in school:

'I told you not to fucking tell anyone our business.'

The sad-looking girl retreated into the house. Her mum followed, fag in one hand, mobile in the other. What he saw made Ryan angry. How did people get like this? Ryan had been brought up in the same area and it hadn't affected him badly. Nor his friend Evan. Maybe it was different generations, but then what about his sister? She'd fled from Townhill in search of a better life, but still lived on benefits even after her move – in a one bedroom flat in London instead of a terraced house in Swansea. She would have had a better deal if she'd stayed.

People didn't appreciate what they had. Everyone had their mobile phones and Sky TV, their designer wear and brand new cars – even if they couldn't afford it. Everything was on credit, until it got called in. And now, because the whole world had been doing the same, it was all coming crashing down.

Ryan thought again of the nomads. They hadn't needed any kind of TV or phone. How would they react if they were put into the current economic situation? He felt sure they wouldn't sit around spending benefit money on cigarettes and alcohol. They would move to a piece of land where they could set up camp, build a fire and look at the sky.

As his thoughts turned more positive, Ryan passed a well-kept house – hedge trimmed, grass mown, house painted. The car parked outside had Latvian number plates. Ryan briefly thought of Kristine. Now that Sandra had left him, he was a free man. But he knew he wouldn't phone her. He respected her as his former employee and that is how it would stay. He thought that the tabloid version of foreigners ruining the country wasn't true, but that the stereotype of East Europeans being hard workers was.

Maybe people would look at those who worked hard and follow their example. But this fleeting hope was extinguished as Ryan carried on down the steep street into town and saw three young men sitting unsteadily on a low wall, all with cans of lager in their hands. One of the men shouted across to Ryan:

'Go on baldy!'

Fury exploded inside Ryan. What gave these drunken yobs the right to shout insults at him? He'd worked hard all his life, paying tax for them to live off Government benefits. Either work and contribute to society or don't bother existing, thought Ryan. But then to his shame, he saw that one of the men was Johnny. He almost stopped, but Johnny wasn't even in a state to recognise him. Guilt flooded through Ryan. Johnny was such a talented young man and now after just a few weeks out of work he was sitting with the dregs of society. But was it Ryan's fault?

He'd given the boy a job in the first place, when there was no other work around. Should he have stopped, though? Taken Johnny back to the house, sobered him up? And then what? What could he offer? Nothing. Besides, Ryan wasn't his dad – he had his own son to think of, and he was proud that Gerard lived enthusiastically in hope of a journalistic career despite the probability that it wouldn't happen.

More despondent than angry now, Ryan reached

the city centre. The first thing he noticed was the old department store on the corner, closed up for over two years but the sign still there – 'Bevans of Swansea, established 1952'. That made the building the same age as Ryan. When he was a kid, his parents would take him there on his birthday, buying a watch one year, running shoes another. Ryan felt bad that he hadn't continued the tradition with Gerard, but his son had been into things other shops sold cheaper. Bevans couldn't cope with the competition. He'd known about the closure but somehow he'd never really taken in the deserted building before now. How had everyone, including himself, let it all go to ruin?

It was as if his eyes were finally open, Ryan now seeing the glass-fronted new build just off the main shopping street. Built about the same time Bevans had closed up, the building still remained empty – the 'To Let' sign hanging uselessly in a top window.

Usually Ryan ran alongside the beach, from his Mumbles home down to the docks and back. He hadn't planned his route this time, but what he saw made him want to stick to the streets rather than be by the sea. He loved the city he'd been born in, but the centre of it was bloody ugly. Bombed by the Germans in World War Two, it had been grimly put together in a very hotchpotch way after that. Maybe it needed to be bombed again. Start from scratch.

Back out of the centre and heading west, Ryan found himself passing his old office – another minor monument to decay. He pounded on along the pavement, wanting to feel the hard concrete under his feet rather than soft sand. He still had a rage inside to burn off.

Every few strides, Ryan had to move to the left or right so that he didn't step in the dog shit that littered the pavement. There was simply no civic pride anymore. It wasn't just about thinking of other people or your own city. You might step in your own dog's shit, so surely it made sense to clean it up. He didn't get it.

Another thing he noticed was that so many cars passed by with a hubcap missing. Had people become lazier than they used to be? Or was it that in tough times, people didn't even have a spare few pounds to ensure they had a full set of hubcaps? He didn't know the answers, just found it depressing.

Ryan knew he'd pass the Mumbles house with the direction he'd gone, but didn't glance at it wistfully – just thought that he still had the keys and hadn't deactivated the CCTV. He should go and do that one day.

Starting to think ahead with his run and knowing the woods was a few streets north, he went that way. Ryan finally relaxed as he ran through the leafy track, trees on either side. Strangely, his mind took him back to Kuwait and the time when he ran after the mine planter.

It was on the Iraqi border, a dusty track that joined two villages, one in each country. Ryan was there with the unit to check it was safe for them to go through, and was getting his equipment ready when he spotted the Iraqi guy hiding behind some rubble.

The guy took off, at pace but not too fast – zig-zagging along the track. If it was the guy who had planted the mines, the unit wanted him – he was more useful alive than dead. Plus, it wasn't safe to shoot in the mined area.

Without thinking, Ryan ran after the man. Ignoring the shouts to stop from his fellow soldiers, Ryan tracked the Iraqi's every step – one foot wrong and he'd lose more than his feet. Sweat poured down his face, he had to quicken his pace so that he could see exactly what pattern the man ran in. The two men came out the other end one after another, the Iraqi wide eyed and incredulous as he looked behind – Ryan rugby tackling the man to the earth.

An uproar started as villagers poured out of their stone houses, but Ryan had his weapon out and the guy held under him. He didn't want to kill anyone, just wanted the man to come with him and show exactly where every mine was so they could be dismantled. It took a good while to get the point across but eventually the villagers dispersed. Ryan's fellow soldiers were amazed when he turned up with the Iraqi and wanted to give the guy a beating. Ryan made sure the man wasn't ill-treated and was released once the track had been cleared.

That was during his first stint, there as the ground troops went in, Ryan pre-checking the land. He was back less than a year later once the war was over, this time to clear any leftover bombs. And that was his two times. Because he'd left the forces once Sandra was pregnant, he hadn't gone to Yugoslavia, Afghanistan or Gulf War Two and had managed to avoid much of the trauma more of the longer-serving soldiers had endured.

He'd done his job twice, both times extremely successfully, and had got out. It had been a practical decision. If he was honest, he'd enjoyed the adrenalin of bomb disposal. He knew he was fearless and good at it. But if he was going to have a family there was no point being an absent father or even a dead one, as no matter how good he was there was always a chance that one day the wiring would flummox him. He regretted nothing, neither being in the army nor leaving it. Though now his son had more or less left home and his wife definitely had, it made Ryan wonder what it was all for.

With that thought lingering, Ryan came out of the woods into upmarket Killay as he knew he would – the wealthy area full of large detached houses and four wheel drives. And just as he knew he would, Ryan could see Huw's house up ahead.

12

Huw's house was the last one before the land turned into the Gower. Using the Harris & Sons removal truck that was parked outside as a screen, Ryan ran fast past the house on the opposite side of the road. Out of sight, he quickly crossed then doubled back to the side fence.

Peering around the end of the fence, Ryan couldn't see into the house but there in the drive were Sandra and Huw's two Mercedes side by side – same age and model, looking like they were meant to be parked together.

Ryan realised he'd been staring at them when he heard voices. He ducked back behind the fence as Jim Harris and his sons came out. He didn't even want to think of the humiliation of being found in this position so flattened himself into the long grass and snaked commando style to the far end of the fence, abutting the railings of an abandoned church. Hiding behind an electricity mast, Ryan noticed the electricity cable running to the back of Huw's house.

It was strange noticing such details, almost like he was back on a recon mission. From his prone position, Ryan saw Jim Harris and his two huge sons move towards the removal van. The younger son stopped:

'I need a piss before we leave.'

The younger son swaggered back towards the house. His dad called after him:

'Just go by the fucking fence.'

The younger son shrugged and changed direction, wading through the long grass. Ryan watched in horror as Jim Harris's son got closer. He just had to hope the lad didn't come all the way back. He had no such luck. It was embarrassing, but Ryan would have to show himself unless he wanted to be urinated on. Ryan rose from the grass just as the Harris lad was unzipping, the young man exclaiming:

'What the fuck?'

At the van, Jim Harris and his older son looked over. They immediately stalked towards Ryan, who was trying to placate the younger son:

'I was just taking a rest…'

The younger Harris lad cut Ryan off as he looked at his father and brother:

'Fucking pervert was lying in the grass, trying to get a look at my dick or something.'

Jim Harris' face got even uglier than it already was:

'You dirty bastard. No wonder your wife left you.'

Ryan tried to calm proceedings:

'Come on Jim, it isn't like that…'

'Oh, Jim now is it? I don't remember we were ever

on friendly terms in school.'

Ryan frowned. What was it with Huw and Jim, had they never got past their school days? He took in Jim and his two sons. No discussion was going to work with them and he was obviously outnumbered in any fight, so it was best just to get out of there.

'Guys, I'm going to carry on with my run.'

Ryan set off, his jog taking him past the Harris men before they could do anything. He didn't get far though, one of the sons thudding him to the ground in a rugby tackle. Dazed, Ryan tried to push himself up, only for two huge weights to land on his back, squeezing the breath out of him. Winded, Ryan heard Jim Harris speak to his two sons:

'You two keep him there. I've got a feeling Huw might enjoy this.'

With the two sons pressing hard on Ryan's spine, it was difficult to catch his breath, especially as his mouth was full of grass. He struggled but only caused himself more pain. He had to think calmly. It wasn't possible to budge the two lumps. He needed to save his energy and wait until the second when they got off him. That was when he would make his move.

Two shoes stepped in front of Ryan's eyes and he heard Huw's voice:

'Well, well, what have we got here, a peeping Tom? What was it you wanted to see – me fucking Sandra or David's dick?'

It wasn't as if Ryan could answer with his face pushed down hard into the dust. Jim Harris instructed his sons:

'Get him up boys.'

Ryan felt the Harris sons get off. He knew they'd reach down to haul him up. Before they did, he lunged forward through the grass and grabbed Huw's ankles, toppling him over. Ryan's plan was to drag himself over Huw, leap up and sprint for it, but a searing pain surged through his balls, which felt as if they were about to pop out of his mouth.

The Harris boys yanked Ryan up, each slamming one of Ryan's arms behind his back. He was still reeling from the kick to his balls, his face white with pain. Huw stood and dusted himself, his face red with anger. As if Ryan wasn't winded enough, Huw pummelled a fist into his midriff. It wasn't much of a punch but it still hurt. Jim stepped in.

'Come on Huw, what was that? You need to get yourself back to the gym mate. Like this.'

Jim smashed one into Ryan's side. Ryan would have doubled up, but he was being held upright by Jim's two sons so the punch hurt even more. His eyes became watery. Huw gleefully noticed:

'Oooh, he's going to cry.'

Ryan squinted through the pain and involuntary tears at his surroundings. The wooden fence blocked any view from the house and the removal van stopped anyone seeing from the road. Nobody was going to help him here. While Jim went to the van for something, Huw asked the two lads:

'You two remember wedgies?'

'Yea, used to dish them out in school.'

Jim Harris came back from the van, rope in his

hands:

'Right, lift him up there boys.'

Ryan used what energy he had left to struggle, but he was already overpowered. He felt himself lifted then roughly lowered onto a tree branch that shoved up his shorts and boxers, the branch twisting his underwear tight around his scrotum. As he once more gasped for breath, his arms were spread out and hands tied to the church railings.

Huw, Jim Harris and his two sons stood back to admire their work, all four of them smiling. Jim's younger son hopped about:

'I still need a piss.'

His older brother pointed at Ryan:

'Go ahead. He wanted to see your dick, so why don't you show it to him?'

The younger son smiled, unzipped and pissed all over Ryan's shorts. His brother pointed at Ryan's piss-soaked shorts:

'Looks like he pissed himself, the dirty bastard.'

The four men laughed.

Jim Harris and his two sons walked back to their van while Huw stayed with Ryan. Huw got out his mobile, talking to Ryan as he messed around with it:

'You being the Peeping Tom that you are, thought you might like to hear me and Sandra in action. I recorded this.'

Huw held the mobile to Ryan's ear, Ryan with no choice but to listen to Huw's grunts and Sandra's moans. Thankfully, it was quickly over. Ryan found enough breath to speak:

'That as long as you can last?'

Huw's face went red as he pocketed his mobile:

'At least I can get it up, which is more than you'll be doing for awhile.'

Ryan watched Huw stomp off to the removals van. The men exchanged handshakes, Huw turned to his house and the van drove off. Now, if anyone drove past, it was possible Ryan would be spotted. But he didn't want to be seen in this humiliating position.

Ryan couldn't get his hands free so he would have to get untied via his shorts. His groin was where the main pain was anyway. He thrust forward, felt his balls pulled tighter, thrust again. The branch cracked and his shorts ripped, slowly slipping to his ankles. He was exposed in his underwear but he was no longer stuck. Pushing himself up the railing, Ryan was able to loosen his hands, untying one then the other. He took several deep breaths, used the rope to tie his shorts up and limped gingerly to the end of the fence.

Ryan wanted to be home. He no longer had one he could call his own, but his parents' house would do. He wanted to get there without being seen. He'd just had a lifetime's worth of humiliation and didn't need any more. If he was seen by Sandra, he didn't know if he would cry or go and find Huw and kill him. Peeking around the end of the fence, he didn't see anyone so he stumbled out and past Huw's house without looking at it. Sandra's voice stopped him cold:

'Ryan?'

Ryan slowly turned. Sandra was getting out of her

Mercedes, travel bag in hand. He hadn't spotted her. She must have been bent down inside the car. She looked at him sadly:

'What are you doing here?'

Ryan's jaw throbbed as he tried to formulate an answer. He should just walk on, but he was strangely frozen as Sandra looked at his shorts:

'And why are your shorts tied with rope?'

Ryan remained silent as Sandra stepped closer. He realised he couldn't be humiliated any more. He'd lost everything. His wife was even moving in with the bank manager who had a hand in him losing everything. And he'd just been kicked in the balls, hung up by his underwear and pissed on. There was nowhere lower to go. So he remained impassive as Sandra screwed up her nose:

'And what is that smell?'

Ryan just stared at Sandra. He wasn't going to answer her. His impassivity was jarred by the front door opening. Huw stepped out and sighed:

'What's going on here?'

Sandra glanced at Huw:

'It's okay, I'll deal with it.'

Huw puffed out his chest as he came forward:

'No, no, this needs to be sorted man to man.'

Huw shook his head as he faced Ryan:

'Ryan, you really have to accept the situation. Sandra and me are together now. So run along to your own home, if you've got one to go to.'

Huw pointed at Ryan's rope-tied shorts:

'You look a bit like a hobo. I know this must all be

difficult for you but you should make an effort.'

Sandra intervened:

'Come on Huw, that's enough.'

Ryan simply listened as Huw went on, Huw crinkling his nose:

'Smell like one too, you've really let yourself go.'

Ryan lashed out with his right arm, his hand grabbing Huw by the throat and lifting him off the ground. Sandra shouted:

'Ryan!'

Ryan released his grip. Huw crumpled to the ground and gasped for breath. Sandra stood uselessly between the men. Ryan raised his palms as he backed away. He turned and jogged off as best he could, the pain in his groin bringing tears to his eyes.

A few hours later, Ryan sat on his parents' sofa, just a towel around his waist. The room was starting to darken. The journey back had been a blur, Ryan just about remembering that he'd taken a shorter route and cut out the city centre detour. He'd washed, but the smell of piss was still in his nostrils.

An ice-pack was between his legs. Ryan wasn't sure if a man's balls bruised, but it was good to numb the throbbing ache. His insides hurt and he wasn't sure if a rib had been fractured, but he knew there was no point in going for an x-ray. A cracked rib simply had to heal of its own accord. He also had a split lip, presumably from thudding to the ground in the rugby tackle. But that was a superficial injury. The real injury was to his psyche. Images of revenge kept flashing through his mind.

He needed to stop thinking vengeful thoughts. To take his mind off things, he picked up the video he hadn't watched – 'Odds Against Tomorrow'. But before he could slot the cassette into the machine, there was a knock at the door – it made Ryan jump, he felt unnecessarily alert from the earlier incident and his nerves were on edge.

He limped to the door and swung it open, surprised to see Evan standing there and looking sheepish. The two of them were silent for a second, both with déjà vu. As kids, Evan used to call on Ryan all the time to see if he was coming out. Evan laughed:

'Like back in the day.'

Ryan cracked a smile back and immediately winced, any movement causing pain inside. Evan frowned, sensing Ryan wasn't right but not seeing why. Emotion almost took hold of Ryan:

'I can't come out to play, but I'm just about to watch one of my dad's old films – you want to come in and watch?'

Ryan held the door open wider, but Evan hesitated:

'I can't stay, Julie's already mad at me because I've missed dinner.'

Ryan frowned. So why was Evan here? Ryan realised that Evan was in his work suit. It wasn't a social call. Searching for words, Evan gestured across the bay:

'Always was a great view from here.'

Ryan pointed to the Sky TV dishes on the house opposite:

'Pity people don't appreciate it. The nomads I saw

in Kuwait didn't need Sky TV or mobile phones. They could live with nothing.'

Ryan faced Evan:

'Maybe we all need to live with nothing, start from scratch.'

Evan became awkward:

'Look, I know it must be really difficult…'

Evan didn't finish his sentence. Ryan didn't help him out. They hadn't spoken since the race nearly a month ago. That was normal, but Evan had obviously spoken with Sandra if he knew the situation without Ryan telling him. And now Evan wasn't behaving normally, speaking with concern:

'I didn't know things were so bad.'

'You mean with the business or with Sandra?'

'Either.'

'Nothing you could do either way.'

Evan nodded uncomfortably:

'I'm here because Sandra called me. Huw wanted to make it official, get a restraining order but she persuaded him not to.'

'Restraining order?'

'Says you were prowling around his house then grabbed him by the throat.'

'I didn't prowl.'

Evan looked at his friend directly:

'You're on CCTV Ryan. And Sandra is a witness.'

'I just went for a jog and ended up that way.'

'You weren't jogging when you grabbed Huw by the throat.'

'He provoked me…'

Ryan stopped mid-sentence. Evan looked him over, concerned:

'Ryan, you okay? If something went on, tell me.'

Ryan looked at the ground. What was he going to say, that he'd been wedgied and pissed on? It was humiliating enough that it had happened. He didn't want to relive it by telling anyone. It would make him a telltale if he did say anything. And how would he prove it? Huw, Jim Harris and his two sons would simply deny everything.

With Ryan refusing to say anything, Evan had to warn him off:

'Okay, so you're going to have to stay away from them.'

Ryan nodded. Evan tried to be conciliatory:

'Look, its better I say this to you rather than it go in as an official police complaint. And as your friend, you want to meet any night, have a drink, just call me.'

Ryan nodded again, slower this time. Evan put his hand out to shake, but seeing that Ryan wasn't making a move patted him on the shoulder instead:

'Call me, yeah?'

Ryan's final nod was barely detectable.

13

Two days later Ryan got another unexpected visitor when Gerard turned up at the door. With Ryan surprised and Gerard bewildered, they gave each other an awkward father-son hug, Gerard's satchel almost falling off his shoulder.

Letting his son inside, Ryan didn't bother with the pretence of asking him what he was doing there, knowing Gerard must have talked to Sandra. Gerard confirmed it:

'I talked with mum.'

In the kitchen, Ryan kept his back to Gerard as he filled the kettle. Behind him, Gerard shook his head:

'I couldn't believe it when she told me. I mean all those years together and just to leave for money. She said it wasn't because of that, but what else can it be? I told her I was coming to see you straight away.'

Gerard shifted uncomfortably, said:

'Dad, I can't speak to her for a while.'

Ryan switched the kettle on.

'Don't be hard on your mum.'

This flummoxed Gerard, keeping him quiet. His dad was eerily calm. He'd always been like a rock in any difficulty. Gerard recalled a time as a kid when he'd fallen off a boulder in Caswell and cracked his head. His dad hadn't panicked, but had instantly picked him up, staunched the flow of blood and driven him to hospital – all the while ignoring his mum's histrionics.

It was just that it was all so hard to take in. A few weeks ago, his dad had called to say he'd lost his business and the house. And now his mum phoned to say they'd split up. How had he not seen it coming? They always seemed like such a stable couple. His parents separating made him feel young and vulnerable.

It was always his mum he discussed things with, especially since his granddad's death, but Gerard had instantly sided with his dad – not appreciating what his mum had done. Gerard guessed it was up to his dad though if he wanted to be mad or not.

While Ryan made the tea, Gerard kept his counsel. It was odd being back in his grandparents' house, the kitchen held a lot of happy memories. It was where his gran used to set out homemade Welsh cakes. The living room was where his granddad would talk about his union days, inspiring Gerard in his teens. If it was strange for Gerard being in the house, how did it feel for his dad, aged fifty, and back in the house he was born in? Ryan turned to his son with a cup of tea in each hand:

'You want to watch a film?'

Gerard wondered if his dad was in denial as this was definitely strange behaviour from him. He couldn't ever remember watching a film together. It had been all climbs and runs as a kid, which was great at the time, but once Gerard became interested in journalism and changing society his dad just didn't seem interested. Gerard shrugged and followed his dad into the living room.

Ryan pointed to the box of old videos:

'I found all these – they were your granddad's…'

'The Robert Ryan ones?'

Ryan looked quizzically at his son:

'That's right.'

Gerard beamed:

'Granddad showed me them all.'

'Oh, we don't have to watch one if you've already seen them.'

Ryan was slightly deflated. But Gerard brimmed with enthusiasm:

'No, I'll watch any of them again – I love those old films. Granddad told me how he named you after the actor, said that you even seemed to resemble some of the characters as you got older.'

Ryan's emotions whirled around inside, now shamed that he'd felt annoyed because Gerard had already seen the films. Gerard had come from London out of concern for his dad. Ryan appreciated this, even if he didn't express it.

Gerard held up one of the videos:

'How about Berlin Express, have you seen that?'

Ryan had watched them all in the last few days. Berlin Express was one of his favourites – Robert Ryan trying to unify post-war Germany. It was how people still carried on with their lives amid the devastation that intrigued Ryan.

'Yea, let's watch that.'

Ryan and Gerard sat next to each other on the sofa, watching the film in silence with their cups of tea – not having to tell each other, but both knowing this was a rare shared father-son experience. Ryan smiled inside, but was still mindful of the time. Halfway through the film he told Gerard he had to go and do his daily run. Gerard pressed the pause button on the video player:

'It's only half way through.'

'You don't have to wait for me.'

Ryan left Gerard perplexed as he went to change into his running gear. Gerard left the video on pause. He didn't get his dad. After setting up a nice activity to do together, Ryan abruptly left. Still, he must be going through hell. Gerard would wait for him to come back from his run.

When Ryan returned, running vest drenched in sweat as he jogged to a stop, Gerard was standing by the front gate. Pointing to the west, Gerard said:

'Did you hear that explosion?'

Ryan regained his breath as he looked at the smoke rising across the bay:

'I saw the ambulance and fire engines go past.'

'Wonder what caused it – was a huge bang.'

Gerard's journalistic instincts were telling him to go and find out what had happened. But he felt torn, he was here to support his dad:

'The film's still paused.'

Ryan patted his son on the shoulder and went in to shower.

In the morning, Gerard had just got out of the shower when the doorbell rang. By the time he threw on his jeans, Ryan had already answered it. Evan was facing him solemnly on the doorstep as he read Ryan his rights:

'…but anything you say maybe used against you.'

Gerard bounded over:

'What the hell's going on?'

Evan glanced at Gerard, unaware that Ryan's son was at the house – secretly hoping this would mean an alibi could be provided for Ryan. Keeping it professional, he turned his attention back to Ryan:

'We can do this here, but it would be better down at the station.'

Ryan nodded, looked over his shoulder at Gerard:

'I'll be back soon.'

Gerard stepped forward:

'No way, I'm coming with you.'

Ryan put a hand out to stop his son:

'It's fine.'

Gerard was left to watch as Ryan ducked into the waiting police car, Evan getting in the front with an officer driving.

It only took a few minutes to drive down the hill

to the city centre police station, Ryan and Evan both silent. Evan hoped he was wrong, but was ready to proceed as any police detective should. Though, by reading Ryan his rights straight off the bat, Evan had in fact given him a heads up.

In the interview room, Evan asked Ryan if he required a solicitor present. Ryan declined. With the tape on and another officer present, Evan began the interview:

'Can you tell me where you were last night?'

'At home.'

'And you have someone who can confirm that?'

Ryan nodded:

'Gerard was there – I guess he must have arrived about six.'

Evan felt a great sense of relief. He might lose his friendship with Ryan for bringing him in but if it helped prove him innocent it would be worth it.

'So your son can verify that you were at home the whole of last night?'

'Sure...apart from when I went on my run.'

The feeling of relief quickly evaporated.

'And what time was that?'

'Left the house at seven, got back about eight thirty.'

Any last glimmer of relief faded. The explosion was bang in the middle of Ryan's run. Evan calmly asked his next question:

'What was the route of your run?'

'Down to Mumbles and back.'

'From and back to Townhill?'

'Yep.'

Even if he didn't know how fast Ryan could run, that was too short a distance for an hour and a half.

'That's quite a lengthy amount of time for such a short distance.'

Ryan kept silent. He hadn't been asked a question. Evan's insides churned. He'd skirted around the issue long enough.

'Last night there was an explosion in Killay. As you were informed earlier, a man's body was found and named as Huw Hughes.'

Ryan didn't blink as Evan looked him in the eyes and continued:

'Last week your wife left you and moved in with Huw. The same day as the move, you assaulted Huw and your wife asked me to call on you and ask you to refrain from contacting them both in the future.'

Evan knew Ryan well enough that he would remain calm under pressure and that unless there was a question, a reply wouldn't be forthcoming, but there were procedures to follow.

'You don't seem surprised by Huw's death.'

Evan let that one hang. Ryan remained silent. Evan thought that, yes, Ryan was a guy who could remain unruffled, but to not even bat an eyelid at someone's death was strange, especially with that person being your wife's new lover. Ryan clearly had motive, had already been warned about his threatening behaviour and had no alibi. It didn't look good. Not to mention that if anyone was capable of setting up an explosion it was Ryan.

Evan hadn't ruled out that the explosion was an accident, but he was pretty sure it wasn't. The house was obliterated by the time Evan had arrived, the fire brigade already there and hosing down the remaining flames. An ambulance was parked nearby but wasn't required as the body was charred beyond all recognition - the man was definitely dead.

The first thing he had to organise was to keep Sandra at bay as she pulled up, back from her zumba. Evan allocated a female officer to escort her away, Sandra having to stay the night in her hotel where she remained in a state of shock.

Evan then spent the rest of the night going through the scene. Accidents happened, but the fire brigade said it didn't appear like a normal house fire and the gas company hadn't reported any leak.

Evan's suspicions increased when he checked the debris of the French window, blown by the blast into the back garden. There were fragments of curtain pole but no remains of any curtain. Sure, the fire could have licked up the material but how had bits of the pole blown out with nothing attached? In a phone call with Sandra, he got confirmation that there had been a curtain. As forensics were going through the body, and sifting among the ash, Evan was willing to bet the burnt remains of curtains would be found on or near the body.

After his officers reported that none of the neighbours had seen anyone suspicious by the house, Evan checked with ADT, the security company that had installed Huw's CCTV. The house didn't have live link up but footage recorded onto the system for any future prosecution in case of burglary. When ADT reported back, Evan was sure things weren't right – the CCTV had gone down ten minutes before the explosion. Evan's suspicions were further confirmed when he found that the electricity line to the house had been cut.

Tracking down a suspect hadn't been difficult, his instincts pointed him in the direction of Ryan's door. And now he needed to get some answers:

'Is there a reason why you are not surprised by Huw's death?'

Ryan shrugged:

'Maybe it was Karma – guy got what he deserved.'

Evan raised his eyebrows:

'You believe in Karma?'

'No.'

Evan's heart sank. Ryan wasn't doing himself any favours, coming across as guilty with every answer. It was time to simply ask the question:

'Ryan, did you...?'

Ryan held up his hand as he interrupted:

'I have an alibi.'

'Go on.'

Ryan shifted awkwardly:

'I didn't think about it earlier because... I was somewhere I shouldn't have been.'

Evan waited. Ryan continued:

'I took a break from my run, stopped by my house – my old house. I never disconnected the CCTV – it will show me in it.'

Evan turned to his colleague, nodded for this to be checked and suspended the interview. Ryan was left alone while Evan took a breather. Ryan was a hard rock to climb, both as a friend and suspect. Evan just hoped the CCTV would put him in the clear.

An hour later, Evan released Ryan from the station, stepping outside with him:

'I had to bring you in.'

Ryan nodded:

'I know.'

Evan offered his hand:

'No hard feelings?'

Ryan shook his old friend's hand.

'No, but you believed I did it?'

'Ryan, doing my line of work as long as I have, nothing surprises me.'

'And I guess a jilted husband comes first in a list of suspects.'

Evan shrugged.

'Not to mention the husband being an ex-bomb disposal expert who happens to show no remorse over the death, it not being murder of course…'

Evan gave Ryan a meaningful look:

'…until proven.'

Evan thought that Ryan was one of the calmest people he had ever interviewed. Still, the important thing was that the CCTC footage proved conclusive. At the time of the explosion Ryan clearly entered his old house before sitting mournfully in the garden. With Ryan's body almost shaking as he held back tears, it was awkward viewing – Ryan obviously pining for his wife and home. But it was better than getting revenge and killing his wife's lover.

As Ryan walked away from the station, Evan was left to pursue other enquiries, still convinced Huw's death was murder. That was okay, it was his job. Out of relief for Ryan, he craved a cigarette. If he started up again though, he'd never catch his friend in next year's race.

Gerard was also relieved to see his dad free, shaking his head in disbelief:

'I can't believe he suspected you, he's one of your oldest friends.'

He had unquestioningly believed his dad innocent, which had proven true. But of course the police had to question him. For all sorts of reasons, Ryan would be the prime suspect.

While Ryan was down at the station, Gerard had found out as much as he could – turning on the news, checking the internet on his laptop and calling the police for any information. Once he'd found out what had happened he'd gone over to his mum, holed up in her hotel in a state of shock.

Gerard had never seen his mum looking so frazzled and never known her to be so quiet. He'd been angry at her for leaving his dad, but as she sat there, vulnerable and sobbing convulsively, he comforted her. It was as if she was the child and he was the adult. When she was able to speak, she alternated between disbelief and self pity, even suggesting it was some sort of punishment for her leaving Ryan.

Neither had mentioned Ryan in connection with Huw's death, maybe both not daring to in case it turned out he had done it. Naturally, it was a huge relief that Ryan was innocent, but it didn't help his mum. The man she'd just left her husband for had been blown up. Even with Ryan innocent, she could hardly go to him for comfort. Gerard broached the subject with his dad:

'I saw mum.'

'How's she coping?'

'Naturally she's in shock. She didn't say much and what she did say didn't make much sense. She started going on about how maybe it was some sort of divine punishment.'

Ryan frowned. He'd never known Sandra to be religious, but Huw dying like that must be hard to take.

'I guess she has to turn to something.'

The two of them lapsed into silence.

Later, Ryan insisted that Gerard get back to London and his final exams. Gerard corrected him:

'It's a series of articles rather than exams.'

He'd done the articles on the anti-bank demos and the people involved – showing them not just to be hippies or troublemakers, but from the whole spectrum of society, reflecting the need for change.

Gerard wondered if there was a better story close to home. Was it possible to work in a personal angle of his mum running off with the local bank manager as soon as his dad was in financial difficulties and then the bank manager getting himself killed? It could be a metaphor for people tempted by greed and the common man fucked over, only for the greedy to get their comeuppance. But perhaps that was all going too far, and he guessed his parents wouldn't appreciate it.

'Glad you're innocent dad, otherwise I might have had to write it up.'

'"Jilted husband gets revenge" isn't a unique story.'

Ryan guided his son to the door:

'If I have a story, I'll tell you before anyone.'

Gerard smiled, knowing this was his dad's way of showing affection. Though Ryan's next words surprised him:

'I'll always be proud of you. Take care of yourself.'

Gerard felt tears stinging his eyes as he waved to his dad and walked off toward the station. Ryan's words had seemed strangely final, but that was probably because he wasn't used to expressing his feelings. His Dad had been through a lot in a short period of time. Gerard exhaled. It had been a crazy twenty four hours, but there was nothing more he could do for his parents and he had a degree to finish.

Ryan watched his son turn the corner before shutting the door. He stretched his neck and checked his watch. It was still too early for his daily run. Besides, he wanted to sit alone for a few moments. He had a headache and the explosion from the day before was still ringing in his ears.

14

Ryan sat heavily on the old sofa. He stretched his neck and pressed his fingers into the side of his head, trying to get rid of the ringing. A run might help, but it was too early. Watching one of the Robert Ryan films would take his mind off things but he'd seen them all in the last few days, Berlin Express twice now that he'd watched it with Gerard.

He wasn't worried about his son. Sure, it must be strange suddenly finding his parents separated, but he was old enough to deal with it. Gerard had had a more privileged upbringing than Ryan – middle-class Mumbles home rather than Townhill ex council house, University fees paid instead of going into the army – and he didn't have the same physical forcefulness that Ryan had, but there was a mental fortitude there, of that he was sure. Even with what was to come, Gerard would be okay.

Wanting to distract himself, Ryan turned on the old TV, the screen emitting sound before finally showing images as the afternoon news flickered on. The BBC was doing a special report on the banking system. It wasn't just about banks being bailed out by the Government. Over five hundred billion pounds of taxpayers' money had been spent on the bank rescue package. Despite this, the banks' CEOs were rewarding themselves with million pounds bonuses. The BBC's reporter spoke to camera:

'Edward Cameron, CEO of South West National, had this to say...'

The image cut to the headquarters of South West National. And there, large as life, was Ryan's former Lieutenant General, the man as pompous as ever:

'The constant refrain of blaming bankers for the country's economic woes is misplaced. The period of remorse and apology needs to end. For the economy to recover, banks need to thrive. It is basic economics. If money circulates on a high financial level, it works its way down to all other levels. If we regulate every penny that bankers make, we will simply impede economic growth.'

Ryan was so furious he couldn't listen to any more of it. The same bank that had put him out of business and taken his home existed purely because taxpayers' money covered its debts - tax that he had contributed every year. So he'd paid to keep a bank afloat that then closed him down. The bank's CEO was none other than his former Lieutenant General Edward Cameron, a man who had humiliated Ryan and refused to help him while he lived on unwarranted bonuses. And now, there he was on TV actually defending the bank's policies. Ryan wanted to put his fist through Cameron's face on the TV screen.

Ryan tried to calm himself, not let it be personal. But on an ethical level, he also felt betrayed. Up to now he had spent his adult life adhering to the economic model of capitalism. A way of living that had gained him a good life through hard work. However, what was happening now wasn't part of the economic system. It was blatantly unfair. Banks were bailed out, then turned around and awarded themselves huge bonuses while liquidating companies that were actually driving the real economy, creating jobs, paying people's wages, and paying taxes that went into propping up their banks and paying their bonuses. It was madness, a circle of cronyism and corruption. Logically, it simply didn't fit. It was okay for a bank to be in debt but not anyone else. And if the banks were in debt, how could its CEOs reward themselves such staggering bonuses?

Ryan wondered if his son had been right with his diatribes railing against the system. After twenty-odd years as a self-made businessman it was hard to admit this, but he was pretty much there, his disillusionment almost complete.

Ryan tried to get a lid on his anger as he refocused on the TV screen. The news had moved onto a response from the Occupy London Movement.

The spokesperson was a well-spoken woman in her thirties, not the hippie type Ryan had imagined, and was all too ready to give her opinion – describing the banks' actions as disgusting and urging reform. She pointed out that it wasn't just the banks that needed reforming, giving examples of energy companies that had fixed prices and forced people to pay bills they couldn't afford. One of the energy companies was Southern Gas and Electric, Ryan remembering that Edward Cameron's MoD chum was the company CEO. At the top, it was a small world, the same few sharing the wealth.

Although Ryan was in agreement with the Occupy woman's sentiments, her speech still grated. He wasn't sure why. Was it because she sounded too middle class to have experienced hardship? Or maybe it was just that for Ryan action spoke louder than words and he couldn't see what hers would achieve.

Behind the woman, Ryan could see a ragtag group of protestors. And looming over them in the distance were the glass towers of The City, police presumably keeping the demonstrators away from the heart of the banking industry.

Whether it was with his dad going on about his union days or Ryan's time in Kuwait, he knew that speaking about something had less impact than doing something about it. This applied to all sides, strikes achieving more than talks and insurgent bombs being more effective than political discussions.

Turning his attention back to the TV, Ryan saw that the news had moved on from national to local – a reporter standing in front of a burnt-down house:

'The dead man has been named as Huw Hughes, a bank manager at the Swansea branch of South West National. At present, police are keeping an open mind, but arson has not been ruled out.'

With neither his nor Sandra's names mentioned, Ryan knew Evan had done everything he could to prevent any leaks to the press. Even if he could no longer be counted on as a friend, he was still a good man. But their names would come out soon enough. As Gerard had indicated, a story that involved a jilted husband and his wife's dead lover was bound to be newsworthy.

And Evan wouldn't stop either. He had been the same in school, always plugging away until he got there in the end. He'd keep on until he found out how the house had burnt-down with Huw inside. Just as every year Evan kept doing the race despite finishing second each time, determined that one year he would catch Ryan.

The first time Evan had come to the door and warned Ryan off had proved useful. From what Evan told him, Ryan knew that Huw's house had CCTV at the front but that behind the fence at the back there was no coverage. And from where he'd hidden, he recalled both the electricity pole and abandoned church – knowing that both of these could be called upon. All of which made Ryan wonder if he'd subconsciously planned things from his very first run by Huw's house, which gave him pause for thought.

Checking maps of the area, Ryan found the old Methodist church that had once stood alone at the start of the Gower approach. But as the suburbs had continually expanded and people went shopping on Sundays instead of to church, it had lapsed into disrepair. With his finger, Ryan traced a route from his old Mumbles home, up through the woods to the church at the back of Killay. It was possible to get to Huw's house without being seen.

When Gerard unexpectedly turned up it didn't deter Ryan from carrying out his mission. If anything, seeing Gerard had made him all the more determined to continue with his plan. After jogging across the top of Swansea and through the woods, he reached the church in good time.

He squeezed though the busted gate, probably done by whoever had nabbed all the slate from the church roof, and collected the backpack he had stashed the day before. He climbed onto the railings and leant against the tree.

As he balanced on top of the railings, the humiliation of being tied there by Huw, Jim Harris and his sons flooded through him. He tried not to think about it as he needed to carry out his task without emotion, although the memory spurred him on. He took out his Steiner binoculars and focused on the windows at the back of Huw's house.

Nobody was downstairs, so Ryan raised the binoculars to the upstairs bedroom window. The binoculars were used by the army, high-powered with night vision and zoom, allowing Ryan to see every detail. What he saw almost made him recoil.

Stark naked, Huw was gyrating his hips while staring at a flat screen TV. Ryan wasn't sure, but it looked like Huw was practicing his sexual moves. Ryan adjusted his vision to see what Huw was watching. On the TV screen, a man and women were having sex, the woman underneath in missionary position. Ryan couldn't see the man's face, but recognised the out of shape body as Huw's. The woman was Sandra.

Ryan put the binoculars away. He felt dead inside. It had to be that way, otherwise he'd puke. He jumped down from the railings and took out what he needed from the backpack – industrial rubber gloves to prevent any shock and bolt cutters to cut the electrics. He didn't have time to fiddle with wires, so simply cut the main cable. With the electrics down, Huw's CCTV wouldn't capture Ryan entering the house. A smile flashed across Ryan's face and vanished. The TV in Huw's bedroom would also have suddenly switched off. That would put a stop to the bastard's wanking.

Backpack on, Ryan grabbed the top of Huw's garden fence and levered himself over – dropping to a crouch on the garden side, then instantly sprinting to the back of the house. The one flaw in his plan was that as he came over he had no way of knowing if Huw was looking out of the house at that moment, but he reached the French windows without being seen. Standing out of sight to the side, he thumped on the glass.

Huw would be aware of the electrics going down and was bound to investigate the sound. The second the French windows slid open, Ryan whipped in, grabbing Huw in a neck hold and hauling him to the floor.

With the air knocked out of him, Huw was

temporarily out of action. Before he could regain his senses and react, Ryan put his knee into Huw's spine – both pinning him down and further winding him - giving Ryan time to take some rope out of his backpack and tie Huw's arms behind him.

Ryan grabbed Huw by his arms, heaved him into the kitchen and sat him in a chair. Seeing who his captor was, Huw spluttered his first words:

'What the fuck Ryan, have you gone mad?'

Ryan wound the loose rope ends around the chair, fastening Huw to it.

'Is that some new bank manager speak?'

Getting over his initial shock at being tied up and manhandled in his own home, Huw was outraged:

'Untie me right now.'

Ryan took black masking tape out of his backpack. The house was detached, it was unlikely Huw's calls for help would be heard, but he might need it if Huw got louder than at present. Huw had suddenly lost his outrage and was trying to reason calmly:

'Come on Ryan, Sandra's going to be here any minute. This is going to be embarrassing for all of us.'

Ryan shook his head:

'Don't think so. Zumba on Tuesdays – benefit of being a husband is you know your wife's routine.'

Huw's face once again contorted in rage:

'Untie me before you regret it. You won't get away with this.'

In the long run, Huw's words might prove true but Ryan was going to carry on regardless. Huw hadn't realised this yet as he reverted to negotiation mode:

'Ryan, harming me isn't going to bring Sandra back. Let's deal with this like adults.'

Ryan hadn't wanted to get into a conversation with Huw, but he couldn't help it:

'You mean like the other day, when you had your old school friend and his two sons with you? Not so tough on your own, are you?'

Huw turned vindictive:

'Sandra's left you, don't you fucking understand that? It's over between you. If you want, I've got a nice video of me fucking her, so you can get it into your head.'

Ryan stepped behind Huw and turned on the gas cooker, opening the oven door wide. Not able to see what was happening, Huw was unnerved:

'What are you doing?'

Ryan didn't answer as he dropped paraffin sticks onto the kitchen tiles. He strode to the back room, ripped down one of the curtains from the French window, and then trailed it into the kitchen, where Huw had once more changed his attitude:

'Look Ryan, let's discuss things. The liquidation and the house, it really wasn't personal. I had no choice but to follow the bank's directives.'

Taking a petrol can from his backpack, Ryan soaked the curtain. Huw was starting to get desperate:

'Ryan, come on, you know I had no option. And with Sandra, it really wasn't vindictive. You know I've always loved her. You know that. Ryan?'

Huw's eyes widened as Ryan wrapped the petrol-dosed curtain around his body and chair. The smell of petrol mingled with the gas from the cooker. Now terrified, Huw pleaded:

'Ryan, please don't do this. Let me go and no-one will ever know – I'll remain forever indebted to you for letting me live. I'll tell Sandra it's over, give you two a chance to get back together.'

Huw really was a schizo, thought Ryan. One moment the man was spitting threats, the next he was almost begging. What had Sandra seen in him? In exchange for his life, Huw was now ready to swap her like some item. Sandra was a grown woman who made her own decisions. And how did Huw think Ryan and Sandra could get back together after all that had happened? And what about his house and business – was Huw going to bring those back?

No, Huw couldn't make up for what he'd done. Ryan understood that he wasn't solely culpable, but Huw's pleas that he was just carrying out the bank's orders didn't excuse him.

Yes, there were others to blame, but Huw was first in line. Ryan had lost his business, his home, his wife. And now it was payback. Ryan couldn't make Huw lose his business as he was just a manager, not an owner. And he could hardly kill Sandra. But he could make Huw lose his house, Huw going up with it.

Starting to feel heady from the mixture of fumes, Ryan didn't have long. He tore off a piece of masking tape and sealed Huw's mouth, Huw's eyes were wide with fear above the tape.

Ryan didn't think about the morals of what he was doing. He'd set himself a task, so that was what he focused on. In the army, he'd been taught to de-emotionalise in tense situations. It had come easily to him. He'd always been able to block out the pain in his legs as he ran across the Gower terrain as a kid.

If he did think about it, Ryan reasoned he was doing the world a favour. Huw was exactly the kind of person it didn't need. Vain, arrogant and self-centred, Huw thought money could buy you everything. Always showing off his wealth, which was minuscule compared to the really rich, Huw was someone who constantly tried to gain the upper hand for no reason. Now, he had no hands he could use. Huw desperately struggled in the chair, his eyes begging Ryan to stop as he mumbled indiscernible words behind the tape.

Ryan couldn't tell if Huw was making more threats or begging for his life. Either way, he didn't care. But did he really need Huw to suffer? With his full force, Ryan threw a right hook into Huw's nose. The chair toppled backwards and Huw's head hit the kitchen tiles hard, knocking him out cold. Satisfied that Huw wouldn't feel the flames, Ryan quickly ripped down the remaining curtain and threw the last of the petrol over it.

Ryan tied the second curtain to a leg of Huw's chair and stretched it from kitchen to backroom. He scattered the paraffin sticks he had left and dumped the petrol can on the sofa. He lit the tapered curtain fuse, nipped out of the French windows, quickly slid them shut and dashed to the end of the garden – hauling himself over the fence as the explosion shattered the glass.

Ryan didn't waste time, climbing over the railings into the church grounds. A quick glance over his shoulder told him all he needed to know – the house was aflame. However quickly the fire brigade got here, it wouldn't be fast enough. He eased through the broken gate and jogged to the woods. Along the track, he dumped his backpack in the undergrowth and picked up speed until he reached his old Mumbles house.

The day before he had gone in and set up the CCTV to stop after thirty minutes. Back outside, he'd sat on the front doorstep, his face naturally mournful as he thought through his plan. A sudden breeze had made him shiver. Checking his watch that half an hour had passed, he'd got up and jogged away.

This time, he quickly unset the alarm and reset the CCTV to start in five minutes. He sat himself in the same position by the door as the day before. He'd worn identical shorts and running vest both days, so anyone looking at the CCTC footage wouldn't initially notice the difference. And whoever checked the footage would find that, going back from when they turned the CCTV off, Ryan was there at exactly the time of the explosion. Only when someone looked into it properly would they see what he'd done. Shaking his shoulders, Ryan upped and jogged back to his new Townhill residence, Gerard waiting at the gate and pointing over to the rising smoke.

The end theme tune of the news on TV snapped Ryan out of his reverie. Still motionless on the sofa, Ryan watched as the TV programme changed to some daytime political discussion. Following on from the bank scandals, ministers were being questioned about Government policies. Not that the Chancellor of the Exchequer seemed to mind, batting off the interviewer's questions about Government cuts:

'In the present recession, caused by the previous Government I might add, austerity measures are unfortunately a necessity.'

The interviewer didn't let it go:

'But how can you reconcile public sector cuts while at the same time bank CEOs are getting huge bonuses? Let's take South West National. Despite being bailed out by the government at a cost of thirty four billion, the CEO Edward Cameron has recently given himself a bonus of one million pounds. How can you justify that?'

The Chancellor waved off the question with a chubby hand as his doughy face puckered:

'It really is time to stop all this banker bashing as frankly, it doesn't achieve anything. A whole industry shouldn't be tarred with the same brush. The British government is trying to reach an agreement with the banks whereby they can lend significant sums to stimulate the economy, but the present economic situation isn't something that can be fixed overnight. As a society, we all need to contribute. The welfare state is being drained by people who refuse to work. This, more than the occasional banker's bonus, is what we need to change.'

The interviewer questioned the Chancellor's stance:

'But can you answer the question? Can you justify those bonuses while there are welfare cuts?'

'Let me finish. Instead of complaining about others, people need to look at themselves. We all need to dig in. Literally. Instead of moaning that they don't have enough money, people could, for example, grow their own food – fend for themselves instead of living off benefits. The new welfare cuts will allow people to break free from benefits dependence and get back to work, thus contributing to the economy.'

The interviewer was almost as thrown as Ryan was by the Chancellor's bizarre and illogical non-answer, needing a second before he asked his next question:

'But aren't banks also living off government benefits?'

Ryan didn't get to hear the Chancellor's answer as the TV abruptly clicked off. Ryan stood and tried the light switch. No light came on. So, the electricity company had cut him off. He was surprised it had taken them this long to work out he had no money. That was fine, he had a lot to do. First, he needed to research Edward Cameron, CEO of South West National – and do it before Evan's investigation brought him back to Ryan's front door.

15

With his plan formulated, Ryan had to be ready before Evan got to him. His old friend wasn't to be underestimated and might be quicker than Ryan thought in working things out. It had been like that at school, the teachers never suspecting that Evan was anything but a steady worker. Yet, he was always there in the top three.

Ryan had left the computer for Sandra to take. Besides, there was no electricity to power it. So instead he jogged around the corner to the local library and used one of the PCs there. Typing 'Edward Cameron' into Goggle search he instantly had a whole list of hits, including Wikipedia, South West National and various British Army websites. Edward Cameron was an easy man to find out about. There were also several newspaper articles linked to his name. 'Lieutenant General in arms to Iraq scandal' was one headline. 'Army General claims innocence in fake bomb detection scam' was another headline.

Ryan didn't bother reading further. He knew shit didn't stick to Edward Cameron. What he wanted was personal information. Of course he knew Cameron from his stint in the army, but at the time he'd simply accepted him as their General. Like all the men, Ryan hadn't respected him much, but he was still in charge. Ryan had never thought to do a background check on the guy.

Ryan started on Wikipedia and discovered that Cameron had royal connections going back a century – no direct lineage, but landed gentry all the same. One of his family ties was with the chancellor's wife. Like his father, Cameron had attended Marlborough private school. Ryan switched to the school's website and under 'alumni' found out that Cameron had been captain of the polo team and head boy. Back on Wikipedia, Ryan saw that Cameron had continued his education at Oxford, where he was chair of the Oxford Union, a position that had later been taken up by none other than the Chancellor, George Oswald.

Basically, Edward Cameron had been born into privilege and was used to being a leader from an early age. After university, Cameron had seamlessly stepped into a high ranking position in the army – rising to Lieutenant General within a few years. No doubt he'd landed the job through family connections. Edward Cameron was born into wealth and privilege.

The switch to CEO of South West National was seamless and also partly due to who Cameron knew, but once again he easily took up the reins. He was simply used to assuming control.

Ryan didn't feel the class hatred his dad would have done. Cameron couldn't help what he was born into. But what Ryan found useful was what he had already guessed from his days in the forces - if it came to a choice between furthering his own career or taking a last stand with his team, Cameron would opt for the former.

Wanting to know more about Cameron's personal life, Ryan found out he had a wife and two daughters. Apart from the fact that he was married, there was no other information on Cameron's wife, suggesting she was a lot less high profile than him. Perhaps something to be noted, thought Ryan.

Edward Cameron's daughters on the other hand got lots of internet hits. Both in their late twenties, one was a newly-crowned equestrian champion and the other was a recently appointed executive of a major bank – the youngest woman to hold such a position. It seemed that, for some, the recession didn't make any difference at all.

Cameron's address obviously wasn't listed, but Ryan was sure he could guess the area. South West National's headquarters were in Bath rather than the City of London as that was where the bank had been founded. Cameron had gone to school in Marlborough. And the horse-riding daughter was based in Cheltenham. So the family home was going to be in the vicinity.

Ryan found the horse-riding daughter's Facebook page. Photos of her from a young girl to an adult, each time on horseback, showed a manor house made of Bath stone in the background. It didn't take long for Ryan to match the image with an address on the outskirts of Bath. Ryan nodded to himself. The first part of his research was done. He now knew where Edward Cameron lived. Ryan wondered if this was the sort of research his son did for his articles. Or maybe it was more like the investigative work Evan carried out, which made Ryan think he better get a move on.

In the Swansea branch of South West National, Evan waited for the list he'd requested. Huw's secretary wasn't prepared to hand it over without Huw's permission, which was obviously impossible with him being dead. The secretary said she'd need the go-ahead from headquarters and that it could take twenty four hours before getting confirmation. Evan gave her one hour, positioning a police car in the street outside and an officer in the foyer to hasten the process.

Not wanting any press enquiries or negative publicity, the bank gave Evan the list in thirty minutes. Looking at it, Evan saw that, just as he thought, Ryan was not alone. Since the start of the year, there had been ten house repossessions and five company liquidations – all signed off by Huw. That meant three possible grudges per month. Dividing the list in half, Evan split the names between the officer and himself.

A few hours later, the two of them reconvened at the station. The people on the list had ranged from devastated to resentful but all of them had alibis.

The last man Evan questioned was a fifty-year-old carpet fitter, who placed the blame for his plight squarely on immigrants:

'Bloody Poles taking all our jobs, and at lower wages, that's what it is. I've been in work since I was sixteen. Never once signed on. And now look, at my age, I've got no choice but to go on benefits. The Government should send them back to their own bloody country, give the rest of us a chance.'

Evan wasn't concerned about the man's political beliefs, just whether he had a hand in Huw's murder. He certainly had the anger inside him, but it was seemingly directed at Polish immigrants rather than the bank. Evan still asked about the man's whereabouts on the night of Huw's death. Without hesitation, the man said he was in his local.

The pub landlord confirmed the alibi, which could also be backed by CCTV. The carpet-fitter had been a man of routine, in the pub at six every night for the last thirty years – even after his company had gone bust.

Telling the officer to take a break, Evan brooded over the case. The scene definitely suggested arson, but anyone with a possible grudge against Huw had an alibi. Huw had never been married or had kids so there were no family to get information from. This left Sandra to fall back on.

Evan drove over to the Village Inn. Sandra was still holed up in her office. She wasn't capable of running the place, but she had nowhere else to go. For the first time in her life, Sandra looked older than her years. Huw had never seen her look so dishevelled. She had gone into herself, hardly greeting him, but he had to persist in asking if she knew of any enemies Huw might have. She didn't mind being questioned but had nothing useful to tell Evan. As they both knew, she had been with Huw a matter of days so simply didn't know who he associated with.

Strangely serene, Sandra had realised that she was more relieved that Ryan wasn't guilty than saddened by Huw's death. She'd loved Ryan not Huw and saw that she had made a grave mistake, forsaking Ryan at a time of need and selfishly turning to Huw. What had happened to Huw was too awful for words, but maybe it was all because of her infidelity. She looked up at Evan:

'Do you believe in divine retribution?'

Evan looked back at her carefully:

'What do you mean?'

'It's awful what happened, but maybe this is God's punishment. I shouldn't have left Ryan. And the more I think about it, it's like divine intervention. Maybe this is my penance.'

Evan simply nodded. He'd never known Sandra to be religious, but people turned to all kinds of things once shocking acts occurred.

What Sandra didn't know was that the electrics had been deliberately cut. Someone had planned Huw's death. And something kept nagging away at Evan. Somewhere there was an inconsistency. He just wasn't sure what.

Thinking there was nothing else to get from Sandra he stood to leave and noticed the calendar on the wall. Routine, everyone had one, like the carpet-fitter who went to the same pub at the same time for thirty years. Sandra didn't know Huw's routine but she did know Ryan's.

Almost as an afterthought, Evan asked Sandra:

'By the way, do you know when Ryan does his daily run?'

'Starts at six, back at seven.'

Having replied without hesitation, Sandra looked puzzled:

'Why?'

Evan's mind reeled and he blurted out a lie:

'Thought I'd try and join him one day.'

Evan quickly got out of the hotel before Sandra could detect his real reason for asking. Rubbing his head as he reached his car, he thought; there was the inconsistency. Ryan went for a run every day at six, as he had done the day Evan warned him to stay away from Huw's house. So why, the night of Huw's death, had Ryan gone for a run an hour later? Behind the wheel, Evan put the car in gear. He didn't like where his thoughts had taken him, but knew he had to pursue it.

What Ryan wanted next were facts. Using various newspaper websites, Ryan found confirmation that South West National had been bailed out by the Government with taxpayers' money to a tune of thirty four billion pounds.

In the last tax year since the bail out, the top executives including Edward Cameron had each received one million pounds bonuses. The total amount of bonuses equalled the bank losses for that year – one point one billion.

During that same period the bank had sacked eleven thousand employees, liquidated just over two thousand companies and repossessed a thousand and twenty two homes. The facts were staggering. And what it confirmed, for Ryan, was that Edward Cameron had debts he needed to settle.

Evan stood over the shoulder of the IT technician as they rechecked the CCTV footage from Ryan's old home. When it had first provided Ryan's alibi, they had simply worked backwards from when the CCTV was stopped by the police. As the footage rewound on the monitor, Evan told the technician to stop when a removal truck appeared on screen. A quick check in his notebook gave Evan the day Ryan and Sandra had moved out. From that point, there should have been three days' worth of footage. The technician clicked on the time slide at the bottom of the screen. It was twenty four hours short. Evan cursed:

'He's bloody doctored it.'

Evan yanked open the door and called to the first officer he saw.

Ryan packed the bare essentials required for a cross country trek – binoculars, maps, and compass. With all his belongings logically boxed from his recent move, it was just a case of transferring the items to his old army rucksack. On impulse, he also took the miniature CCTV camera that he'd kept when

Morgan's was liquidated, thinking it might prove useful down the line. He didn't waste any more time in the house and strode outside to where the hired car he'd paid for in cash was parked. He'd deliberately chosen a national company. When the car didn't come back and they tried to reclaim the money from his account, they'd find it was empty.

With one hand, he bleeped the nondescript Ford Focus to unlock. With his other, he put the house keys through the letter box. Thirty two years after he first left home to join the army, he was leaving again – embarking on his final mission.

Instead of using his unmarked detective's car, Evan grabbed the officer's keys and jumped into the driver's seat of the patrol car. The officer slid into the passenger seat. Evan drove through the side entrance, the engine revving, and the car swerved toward the edge of the road. Siren on, he found a gap and motored up the hill.

Swerving left at the top of Townhill, Evan screeched to a stop outside Ryan's parents' house. Out of the car and through the garden gate, Evan pounded on the front door as he called Ryan's name out. With no answer, Evan motioned for the officer to go around the back. But a quick peak through the letterbox told Evan that it was too late. The door key was on the doormat inside. Ryan had gone.

Ryan drove over the Second Severn Crossing, the estuary lit up below by the setting sun. In his rear view mirror, the last of the light blinked at him through the diagonal metal struts of the bridge. With Wales left behind, England was calling. Sandhurst would be Ryan's first port of call.

16

Ryan arrived at Sandhurst at the same time as he had when he'd gone with Sandra to the reunion. As he'd hoped, the same officer cadet was on night sentry duty. Ryan stopped the car in front of the gate and waited for the young cadet to come over. Ryan leaned out of the window:

'Still got you on night shifts?'

The sentry was instantly put on the back foot, trying to place Ryan, who helped out:

'I was here two weeks ago for the reunion – in my wife's Mercedes that time.'

The sentry remembered now. The wife had been driving. It was her who had done the talking, Ryan silent and brooding. And they'd left early. Seeming to read his thoughts, Ryan said:

'Bit strange for me that night, being back after ten years.'

The sentry recalled how apparently Ryan had been a legend in his day, despite his short stint. Deferential now, but still doing his duty, the sentry asked:

'How can I help you, sir?'

'Forgot my jacket at the reunion. I called and apparently it's hung up in the mess hall. I'm on my way to London, so I thought I'd stop by to get it.'

The sentry handed a clipboard with a form on to Ryan:

'If you can sign here. And I'll need some ID – protocol.'

'Wouldn't expect anything less.'

Ryan signed and showed his driving licence. The sentry asked:

'You know the way sir?'

'As if I was still based here.'

The sentry raised the barrier and Ryan drove through, parking in the visitors' bay. After inserting a large folded plastic bag inside his shirt, Ryan strode into the complex and headed towards the mess hall. But the second he was out of sight of the sentry, Ryan altered direction.

It was impossible to breach security at Sandhurst without permission to enter, but once you were inside it was a different matter – as long as you knew where you were going and could be quick. At the reunion, Ryan had noticed that the bomb disposal unit was still located in the same building. The thing with bomb disposal was that you needed explosives to work on, and that was exactly what he required now.

Checking no-one was looking, Ryan cracked the lock on the door with bolt cutters from his bag. Inside, he worked fast, spotting what he wanted with his torch. He bagged several blocks of PE4 explosives, detonator cord and a handful of remote detonators. With enough for several hits, he left the building.

In the parking bay, Ryan popped open the boot and placed the bag of explosives inside. He took out his jacket and dropped it on the front passenger seat. Back at the gate, he held up the jacket to show the sentry, who raised the barrier. Ryan saluted and drove off.

Ryan drove back along the M4 towards the turning to Bath, the roads with hardly any other traffic that late at night. He didn't wait for the junction but turned into a service station beforehand. The place promised a welcome break, at an extortionate price no doubt. Ryan cruised past the mini shopping mall and petrol station, taking the service road out the back. He bumped along the uneven tarmac until he came to a proper road – one way leading to Bath, the other to the countryside. Ryan took the latter, driving slowly until he spotted a secluded track through woods.

His presence at Sandhurst would eventually be discovered, as would where he left the car, but he could buy some time. Parked at the beginning of the woods, Ryan transferred the explosives into his army rucksack. As well as survival essentials, he also had two sets of clothes – walking gear to make him look like a rambler if he met anyone in the woods during the day, and his shirt and trousers as owner-manager of Morgan's for when the ground war started and he needed to look like a civilian.

Rucksack on, Ryan studied the ordnance survey

map, checked the compass and headed through the trees, torchlight illuminating the way.

After half an hour, Ryan reached his destination. Edward Cameron's Manor House could be seen clearly through the trees. Ryan found a mound of earth that both gave him a good vantage point and kept him hidden from view once behind it.

Taking out his binoculars, Ryan lay on his front and focused on the house. A grand building made entirely of Bath stone, it stood in the middle of the grounds – a small stable and riding field to one side, immaculate lawn and gardens to the other. Bordered by the woods and farmland, there was no security to stop anyone from simply climbing the fence into the grounds. But as Ryan roved the binoculars across the stone face of the house, he saw that it had top notch alarms and CCTV provided by ADT. You might get onto Edward Cameron's land, but you wouldn't get inside his house quite so easily.

Ryan scanned the drive. Two cars were parked there – a Bentley and BMW, the latter with a dent on the side. Ryan didn't see Edward as someone who drove around with a damaged car so guessed the BMW must be his wife's.

Ryan knew Edward wasn't away because he'd made a fake phone call to the number on Edward's business card, a secretary explaining that although Edward was in Bath, he had no free time to meet that week as he was in meetings.

Ryan stretched out below the mound, ready to rest. He closed his eyes, but his mind was restless. He found himself thinking of Sandra, wishing he was next to her in bed. He wasn't bitter at her betrayal, just sad. He'd always thought they'd be together forever. He genuinely hoped she recovered from the shock of Huw's death.

Ryan wondered if he was being completely honest with himself. Had Huw's murder been necessary and not simply vindictive revenge? The only way to justify it was to logically pursue his plan. Working his way up the chain, everyone responsible for his losses would pay. But it wasn't purely personal. This was for society as a whole. The people he was targeting owed society and had no intention of paying their debts. Who was going to hold them to account? No-one else was taking action about it, so he was. Feeling justified, Ryan's mind finally calmed enough to let him sleep in peace.

Ryan woke with the birds. As they chirruped their morning songs, he noticed the dance of sunlight through the leaves. Stretching his long stiff limbs, Ryan felt more alive than he'd felt in a while. He hadn't camped out for a long time. After leaving the army, there'd been a few times when Gerard was a kid, but Sandra had always wanted hotels when they went on holiday. Sleeping under the sky was the real thing. It was uplifting to know you could survive with the bare essentials. He took out his flask and gulped some water. He was ready to start the day's surveillance.

With the front of the Manor House in his clear line of sight, Ryan saw curtains pulled aside in an upstairs window. A minute later, blinds went up in a downstairs window. Zooming in, Ryan could see Edward in the kitchen, in his suit, as he quickly drained a glass of juice. He then watched as Edward strolled out of the front door and got into the Bentley, which pulled out of the drive.

Ryan turned his attention back to the house. A different set of curtains were pulled open upstairs, Ryan noticed that Edward and his wife slept in separate bedrooms. He tracked the wife down to the kitchen, where she spent more time than Edward. First, she downed some medicine, Ryan unable to see what. Then she blended fruit to make fresh juice, nonchalantly adding a drop of vodka. Ryan checked his watch. It wasn't even nine yet.

Ryan knew that the only way to get inside the house was while Edward Cameron's wife was at home so that alarms weren't set, but he guessed that, with the house and garden as spotless as they were, there had to be help. Sure enough, just after nine, a gardening van turned up, followed shortly after by a cleaner pulling into the drive.

Ryan waited. He watched Cameron's wife drive off at about ten and come back an hour later, a bag from Waitrose in her hand, the top of a vodka bottle sticking out. By midday, the gardeners and cleaner had left. Ryan put one block of PE4 explosive in a smaller backpack and made his way down to Edward Cameron's Manor House.

Looking through his binoculars, Ryan moved along the fence until he caught sight of Cameron's wife. Eyes half closed, she was lounging in a glass conservatory at the back, book on her lap and drink to the side – almost empty. From an unseen position, Ryan swung over the fence and strode to the open kitchen window.

Once inside, Ryan inspected the blender full of juice, bottle of vodka on the counter beside it. Having seen Cameron's wife take some kind of medicine in the morning, Ryan searched the cupboards until he found her Valium, plus painkillers and sleeping tablets. Taking a few of the tablets, he ground them into the juice mix then went in search of a place to wait.

As they had a cleaner, Cameron's wife wouldn't go looking in the closet where the equipment was kept so he stood next to a mop and watched through the keyhole as she helped herself to another cocktail mix. Giving it an hour, Ryan stepped out and sneaked a look at her. She seemed fast asleep but he made a sound just to be sure. There was no movement so he moved in.

Heaving Cameron's wife over his shoulder, Ryan carried her to her bedroom and lay her down on the bed. As long as Cameron didn't come home too late she'd be out for the count. He'd been prepared to restrain her, but circumstances had allowed him to improvise.

With the house to himself, Ryan explored. The living room was a Laura Ashley museum and didn't interest him. However, the wood-panelled study with heavy furniture did. Looking for anything that could be used as leverage in dealing with Cameron, Ryan found just the thing – a safe behind a large-framed painting. Bit of a cliché to hide it like that, thought Ryan. But what he also thought was how strange it was for Cameron to have a safe. As CEO of a national bank, he presumably had access to the most exclusive accounts in the world, so why did he have a safe in his home? Ryan shrugged and sat in one of the armchairs. He'd soon find out.

17

Edward Cameron eased the Bentley to a stop by the wooden fence. With the window down, he watched his daughter jump the bars on the grey mare. The horse was a pure breed Trakenher. He knew the type of horse well because it was on the logo of South West National.

The sun was rising and flowers sprouting. Edward Cameron could literally smell spring turning into summer. It was at moments like this that he felt everything was still all right with the world. He got out and waited by the fence as his daughter came trotting over on her horse:

'Morning daddy, did you see how well she jumped?'

'Majestic darling.'

'I think she has an awfully good chance of winning.'

'With you at the saddle, how could she not?'

Edward Cameron winked at his daughter. She gave him a childish smile. She was nearly thirty, but still his little girl – needing to please and be admired.

'We're going to do one more circuit. Care to watch?'

'I'd love to darling, but must dash. Very important meeting this morning.'

His daughter pouted as she talked to her horse:

'Oh, isn't daddy silly Millie, can't watch because he has a "very important" meeting.'

Edward Cameron sometimes wondered if his daughter was a little simple. She'd always been horse mad, that was okay, but she didn't seem to realise how she had been able to turn her pastime into a way of life. Being an equestrian champion brought recognition within in its own small insular world, but it didn't bring in any money. It certainly cost a lot though. The Trakenher alone had cost a little over ten thousand pounds.

As his daughter turned the horse around, Edward Cameron got a nice view of her rump. He gave it a smack and she looked coyly over her shoulder:

'Naughty daddy.'

Edward Cameron watched his daughter trot off before getting back in the Bentley, adjusting his trousers around his erection. He put the car in gear and drove away from the converted stables. Half the stables were still in use. The other half had been turned into a country bungalow for his daughter. A few miles from the Manor House, he'd bought up the land as an eighteenth birthday present for his daughter. She'd been living there for almost ten years, everything paid for by Daddy.

Thank heavens for George coming through, was all Edward Cameron could think. It was only a short while ago that things had looked pretty bloody drastic. If the bank hadn't been bailed out, they would have owed untold billions. For the common account holder, it would have been a case of tough cookies. But there were some serious players who could have filed serious lawsuits.

Back in 2008, at the start of the crash, things had been pretty touch and go. Financial institutions around the world had faced the threat of total collapse.

It had been a different government back then and Cameron hadn't been sure how the emergency meetings would turn out. Cameron and the other bank CEOs went into scaremonger mode, said the only solution was bailouts and the chancellor had agreed. No chancellor needed a financial crisis. It had been amazingly easy.

That was before the Libor scandal broke. The Libor rate manipulation had been going on since well before the 2008 crash. Cameron had no actual hand in it, he left that to the traders. But of course he'd unofficially sanctioned the whole business. It was how the banks made money. Initially, the banks falsely inflated rates to profit and then later simply to appear creditworthy. Reports of fraud had started leaking in 2008 but it had taken another four years before the scandal broke.

The problem now was the public backlash. Governments worldwide were being forced to take action. Bankers were being made to resign left, right and centre. Starbucks, Google and Amazon were all being taken to task for tax avoidance. Tax havens were being investigated.

Edward Cameron had started stashing cash instead of putting the money in his off shore account when it had looked like the entire system was about to come crashing down. Now, he continued to do so because with the public outcry against tax avoidance and government measures being put in place, he didn't fancy his chances in any legal proceedings. He'd got away with the arms to Iraq and fake bomb detectors. He didn't want to go to prison over a case of tax evasion. So, to avoid any investigation, his latest bonus had gone straight into his safe with the rest.

Owen had held off, but knew he had to bite the bullet. Until he found another job, he had to sign on. He had a family to support, kids to feed.

He knew he took his anger out on Sarah and couldn't help it. He loved her and the kids. He'd been the guy who'd brought in the bacon and now he was going for government hand-outs.

The forms killed him, pages and pages of them, all stacked up on the kitchen table. Sarah had offered to help and he'd snapped that he was able to do it. But a few minutes later, he'd thrown the pen on the table in disgust, and said if she was so clever why didn't she do it. So she did.

It turned out that they could claim quite a lot, not only jobseekers allowance and housing benefit but also care for Rhys. There was no chance of him going to the live-in centre now and Owen was at home to deal with the boy when it was too much for Sarah, but he still needed assistance.

On his way to the job centre, Owen felt relief that his family were being given a lifeline, but sick that it wasn't from him.

The young job centre officer looked over the forms, gave Owen an agreement to sign – explaining that Owen had four weeks to take up one of the jobs on offer or face having the benefits cut. Owen didn't like the officer's tone, but thought fine, he'd have a job within a month.

The officer handed over a list of jobs. All of them were cleaning, sixteen hours per week, on minimum wage. It didn't make sense. If he took up one of the jobs, he'd lose all the benefits and have less money. The officer smiled as he explained - if Owen didn't take the job, his benefits would be cut anyway.

Like Edward Cameron, the six suited men around the table were all in their early sixties. They waited for Pam to finish taking the minutes. A sexy thing of twenty, Cameron had tried unsuccessfully to bed her on numerous occasions. Maybe she was a lesbian, although watching her sashay out of the room, he was sure she wasn't. Perhaps she was just a clever girl – give the men a hard on but don't put out because as soon as she did, she'd lose respect.

The whole roomful of men had been looking at the girl's bottom, Oliver saying:

'I'd like to give that a spank.'

James joined in:

'Rather she spanked me.'

Edward Cameron tapped the table to get attention:

'Gentlemen, if the spanking can be left until later, we can get down to the real business we need to attend to.'

The minutes Pam had taken covered the official board meeting, complete with monthly figures and future strategies. Now that the secretary was out of the room, they could speak about more important matters off the record.

The six men all sat to attention. Three of them had gone to the same boarding school as Edward Cameron, the other three he'd met at Oxford. Cameron had always been head boy, so they naturally deferred to him. The meetings were essentially a grown up version of the boys clubs they'd started in school and continued in university.

They'd kept the old school ties, and certainly didn't want any outsiders muscling into their cosy little club. Yes, they let the brash young guns in the City deal with investments, but they'd kept the headquarters in Bath to preserve the bank's name and reputation, and add a little distance between themselves and the thugs in the city. This reputation was the reason Edward Cameron had called the meeting:

'As you are aware, we must be grateful to our friends.'

Oliver chimed in:

'Good old George.'

Cameron silenced Oliver with a stern look before continuing:

'Unfortunately the press have got wind of this and would like to blow it into a storm. We know that we jolly well deserve those bonuses, but we need to be discreet.'

Cameron glanced James' way:

'That means no more pictures of you getting blow jobs in your Aston Martin from some prostitute.'

Chastised, James bowed his head in acknowledgment. Edward Cameron went on:

'Last thing we need is some bloody hippies turning one of our branches into a library. It's a very simple equation. Bad publicity equals loss of value, something we cannot afford.'

Oliver piped up:

'What about that branch manager who died? Is that anything to worry about?'

Cameron waved it off:

'As I understand, a local man was arrested – some kind of jealous revenge scenario. Nothing to do with us anyway.'

With the room nodding sombrely, Edward Cameron held back a smile:

'So I suggest we adjourn to a certain discreet club where we can participate in as much spanking as we choose.'

Kristine had a few weeks before the money from Morgan's ran out. She was grateful to Ryan for that. She knew he hadn't left much for himself.

She'd cut back on all the non-necessities, curbing the Friday nights on Wind Street and cancelling the gym membership. The problem was that both of those were small costs. It was the rent that was the problem.

She needed to find work soon. In her last gym session she went up to the older guy who'd asked her for coffee. Richard was his name, and she remembered that he'd said he owned a restaurant and bar.

Kristine wasn't innocent. She knew what she was doing by agreeing to the coffee and telling Richard about her plight. In Latvia, she'd often seen young attractive women in cafés with richer older guys. It was a way of surviving when there were no jobs.

It turned out that not only did Richard have a bar position going, but he also had a room above the bar he could include in the deal, rent free. When he asked if she'd like to see the room, Kristine knew she'd be doing more than showing a flash of cleavage.

Looking around the self-contained room, Kristine kept up her confident appearance despite feeling her heart sinking. She weighed up the situation. She didn't really find Richard attractive, but he was fit and seemed genuine. Nothing crass had been said, but the deal was clear. He could give her a job and rent free room. In return, she'd be his weekend mistress.

It meant any feminist ideals went out the window, as did her hard fought independence. But she had no job and in a few weeks no flat. She couldn't face cleaning again and that was the only other job out there. She could make the room her own and after some months she should have enough money from the bar work to move out if she needed to.

Forcing herself to smile, Kristine stepped towards Richard and unzipped his jeans.

The club was so discreet, it appeared to be a normal Bath town house. The seven men had pooled together when they were at Oxford. One room had been converted into a bar, there were three bedrooms if you wanted privacy and a lounge for more public affairs.

The girls were from a high class agency Edward Cameron had used on many occasions. Each one was a buxom treat and they all knew what to do, aware that if they played their cards right they'd get tipped handsomely. A few of them didn't speak very good English, but that didn't matter.

Cameron didn't employ anyone to work the bar as he didn't want any witnesses who could go about spreading tales of debauchery to the press. Besides, he enjoyed playing host, ensuring that several bottles of champagne were on ice. With the party in full flow, he paused to watch proceedings. Oliver gleefully had one naked woman over his lap and was heartily spanking her. James was bent over an armchair and getting spanked.

All this could end any minute, thought Edward Cameron. Thankfully, not only had George come through, but the masses seemed to just accept matters. Good thing Britain wasn't like Iraq, people rising up and killing each other all the time. But look at Greece, the heart of ancient civilisation, now on the brink of civil war. Mind you, they always had been a volatile lot. What was the joke, the peasants are revolting? Yes, they are. More worrying than any uprising was that the whole banking system was so close to the brink of collapse.

Edward Cameron's ruminations were interrupted by Oliver shouting over at him:

'Come on Eddie, join in the fun.'

This is what he'd been waiting for, a call to arms. He'd set up the party and needed to be cheered into the fray. One had to lap it up while it was on offer.

Johnny vomited onto the sand. He'd always hated being sick, vividly recalling times in his childhood. He did everything he could to hold it back despite his mum telling him to let it out. He guessed she was right, there was some kind of relief once it was over.

He swayed in the sea breeze. The other two, Frank and Dan, were back in the dunes, drunk on cans of Carling. Johnny had said he was going for a piss, not wanting them to see he was going to puke. He'd at least had enough sense to do that.

He couldn't face going back to the two of them. They weren't mates, just took his money and spent it on drink. He wanted to go home, but didn't know where to go. Townhill was a long hill to go up. Even if his mum let him in, she'd just bawl him out.

His bed in the house-share was inviting, but he knew that in the morning nothing would have changed. He'd wake up with his head and stomach hurting, would drink with Frank and Dan to numb the pain, the days merging into one long drunken stupor.

He found himself on Walter Road, felt his feet taking him to Morgan's Security Systems. He stood unsteadily outside the frontage and looked inside. It was empty, but it was where he wanted to be. He tried to focus his muddled mind, work out how he could get in. It was simple – break in, the place didn't have security cameras anymore.

Johnny stumbled into the cordoned off alley at the back. The rocks from the old stone wall that had fallen were still on the ground, so he picked one up and threw it at the small toilet window at the back of Morgan's. He appraised the successful smash, then clambered over the rocks and squeezed through the hole in the window. Shards of glass sticking out from the frame cut into him but he was numbed to the pain. With most of his body inside, he held onto the toilet tank as he pulled in his legs. His hands slipped and he crashed head first onto the floor, where he lay prone.

18

When Edward Cameron came home, it was past midnight. As soon as he heard the front door, Ryan was alert. He switched on the lamp next to him and sat there relaxed, though ready to spring. As expected, the lamplight brought Edward Cameron into the study. On seeing Ryan, Edward Cameron literally jumped:

'Good God.'

Ryan put up a peaceful palm:

'Your wife said I could wait.'

Edward Cameron tried to regain his composure, but was still dumbfounded:

'That may well be. But pardon my French, what the bloody hell are you doing in my home?'

Ryan held up Edward Cameron's business card:

'You said I could get in contact.'

'Not at my house in the middle of the bloody night I didn't. Can't it wait until morning?'

'I called your secretary but she said you were busy

all week.'

Wherever Edward Cameron had been, it wasn't a business meeting. Ryan could smell the mix of champagne and perfume. Edward Cameron was getting impatient:

'Look, it's been a long day. Leave me your number and I'll schedule you in tomorrow.'

Ryan ignored him:

'What's in the safe?'

'I beg your pardon?'

Ryan pointed to the safe in the wall, the painting neatly placed on the floor:

'The safe. What's inside?'

Edward Cameron looked over at the safe, flabbergasted. Before he could take any action, Ryan sprang. Yanking Cameron's right arm behind his back, Ryan shoved Cameron face down into the carpet. As Ryan took some flex out of his backpack, Cameron put up a struggle, but was no match for Ryan, who soon had him firmly tied in the armchair. Ryan removed Cameron's mobile and wallet as he said:

'Your wife's going to be asleep until morning so don't bother shouting for help.'

Edward Cameron was incensed:

'Have you gone stark raving mad? You can't just come into a man's home and...'

'Bad show.'

'Pardon?'

'That's what you said to me when I told you my business was liquidated – by your bank.'

'Now come on old chap, you don't hold me

responsible for that, do you? There are hundreds of companies liquidated each week. I don't oversee them all, if any.'

Amazing, thought Ryan, Edward Cameron was oblivious to what his words had just indicated. The man was so cocooned in his own wealth that he didn't see that the blasé liquidation of companies lost people their livelihoods. Ryan asked:

'So what exactly do you do to earn your one million-pound bonus?'

Edward Cameron opened his mouth, then closed it abruptly. Ryan spoke instead:

'No comment? The bank manager in Swansea said it wasn't his fault either, said he was just following bank directives. You know the guy I'm talking about, the one who died.'

Edward Cameron slowly nodded, apprehensive now:

'Yes, I recall it.'

'Unlike you, he didn't get a choice.'

'What choice?'

'Between your money or your wife.'

Ryan took a card out of Cameron's wallet:

'Lucinda's Escorts eh?'

Just then, a message bleeped on Cameron's mobile. Ryan picked up the mobile and tapped the screen, bringing up the message 'Splendid night Eddie old boy. Here's a memento.' He clicked on the attached video. The unsteady image showed Edward Cameron pouring champagne over the breasts of a naked escort, who lay on her back. The mobile phone camera panned around what looked like the back room of a Gentlemen's Club. Several other men in their sixties were getting blow jobs from other escorts. Ryan stopped the video.

So while people desperately tried to survive, Edward Cameron partied lavishly – all paid for by the taxpayer. Ryan shook his head as he chucked Cameron's wallet and mobile onto the desk.

'What's in the safe?'

Edward Cameron kept his mouth closed. Ryan took out the block of PE4 from his backpack and placed it on the desk:

'You know what this is.'

'Money, there's money inside.'

'How much?'

'A fair amount.'

'Edward, or should I call you Eddie? I don't want your money. I just want to know if you'd like to keep it.'

'Yes, I would like to keep it.'

'So how much is there?'

'My last three bonuses.'

'I would have thought you kept it in some off-shore account.'

'You don't understand how precarious the whole banking system is. It could all collapse any day. Even the safest accounts could be suddenly wiped out. In case of emergency, I have cash back up.'

'I understand. You're looking after number one. What I don't understand is why my company gets liquidated and your bank gets bailed out. How is that?'

'It was all above board I can assure you.'

'Nothing to do with you having family ties with the Chancellor or both of you going to Oxford?'

Edward Cameron laughed nervously:

'We all call on friends in a time of need.'

'Or greed.'

Ryan shook his head in disgust:

'What's the code?'

Edward Cameron's shoulders slumped, resigned as he answered:

'Lucinda.'

Edward Cameron stared at the carpet. Ryan opened the safe, took out a briefcase. Cameron looked up as Ryan stood in front of him, briefcase in one hand and the explosive in the other:

'Here's your choice. You can drive off with the money but you won't see your house and wife again. Or, you can stay with your wife, keep the house and lose the money.'

'That's absurd.'

Ryan shrugged:

'That's your choice.'

Edward Cameron gulped:

'I'll take the money.'

'So you're choosing the money over your wife and house?'

'You gave me the choice.'

'Just making sure you understand.'

'Yes, I bloody understand.'

Edward Cameron was so indignant now that he didn't care that Ryan had him tied up. Ryan shook his head:

'You still don't take responsibility. Just like in Kuwait – you've never admitted it was your fault those men died. You ignored our warnings, made us drive into that death trap and then you had the nerve to suggest we'd fucked up.'

'It was a war. I can't be responsible for every casualty.'

'You ordered the unit to go in.'

'So why have you never said anything? No, you were happy to receive your bloody medal.'

Ryan had to exert considerable control to keep from hitting Edward Cameron:

'I never said anything out of loyalty, something you obviously don't understand. All you've ever thought about is your own profit, selling arms to Iraq and buying in fake bomb detectors.'

'My name was cleared on both accounts.'

'That doesn't mean you're innocent.'

Pocketing the explosive, Ryan hauled Edward Cameron to his feet and frogmarched him out to the Bentley. Resting the briefcase on the car's roof, Ryan unlocked the driver's door and shoved Cameron into the seat. He flicked open a penknife and cut the flex that tied Cameron's hand behind his back. Reaching for the briefcase on the roof, Ryan quickly pressed the PE4 into the lock. He chucked the briefcase onto the passenger seat and said:

'Here's your money. I hope it kills you.'

Ryan shut the driver's door and slapped the roof of the Bentley. As Edward Cameron turned the engine on, Ryan stalked off. He heard the tyres on the gravel as he leapt over the fence. Flattening himself to the ground, he pressed the detonator.

Flames from the exploding Bentley lit up the night sky. Ryan switched his view to the house. A light had gone on in a top window. In the frame, Edward Cameron's wife looked out, dazed. Her gaze fell on Ryan as he stood. He gave her a nod, thinking he'd done her a service. It looked as if she nodded back, though he couldn't be sure. Ryan jogged up the hill to where he'd left his rucksack, threw it over his shoulder and slipped away through the darkened woods.

19

As soon as Evan received news of Edward Cameron's death, he was sure there was a connection with his own case. Edward Cameron had been in the news recently as one of the CEOs that received a huge bonus despite the bank being bailed out. More importantly for Evan, it was the same bank Huw had been branch manager of. Was it a co-incidence that the branch manager and CEO of South West National had both been killed in the same week? And it was strange how Cameron's death coincided with Ryan going on the run.

Once he'd found that Ryan had abandoned his Townhill residence, Evan had wanted to put out a photo fit around every UK police station. The problem was that although Evan knew Ryan had doctored the CCTV, he had no hard evidence to show Ryan had killed Huw. The doctored CCTV didn't prove anything except that Ryan had lied. Besides, Evan knew it would be dismissed as just a local Welsh case.

Trying to track Ryan, Evan had phoned Sandra to see if she'd heard from him. If she hadn't suspected Evan's intentions earlier, she did this time:

'You still think he's guilty.'

'Sandra, all I know is that he's vanished. For various reasons, I'm worried.'

'It wasn't him.'

It was strange thought Evan how she was so adamantly defending him now. Maybe if she'd been more supportive when Ryan had needed her, nobody would have been killed. But Evan kept his thoughts to himself and instead asked for Gerard's number.

Ryan's son also hadn't heard from him. But unlike Sandra, Gerard went quiet instead of protesting Ryan's innocence. Evan had asked if Gerard knew something. Gerard had said:

'No. Just he was more emotional than I've ever known him. I hope he isn't going to harm himself.'

Evan was more worried about what harm Ryan was capable of inflicting on others. As with Sandra, he asked Gerard to call him immediately if Ryan got in contact.

Sitting at his desk, Evan made his deduction. The branch manager and CEO of the bank that had put Ryan out of business and taken his home had died. Was Ryan on some kind of revenge spree?

The news of Edward Cameron's death was low key and vague. Whoever was in charge didn't want Cameron's death splashed over the front pages. What Evan did know was that Bath was the nearest headquarters to where Cameron had died.

Not optimistic about getting any answers from Bath, Evan phoned through anyway. At the other end, they could see he was calling from Swansea police station but still treated him as if he was a random caller, putting him on hold for ages. When the officer on desk duty finally got back on the phone it was to say that there was no-one available to speak about the case. Evan was insistent:

'Who's in charge of it?'

'Afraid I can't divulge that information.'

'Look, I'm phoning because I might have a suspect.'

Evan was put on hold again. After a while, a new voice came on and identified himself as DCI Chisholm. Evan asked if he was in charge of the Edward Cameron case. Chisholm's response was non-committal:

'You want to know because?'

'I might have a connection to a case of mine.'

'Yeah?'

Evan took a breath, telling himself not to presume any anti-Welsh prejudice:

'A manager of the Swansea branch of South West National died in what we think was an arson attack two days ago.'

'No offence, but some local bank manager in a small Welsh town is bit different from the case we've got here.'

Evan shook his head in dismay. He shouldn't have bothered trying to be open-minded. Bath was smaller than Swansea for God's sake, so what was with the "small Welsh town"? To calm himself, Evan doodled a quick map of Britain as he tried again:

'Both victims worked for the same bank and both deaths are from explosions – I'd say there's a connection.'

'You have a suspect?'

On his map, Evan drew a big circle where Swansea was and wrote 'Small Welsh Town' as he answered:

'Uh huh.'

'And?'

Evan drew a smaller circle where Bath was on the map and wrote 'Big English City' as he replied:

'And tell me who's in charge and I'll give over my info.'

This got a resigned laugh at the other end:

'Well you can try but I was only on it for a few hours before MI5 appeared on the scene, so good luck.'

'MI5? Is it considered a terrorist attack?'

'The guy was a banking bigwig. That, and it looks like the car was rigged with explosives.'

Evan nodded into the phone. The only reason Chisholm was telling him was because he was disgruntled at being taken off the case. But he wasn't going to tell him anything else.

'And no, I don't have a number to give. Try their website.'

The line went dead before Evan finished saying thanks but he paid it no attention. If he got in contact with MI5, first they'd tell him nothing and second he still had no evidence that it was Ryan.

The website suggestion gave Evan an idea. Typing in Edward Cameron's name, Evan froze when he saw that Cameron had been Lieutenant General in the British Army at the same time Ryan had been in the forces. That couldn't be a coincidence.

Evan put himself in Ryan's shoes. He loses everything so enacts revenge against those he sees as responsible. Huw is killed in a homemade arson attack that uses what's at hand. But Edward's death is caused by a car exploding. For that, some kind of device is needed. Ryan would have to get explosive from somewhere. It seemed to Evan that Ryan was on a mission. Where did a soldier go at a time of need? He went back to his Army base.

Evan made the call to Sandhurst. As with Bath police, he got put on hold. He knew he had to tread carefully. The Army wouldn't want the police to look at one of their own. So there was no point in asking if any explosives had gone missing recently as they simply wouldn't give out that kind of information. When a Major Jenson finally came on, Evan repeated that he was from Swansea police, but said he was calling on a personal matter:

'Ryan's an old friend of mine. He's been under a lot of strain recently and he's gone AWOL. On behalf of his family I'm trying to locate him, I wondered if he'd been back to Sandhurst at all.'

'Soldiers are good at looking after themselves.'

'I don't doubt this. Like I said, people are concerned so I'm just trying to check his whereabouts.'

'There was a reunion two weeks ago. He may have attended that.'

'Is it possible to check?'

'Someone will call you back.'

Evan knew he was being fobbed off but he gave his number and thanked the Major all the same. It almost made Evan wonder why he was bothering. Why should he care about some rich English guy's death, especially as it wasn't even in his jurisdiction? Not to mention that the person he had down as the suspect was his old friend. But he knew he wouldn't stop. It was his job.

Fuck it, thought Evan. The only way to find out if Ryan had been to Sandhurst was to go there himself. Grabbing his car keys, he went out to his unmarked Ford.

After a three hour straight drive, Evan turned off to Sandhurst. He parked off road rather than going up to the gate. On the way he'd been thinking how to play it. The Major might admire his perseverance and see him, but more likely, he'd think something major was going on for Evan to come all this way, maybe refusing Evan admittance and wasting his journey.

Deciding to bluff it, Evan walked jovially up to the security booth and smiled at the officer cadet on day sentry duty as he showed his police ID:

'Spoke with Major Jenson earlier, he said he'd leave information about a friend of mine, Ryan Morgan, at the gate.'

The cadet almost frowned:

'I don't think that's possible.'

Evan ignored the cadet's scepticism as he leant in the window and gestured around the counter:

'Sure it's not just here?'

'Be against protocol sir.'

Evan gestured to an internal phone on the wall:

'Okay, well is it possible to call the Major, tell him I'm here?'

The cadet weighed it up. The police detective's unannounced arrival was unusual, but then he had the Major's name. The cadet went to the phone. As he did so, Evan instantly took the opportunity. He'd already spotted the logbook. Leaning in the window, he quickly flicked back until he found it – Ryan Morgan, with a car registration Evan didn't recognize but quickly committed to memory.

His face stony, the cadet finished his call and turned back to Evan, only to find he'd vanished.

Jogging back to his car, Evan got in, wrote down the registration and drove off. With the mobile on hands free, he made a call and found out that the car was hired. Another call, this time to the car hire company, confirmed that Ryan had hired the car. Evan didn't often get a chance to bet on the horses, down to Chepstow maybe once a year. But he was willing to put money on Ryan's hire car being spotted in the vicinity of Bath. He knew he wouldn't be welcome but decided to take a detour on his way home.

The drive to Edward Cameron's Manor House was cordoned off, police officers guarding the remains of the exploded Bentley and keeping the press firmly away from the scene that was being worked on by techs.

Evan found a lone officer and flashed his ID. It was against his nature to come across as arrogant, but he needed a ruse:

'Don't ask, got a call to come here from the MI5 guys – apparently there's a case I'm on in Swansea that connects. You ask me, I think mine's just an insurance scam, but there you are. Orders are orders.'

The officer pointed up to the woods above and beyond the Manor House:

'By the car they found. Best bet is to go around the side of the house.'

The officer led the way past the crime scene, the press annoyed that Evan had gained admittance and the techs ignoring him as they carried on with their work.

Evan nodded his gratitude and headed off. After all the driving, he was glad of the trek. In the breeze, a tiny bit of paper drifted against his face. He caught it and frowned as he saw it was a corner of a fifty pound note.

Evan stopped at the top to get his breath back. To the side was an earth mound from which there was a great view of the Manor House. The mound had clearly been marked and checked for evidence.

Evan scouted a small track and jogged along it, branches snapping under his feet.

He jogged to a stop as two MI5 officers in sharp suits came into view, the male officer in his early thirties, the female officer maybe forty. The female officer nodded at the male officer to deal with Evan and turned back to the techs who were examining a parked car. Evan put up two peaceful palms, his ID in one. The gruff-looking male officer inspected the ID, his surprise genuine:

'Swansea? What are you doing here?'

Evan pointed to the parked car:

'Ford Focus, hired by Ryan Morgan.'

'And how do you know…?'

The female officer stepped forward, interrupting the male officer:

'What was the name you said?'

Evan repeated Ryan's name. The female officer asked:

'You're sure of that?'

Evan nodded:

'Uh huh. Just got it from the hire company.'

'How do you know him?'

'He was a friend, now he's a suspect.'

The female officer and Evan eyed each other. With her sandy hair tied back and red in her cheeks from the fresh air, she was an attractive woman who looked like she would easily cope with a country hike. The way she firmly shook Evan's hand showed she was firmly in charge:

'Angela Stephenson. We need to know where he's gone.'

Evan followed Angela to her car so they could confer. It could have just been a chill in the woods that had made her eyes widen and prickle her arms with goosebumps, but she was obviously someone not easily put out. Evan doubted he'd find out, but he was pretty sure Angela had reacted to Ryan's name.

20

Ryan trekked north east until he heard the rumble of motorway traffic. As soon as the M4 was in view, he headed east alongside it. He had a compass but as long as he kept parallel to the motorway he'd eventually get to London.

Obviously it would have been a lot quicker if he had driven but he simply didn't know how long it would take for the hired Ford Focus to be traced. He didn't want to get stopped by some patrol car that clocked his registration plate. By vanishing into the British countryside, it should eradicate any sight of him. Besides, he wanted to hike so he could clear his mind and plan his next move.

He went in as straight a line as possible, but altered his route slightly to steer clear of any built up residential areas. Sometimes there was a tractor track to follow along the edge of a field of rapeseed, with a gate at the end. Other times, he just trod over earth clomped up by horse hooves and scrambled through hedgerows.

His rucksack weighed heavily on his back but he felt in good shape, taking a sip of water when he needed to and picking wild blackberries. He wasn't a spiritual guy but it felt as if his whole life, until now, had been a blur of existence, a treadmill. This walk, out in the open, was what life was for.

In a couple of places it wasn't possible to avoid skirting close to residences. Around Swindon, the town had expanded right out to the motorway. Ryan circumvented the identical detached red brick houses that lined a suburban crescent. People presumably lived there so they could commute easily, computer programmers maybe who earned good money doing jobs around the country. But suburbia wasn't the ideal it once was.

As he passed, Ryan saw a brand new Audi being towed away. A man in his early thirties with white shirt, untucked, looked on forlornly. The man seemed lost and dumbstruck. Stopping to adjust his rucksack, Ryan watched as a woman came out of the house, a toddler in her arms. She placed the child in the back seat of an old estate, packed with belongings. This wasn't a family holiday but a moving out. The man still hadn't moved. The woman, the man's wife, Ryan guessed, steered the man into the front passenger seat and put herself behind the wheel.

Job losses and house repossessions were happening everywhere, thought Ryan. Maybe he should be grateful that he'd reached fifty with his son about to finish university. This family had to re-plan their whole future. But at least the man had a wife who was taking control of the situation. Ryan wanted to step forward and tell the man that he should appreciate the woman's support. But the estate drove off and Ryan carried on his way, ever more determined.

The system was broken. It wasn't working anymore, not for the majority of people anyway. If you were part of the cabal of gilded bankers and politicians you were oblivious, uncaring. The sheer unfairness and inequality stung Ryan's eyes. Someone had to make a stand, someone had to shake the rotten structure to its very foundations and bring it all tumbling down.

Ryan continued east, along the verge of an old Roman road. He couldn't cut across the farmland as it was fenced off, security signs on the wire mesh. Through the gaps, Ryan saw fields of strawberries that were unpicked. As he reached the farm entrance, he found out why.

Two transit vans were parked side by side in front of the farm's metal gate. By each van, a crowd of people were engaged in a standoff. Unnoticed, Ryan climbed into the crook of an old oak tree and took in the proceedings.

One vanload of people was Chinese, ten of them. How they had all fitted into the van, Ryan didn't know. The other set of people were maybe Albanian. There were only seven of the Albanians, but they were a bit bigger than their Chinese counterparts so it made for an even match. The two sets of nationalities were shouting at each other, sometimes in their own languages, sometimes in broken English. One of the

Albanians stepped toward one of the Chinese and pointed down the road:

'You fuck out of here.'

The Chinese retorted an imitation, in his own accent, his English slightly better:

'You get fuck out of here yourself.'

The Albanian gestured to the front of the vans:

'We are here first, it's our job.'

The Chinese man's face was a picture of incredulity. Pointing at the Albanian's van with a bewildered expression, he said:

'You here first? By your bumper?'

'That's right.'

The Chinese man suddenly ran forward, leapt into the air and landed with two feet on top of the bumper. It crashed off the front of the van with a metallic groan. He faced the Albanian triumphantly:

'Now we level, huh.'

In a flash, both groups were at each other's throats, the scene erupting into a mass brawl. Until a shotgun blast fired into the air put a halt to proceedings. Everyone froze in their entangled positions. On the other side of the gate, a farmer stood with smoking shotgun in one hand, a Rottweiler on a leash in his other. He was flanked on either side by two security guys who looked like they were bouncers from a nightclub. In his Southern Counties accent, the farmer snarled:

'I'll be the one who says who works and who doesn't.'

The Chinese and Albanians regrouped back into

their two sets as the farmer set out the conditions:

'The pay is twenty pounds per hour per group. You pick ten baskets per hour. One pound is deducted for each basket less.'

The Albanian leader spoke up:

'Last time was thirty pounds.'

The farmer shrugged:

'Times are changing.'

The Chinese leader gestured to his group:

'We have more people, means less money each.'

The farmer smiled:

'Means you have more chance of picking ten baskets.'

The Albanian leader glanced at his group, turned back to the farmer:

'We do it.'

The Chinese leader immediately intervened:

'So do we.'

The farmer nodded:

'Chinese it is then, they've got more manpower.'

The Albanian spoke up:

'Wait, we do it for fifteen pounds.'

The Chinese leader said:

'We too.'

The Albanian looked at his compatriots, who shrugged despondently, so he kept his mouth sullenly closed. The farmer nodded to his two security guys:

'Let the Chinks in.'

The gate was opened. The Chinese packed into their van and drove in. Downcast, The Albanians picked up their broken bumper, got in their van and drove off down the country road.

Ryan extracted himself from his tree seat. He hadn't known whether to laugh or cry at the situation. If it was on TV, it would be funny but this was real life. People were bargaining to see how little they could be paid and coming to blows over who could get scraps of work. They were venting their anger on fellow workers rather than on those responsible.

By late afternoon, Ryan reached the edge of a village called Little Hungerford. Tired and hungry, he thought it was time to rest, maybe find a place to stay for the night. Before the village proper started, an old farmhouse was set back off the road. A 'For Auction' sign had fallen to the wayside and the overgrowth showed that no-one had inhabited the house for at least a few months.

Ryan crunched over the weed-covered gravel, checked there was no security. The front door was locked but a side window didn't even have glass, so he climbed inside.

It was as if someone had started to renovate the place then ran out of money. Most of the house was gutted, the floorboards up and plaster hacked off the walls. The only room that had been completed was the kitchen, resplendent in immaculate country house design style. There was no cooker or fridge, but that didn't matter as the gas and electric wouldn't be connected. Ryan tried the taps and water gushed into the big ceramic sink. He checked the cupboards and in one of them found tins of Mexican beans and a packet of tacos. He nodded in satisfaction.

The only other room which had a semblance of life was an upstairs bedroom. It was bare but the floorboards were down and the walls were plastered. Against the walls were three camp beds. Ryan shrugged. He had all he needed.

Looking out of the window, Ryan saw the rest of the village up ahead around the curve of the road. The houses were red brick rather than old stone. Ryan guessed that land around the farmhouse had been sold off to property developers after the Second World War.

An anguished cry drifted up in the breeze. Outside one of the houses he could just about make out some kind of altercation. He took out his binoculars to get a better look.

A woman in her early twenties was pleading with two burly bailiffs who were carrying a sofa from the house. Two young boys hung onto her skirt. She in turn grabbed hold of the moving sofa. But the men just walked on towards a waiting truck, dragging the woman and boys with the sofa. Reaching the truck, one of the men kicked out at the woman, sending her and the two boys sprawling in a sorry heap to the ground. Ryan didn't wait to see the men throw the sofa into the truck.

Enraged, he strode out of the farmhouse.

As Ryan came around the curve in the road, he saw the woman and her two small sons huddled together on the pavement. The woman was pleading with the two bailiffs:

'You can't just throw us on the street. Where will we go?'

The bailiffs ignored her as they padlocked the front door of the house. In nearby houses, curtains twitched, but no-one came to assist the mother in distress. The woman was on her knees on the pavement, begging:

'Please, don't do this.'

The bailiffs just looked at her in disgust. Getting closer, Ryan saw that one of the bailiffs was a skinhead while the other had his arms covered with tattoos of naked women. The woman's two boys huddled close to her. One was maybe eight, the other six. The oldest son put his hand out to his mum and tried to raise her:

'Come on mum, let's go.'

Ryan felt tears of fury sting his eyes. The woman had been kicked out of her home and completely humiliated. Nobody had helped, the neighbours shamed by an eight year old boy's act of responsibility. Ryan had to do something. The suburban family and Albanians could fend for themselves, but this unit could do with a hand. He stepped forward and asked:

'Is it only women and children you pick on?'

The two bailiffs looked dismissively over at Ryan. The skinhead said:

'Fuck off old man.'

Ryan took stock of the situation. It was two against one and both bailiffs were bigger than he was. Not only that, he'd given away any element of surprise. What he had to do was utilise their arrogance, the two men thinking he was too old. He nodded sadly.

Dismissing him, the two bailiffs turned their attention to a remaining kitchen table on the pavement. The skinhead bailiff said to the one with tattoos:

'Just chuck that in and we're done.'

The skinhead bailiff got in the driver's seat of the van while the tattooed bailiff picked up the kitchen table. It didn't fit easily into the back of the van, so the bailiff rammed it inside, one of the legs breaking off. Ryan suddenly strode up to the bailiff, the guy looking over his shoulder.

Ryan grabbed hold of the van door and slammed it into the bailiff's face, the bailiff falling awkwardly into the back of the van. Before the bailiff could get up, Ryan stamped hard onto the guy's knee, the bailiff groaning in pain as he slid to the ground. Ryan kicked down hard again, making sure the bailiff's leg was broken, the bailiff screaming out. Ryan said:

'A leg for a leg.'

Ryan picked up the broken table leg and used it to choke the bailiff.

Roused by the commotion, the skinhead bailiff got out of the driver's seat and came jogging to the back of the van. Ryan faced him and said:

'Get back in the van.'

The skinhead bailiff saw the hardened look on Ryan's face, saw his mate was in extreme pain and in that instant knew Ryan could inflict it on him too. He backed off quickly.

Using the table leg as a choke hold, Ryan dragged the tattooed bailiff into the back of the van, shoving him between the furniture. Ryan let go of the table leg and the bailiff gasped for breath. Ryan jumped out of the van, slammed the doors shut and turned to face the skinhead bailiff back in the driver's seat.

The skinhead bailiff understood, quickly put the van in gear and screeched off down the road. Ryan turned to the woman and her two young sons.

The two boys were staring at him in amazement, but the woman's gaze was fixed on the van, until it vanished out of sight. Gathering her bags, the woman set off with her two boys, each carrying a small backpack. As they moved past Ryan, the boys glanced his way, but the woman didn't even look at him.

Ryan realised that his action man heroics hadn't achieved anything. The woman and her two sons had still lost their home and possessions. Catching up with the woman and her kids, Ryan spoke as gently as he could:

'Do you need a place to stay for the night?'

The woman stopped and stared at Ryan. Anger had replaced her despair:

'The last thing I need now is some pervert hitting on me. You think because you just beat up those two bastards I'm yours for the night?'

The woman drew her kids close and carried on her way. Ryan frowned. He guessed she needed to vent her anger at someone. He also realised he was sweaty, unshaved and had been wearing the same clothes for the last three days. As they walked away, the older boy looked back sadly over his shoulder. Deciding he shouldn't give up, Ryan called out:

'I lost my house too. I found a good place to stay tonight though. If you want to use the place as well, you're welcome.'

Without looking back, Ryan walked to the old farmhouse.

A few minutes after he'd gone in, the older boy's face appeared at the window:

'My mum says the door's locked.'

Ryan cracked a smile:

'You have to climb in through the window.'

The boy waved his mum and brother over, then scrambled inside. The woman looked warily at Ryan, but held up her youngest son for him to lift in. Ryan put the boy down and offered his hand to the woman but she climbed in of her own accord.

Ryan showed them around the house:

'There are three camp beds upstairs you can sleep on. There's no cooker but I'll make a fire later. I found some tinned food in the kitchen so we can heat it up.'

Around the back of the house, Ryan got the two boys gathering twigs. He scrunched up a newspaper the woman had taken from one of her bags and showed the oldest boy how to wigwam the twigs over the paper. Together, Ryan and the boys put bricks around the wigwam and got bigger sticks ready. Ryan lit the fire. Once it was steadily alight, he balanced the cans of beans above the fire across the bricks.

With beans and tacos on plates, the boys looked to their mum before eating. Ryan saw their hesitation:

'Afraid that's all there is.'

The woman smiled:

'No, it's just I don't let them normally eat beans, but I think on this occasion, it's ok.'

The boys tucked in.

After they'd eaten, Ryan stacked the used plates and empty tins. Half asleep, the two boys cuddled their mum, the three of them watching the fire as it flickered to its embers. Ryan felt the glow of the woman's love for her children and for a second he felt at peace. The Robert Ryan film On Dangerous Ground came to mind. In the film, the blind woman's compassion had shown the bitter detective another way of life, a different path to his capacity for violence. Could this woman and her children do the same for Ryan?

The fire dwindled, died and broke the spell. Ryan carried the youngest boy up to the bedroom. He turned to the oldest:

'You'll remember how to make a fire?'

The boy nodded sleepily. Ryan left the woman to say goodnight to her sons.

Down in the kitchen, Ryan guessed he'd be sleeping under the stars again as he'd given away the beds. The grass outside was probably more comfortable than the kitchen tiles. He thought about the woman upstairs. She'd obviously had kids at a young age, but she wasn't uneducated. She was articulate and had brought up her sons to be bright and polite. A blind anger at the people responsible for her situation rose up in him.

When he reached the bedroom doorway, the woman was already at the ready. Sat up on one of the camp beds she had a knife held tightly in her hand. Surprised, Ryan held up his palms:

'I just wanted to ask you a question.'

The woman eyed Ryan suspiciously. The camp beds, fire and food had been more than welcome. But she'd suspected that in the end he'd want something in return. Still not knowing if she could trust him, she said:

'About what?'

Ryan remained in the doorway:

'About how you got in this situation.'

The woman held back tears. Ryan seemed genuine. Lowering her knife, she told him everything, starting with her name, Laura.

At the age of sixteen, Laura had run away to live with an artist in Ireland. The first few years had been wonderful and she'd given birth to her two sons in quick succession. But it soon turned sour. The guy's art stopped selling, he turned to drink and took it out on her. So she ran away again, with the kids, back to England. She'd set herself up in the village, worked in the local nursery and was doing teacher training by distance learning. But each month, she paid out more money than she earned. She couldn't keep up with all her payments and had been evicted. Reaching into her bag, Laura tossed over an official letter.

'Even if we'd managed to stay it would have been no use as they were just about to cut us off.'

Ryan read the letter from Southern Gas and Electric. Rather than direct his anger at the local landlord who had evicted Laura, Ryan turned it on the energy company as he remembered who was CEO of Southern Gas and Electric. Edward Cameron's chum, Sir Howard fucking Pilkington, that was who.

At the reunion, Jack Jones had told Ryan all about Howard Pilkington, how he'd been in the MOD and been complicit with Edward Cameron in the arms to Iraq scandal. And in the news, the energy company had been named along with the banks. Ryan recalled that Southern Gas and Electric had been accused of price-fixing so as to make customers pay more. Just like the banks, the energy companies had been ripping people off left right and centre, sheer profiteering. Pilkington even had the gall to give an interview, the self-righteous prick claiming that nothing illegal had occurred and that senior executives had to be rewarded to ensure such vital services could be provided to the public.

It made Ryan sick. He took another look at the letter from Southern Gas and Electric and noted that their headquarters were in Reading. It would mean a small detour, but it was on his way anyway.

21

Wayne Johnson parked his Porsche next to Sir Howard Pilkington's BMW in the Travel Lodge car park. Sir Howard had named the time and place, informing Wayne that the meeting was clandestine. Wayne wound his window down and Sir Howard handed over a folder:

'Here's the OFT report. Papers will get news of it by the weekend, if they haven't already.'

'How did you get hold of it?'

'Friend of a friend.'

Old Boys' network no doubt, thought Wayne as he opened the folder. The first page made him focus:

'Fuck.'

'My thoughts precisely, which is why I'll be handing in my resignation at the AGM tomorrow.'

This was news to Wayne, making him look up from the folder. Sir Howard said:

'Two years earlier than planned, but with severance pay it will still be a pretty good deal.'

'Too right it will be a bloody good deal because you won't have to deal with the fall out.'

'Way the cookie crumbles I'm afraid. Won't just be the media either. The board will turn.'

'I've made you all shitloads of money.'

'That you have, which is why I am providing you with the dossier. I don't want to appear ungrateful. I'm sure a bright spark like yourself will think of something. See you tomorrow.'

Before Wayne could offer any further reply, Sir Howard reversed his BMW. Sir Howard was playing it blasé, but in fact he was distracted by a number of things. The shit was most definitely about to hit the fan. Under public pressure, the government was being forced to bring in new laws. From what he'd heard, senior executives at Shell, Barclays and Goldman Sachs all faced jail for various price-rigging scams. Sir Howard didn't want to be caught up in that.

Then there was the matter of Ed's death. It all sounded very mysterious. MI5 were trying to keep a lid on it, so something was fishy. Ed was under a lot of pressure too with the bail out. Had he taken his own life? But over the years, there were a lot of people who would bear a grudge if they knew the truth about the arms to Iraq and other business Ed had been involved in. Ed's car had exploded and that suggested a bomb and murder. And if someone had targeted Ed, thought Sir Howard, they might also come after him. It was time to get out of the game, take the wife on that yacht tour from Monaco to Montenegro. He had a Russian friend who had a villa there. Alternatively there was

Dubai, although that was probably best without the wife. Either way, Sir Howard was planning to leave old blighty for a while.

Wayne watched in disbelief as Sir Howard drove off. The bastard had dropped him in it.

Wayne studied the folder on his lap, sat there in the car park as he read every word. Along with other energy companies, Southern Gas and Electric were shown to be deliberately misleading customers for pure profiteering.

Wayne wanted to say, so what? Of course the company had been profiteering. The whole point was to make money. They were a private company not a fucking charity. The problem was the manipulation of prices. Wayne knew full well that they'd made it seem gas wholesale was more expensive than it was, just as they'd worded letters to customers to make it seem they would pay less than they actually did. On top of that, all the companies had been in cahoots, ensuring customer prices could only go up and never down.

There had previously been an investigation by the energy regulator Ofgem, but it had been half hearted, the regulator taken care of. Southern Gas and Electric were so used to getting away with it, they'd become too sure of themselves. The OFT report had concrete 'evidence that the companies colluded in distorting prices so as to raise customer bills.'

Yes, Wayne had been behind most of that manipulation, but nobody had complained as they were raking it in. He just knew the board were going to turn on him tomorrow, especially with Sir Howard bailing out. It was alright for Sir Howard, he was retirement age anyway and would get a huge pay off. Wayne wasn't forty yet, he needed to further his career, not pull the plug on it.

He sped home to the riverside pad in Henley on Thames, cursing all the way. He found Jade towelling herself by their indoor pool. Fuck, she looked good. And the news he'd just had, a fuck was exactly what he needed. Not wanting to show his stress, he ambled over, slipped his hands around her. She frowned:

'You're all sweaty.'

'How about I take a shower and we go to bed?'

'You can do whatever you want, but I'll be sleeping.'

Wayne refrained from grabbing his crotch, but his hands were out in desperation:

'Jade, I'm pretty full here.'

'Then do some DIY.'

Jade went off to bed, leaving Wayne frustrated. They hadn't had sex for months. Whenever he brought it up, she always used the same phrase. She wasn't suggesting he do work on the house. Their house was exactly what the problem was. Yes it was pretty suave, but it wasn't Chelsea.

Every bloody weekend, they traipsed around Chelsea and South Ken, looking at property. Other couples Wayne knew lived in their huge Surrey houses and commuted into the City to work. Wayne and Jade lived and worked in the Reading area, going into London to dream of where they would live and work.

He'd wanted Jade since Business College in Swindon, the two of them studying together. She'd acknowledged his acumen, but she was out of his league and he knew it. His rapid rise through the ranks at Honda had impressed her. She'd initially done well at Anchor Butter, but got stuck at senior management level. She didn't want to be bitter but she was pretty sure it was because she was a woman. Still, she could see how well Wayne had done and they'd make a great team, so she'd married him.

With Wayne headhunted by Southern Gas and Electric, she'd been all for it, though equally jealous. It meant they had more money, but that he had risen quicker than her. It was the same now that he finally had the Goldman Sachs interview lined up. She envied him, but also pushed him as hard as she could to get the position.

The work he'd done at Southern Gas and Electric was what went on the CV, but it was the behind the scenes work that had got him the interview. It was Jade who had done the research, getting information through a friend of a friend on a senior partner at Goldman Sachs. It had cost her a blow job, but had been well worth it as the information was priceless. The senior partner had passed inside information to the buyer on a takeover deal and, with the new laws in place, could easily be convicted. Jade had no interest in the guy going to prison, instead using the information as leverage to get Wayne the interview, not that Wayne was aware of that. Pretty much all Wayne had to do now was turn up for the interview.

But just to make sure he didn't fuck up, she was withholding sex until he had the job at Goldman Sachs and the house in Chelsea.

Wayne had his suspicions that Jade had occasionally been unfaithful, but he couldn't divorce her for a couple of reasons. First, she was too fucking clever and had made sure the pre-nups were well in her favour. Second, he'd never have a woman as attractive.

So, it was simple. Get the property in Chelsea and all would be well again. He'd been on track, had the interview with Goldman Sachs lined up, was ready to show how much profit he'd made for Southern Gas and Electric. And now he was about to be vilified for it.

He listed his options. If he made it look like it was others who'd been behind the manipulation then it would also look like those people had made the profits. So that option was no good.

Perhaps he could find a way to discredit the findings. The problem there was that the gas wholesale guys weren't going to lie for him or be bribed – they were richer than he was.

By the early hours, Wayne reckoned he had the solution. He would alter the minutes of previous meetings, making it seem that along the way gas wholesale prices had been mistakenly entered as higher than they were. The board had only now discovered the error and as a gesture of goodwill would forfeit their end of year bonuses. Privately, they would make up for the lost money by being given new company cars that could be sold. Publicly, they'd look contrite.

And to Goldman Sachs, he'd appear as the guy who made everyone happy, both able to make and save a company vast amounts.

Jade would get her Chelsea penthouse and sex would be back on the menu. Leaving his wife to get her beauty sleep, he strode to the bathroom. Locking the door, he pumped one off into the toilet bowl.

22

Ryan arrived at Southern Gas and Electric headquarters before anyone had started work. Situated in an out of town business area, it was nearer to the motorway than the city centre so had been easy to find.

On the way, he'd passed a gardening centre and DIY store, the first with a huge 'Everything Must Go' banner, the second emblazoned with 'Huge Summer Sale' posters. The gardening centre was obviously on its last legs and the DIY store would no doubt soon follow suit.

The wide parallel streets were each dotted with identical two-floor office blocks, all designed in the same Meccano fashion. Ryan reckoned it must have all been built in the early nineties at the height of an economic boom. Right now, half the offices were empty and out of use.

The set of offices opposite Southern Gas and Electric had a skip parked outside, filled with desks and swivel chairs. The blinds had also been removed from the windows so that Ryan could see right through the building. His eyes roved over the front wall until they stopped on an ADT alarm box with CCTV camera above it. After scrutinising it for a minute, he noticed no red light flashing. With the office vacated and whoever had been in it out of business, nobody was paying for security.

Ryan walked through the empty parking at the side to the back of the offices. In the narrow drainage space between the back of the building and a wire mesh fence was a metal fire escape that went up to the second floor. Beyond the fence was long grass with wild flowers. As Ryan climbed the metal stairs, he saw that a stream meandered through the greenery. He stopped and checked his map. If he was right, the stream joined a river and would lead him back out to the motorway. It was a useful alternative escape route.

At the top of the fire escape, the exit was locked and not easily opened. Instead, he smashed the glass in the nearest window. He carefully removed the sharp edges, then heaved himself inside.

His steps echoed in the empty offices, bits of stationery littering the floor. With no partitions, it must have been open plan. Now that it was bereft of desks, chairs and computers it looked more like a warehouse. On the remote chance that anyone was watching from Southern Gas and Electric across the way, Ryan stuck to the walls as he made his way to the only partitioned area in the building – the toilets.

As with the old farmhouse, the water was still on. Ryan took out his folded trousers and shirt. He changed out of his jeans and flicked water on his shirt. With one hand, he held the shirt against the wall. With the side of his other hand, he pressed hard downwards several times. When it was as un-creased as it was going to get, he put it on and looked in the mirror. He still looked slightly crumpled but that could be put down to a long drive. As long as he acted like a businessman, he would be presentable enough.

He'd washed and shaved earlier that morning in the old farmhouse, up well before Laura and her two sons. He'd left a note telling them to keep a low profile if they were going to stay there. He'd shown them how to find a place for the night and build a fire. What else could he do?

Ryan took out Laura's letter from Southern Gas and Electric, folded it and put it in his trousers pocket. He checked he had 'Morgan Security Systems' business cards in his wallet. Finally, he placed two blocks of PE4 explosives on the hand washing counter.

He wasn't sure of his exact plan yet. First he had to gain entry to the offices, scope the layout and try to find out when those at the top would be in. After that, he'd have to see. He was thinking something along the lines of how it had gone with Edward Cameron. Maybe lure the chief executive Sir Howard Pilkington out to his car and give him a quick choice, help out Laura and her two sons or face the consequences.

Binoculars in hand, Ryan edged along the wall to one of the front windows. He focused on Southern Gas and Electric's building and saw that they had a fully functioning alarm and CCTV system. There was also a security guard, a tall African-looking guy who unlocked the front entrance from inside at eight thirty.

The first car arrived a minute later, a Renault Clio parking in a bay marked 'staff'. A young blonde woman got out and smiled a good morning to the security guard as she entered the offices. Next in was a brand new BMW, easing into the slot marked 'Sir Howard Pilkington, Chief Executive'.

Through his binoculars, Ryan watched Sir Howard with disgust. With his steel grey hair and pinstriped suit, Sir Howard strode purposefully towards the entrance, his stern face not even acknowledging the security guard's presence. Ryan remembered how, at the reunion, Sir Howard had been incredibly condescending. The man thought anyone below his class was inferior, assumed it was his right to exploit them and never gave a thought to being caught out because he was too well connected.

Lieutenant General Edward Cameron, Sir Howard Pilkington, Chancellor of the Exchequer George Oswald - they were all part of the same old boys network, each helping the other maintain their inherited wealth while ripping off the rest of the country.

By nine, the car park was full, a mixture of Ford Fiestas and Vauxhall Corsas driven in by office workers, Audis and BMWs by management. With everyone seemingly in, the security guy stepped outside the building to stretch.

A bright yellow Porsche cruised past the security guard, some young guy flicking his cigarette butt out the window. The butt landed at the feet of the security guard. He looked down at the butt, then up and across at the now parked Porsche. Nonchalantly getting out of his car, the young guy hadn't even noticed.

Ryan focused on the Porsche parking bay and read the nameplate 'Wayne Johnson, Senior Partner'. Ryan would see what Wayne had to say for himself, but he was already sure the guy was going to be an arsehole.

While many people could no longer afford to pay their bills and had their gas and electric cut off, the top brass were driving around in expensive cars. This of course was only the tip of the iceberg, but it seemed symbolic to Ryan. He'd heard Sir Howard speak on TV. The sheer hypocrisy was galling to listen to, the man somehow defending the price hike of customer bills as necessary. Yes, it was necessary so that people like Sir Howard could continue living the life of riley while people like Laura weren't able to pay their bills.

Ryan kept his binoculars on the building for a few more minutes to see how it was set up inside. It seemed that the ground floor was open plan office space, whereas the second floor was for individual management offices with a boardroom at the end.

Turning his attention to the vacant offices he was crouched in, Ryan scanned the floor for any stationery that could be used. Among debris in one corner, he spotted an A4 envelope. He took the envelope, put a few pages from a torn notepad inside and sealed it. In the toilet, he placed the two explosives in his jacket pockets and draped the jacket over one arm. Envelope in his free hand, he was ready for action.

Ryan crossed the street, nodded at the security guard and entered the headquarters of Southern Gas and Electric. He flexed his neck as he walked up to the receptionist, recognising her as the blonde woman who had been first in. Ryan wasn't worried about being identified himself. The night before, he'd checked the newspaper he'd used to start the fire. There had been an article about Cameron's death but no details, no link to Huw and no mention of Ryan. Maybe nobody had made the connection yet, or maybe the police were making sure before releasing his photo fit as a wanted man. Either way, his face wouldn't be known by office workers in Southern Gas and Electric.

The receptionist smiled up at him and he placed his envelope on the counter:

'On my way back from London to Cardiff, so I told Howard I'd drop this off.'

Ryan checked his watch:

'I can't stop as I need to get moving if I'm going to make the next meeting. Besides, he's a busy man, probably in some meeting himself...'

Ryan looked up:

'He is in to receive this though?'

The receptionist nodded:

'He's in board meetings all morning. I'll make sure he gets it.'

'Thanks.'

'Who should I say it's from?'

Ryan cracked a smile:

'Must be getting old and forgetful, or tired from the early drive.'

He handed her one of his redundant business cards. Ryan nodded his gratitude and turned to leave, before turning back again. He frowned as he spoke in a low voice:

'You wouldn't have a bathroom I could use? Just that I'm not sure when the next service station will be.'

'Er, yes, go up the stairs and it's on your left.'

'Appreciate it.'

Striding up the stairs, Ryan nodded at a passing office worker. Ignoring the toilet, he carried on towards the boardroom at the end. Up ahead, Wayne Johnson nipped out of his office and used a fob key to open the boardroom door. Ryan stretched his legs and caught up with Wayne as he was halfway through the door:

'Howard in there? Said I'd have a quick word before the meeting started.'

Wayne frowned at Ryan, not knowing who he was, but on the other hand he seemed to know Howard, so kept the door open:

'Sure.'

Ryan stepped in after Wayne, the door clicking shut behind him. Casually draping his jacket over a spare chair, Ryan took out one of the explosives. At an oval table in front of him were four men in suits. Two of them were in earnest conversation, Wayne was taking his seat and Sir Howard was looking up at Ryan, trying to place him.

'Can I help you?'

'You don't remember me, do you?'

'Should I?'

'We met only a few weeks ago.'

Sir Howard let out a dismissive laugh:

'I meet a lot of people.'

Ryan nodded:

'At the reunion. I was in bomb disposal - served in Kuwait under your old pal Edward.'

Sir Howard frowned, vaguely recognising Ryan now that his memory had been jogged.

'That may be. But what are you doing here?'

'I'm interested in how you became Sir Howard. I don't want to appear insolent to my superior, as you called yourself, but did your services to industry include selling arms to Iraq? Or perhaps ripping off your customers so you could make more money and feather your nest?'

'I was granted my knighthood because I bloody well deserved it so cast your aspersions elsewhere, you frightful little shit. In fact, if you don't leave the premises immediately, I'll have you removed by security.'

Sir Howard made to reach for a telephone, but stopped when Ryan said:

'I also came to tell you Ed is dead.'

There was something in Ryan's dry tone that made Sir Howard uneasy, but he still needed to appear superior.

'I am aware of that, I can read the newspapers.'

Ryan casually took out the block of PE4 from his jacket pocket and said:

'But are you aware you might also die?'

Ryan placed the block of explosive on the table:

'PE4 explosive, basically the same as semtex, as I'm sure you know.'

He displayed the detonator in his hand:

'I just press the wireless detonator and we all die.'

The conversation between the other men stopped. Sir Howard looked at Ryan:

'Is this a joke?'

'No joke. I want you all to put your mobiles and key fobs on the table.'

Sir Howard looked at him with incredulity. Ryan's face hardened.

'Now.'

Still not knowing if it was for real, but hedging their bets, the men put their mobiles and key fobs on the table. Ryan pointed at Wayne:

'Scoop them all into the bin.'

Wayne mulled this over for a second, then turned to Ryan, holding him with a steady gaze:

'Fuck this...and fuck you, Tarzan.'

Ryan had been waiting for Wayne's arrogance to work itself loose, ever since he'd spotted him flinging his cigarette butt out of his Porsche window. Yes, he was younger than Ryan and looked like he went to the gym a few times a week, but Ryan was on the front foot. In one stride, Ryan was over Wayne, grabbed him by the hair and smashed his face into the table, blood spurting out of his nose onto his shirt.

Ryan quickly stepped back and glanced at all the others, one of them halfway to reaching for his mobile. Ryan raised his detonator-attached hand once more.

'Believe me...you don't want that explosive to go off, just do as I say.'

The men sat back and glared at Ryan, not used to having someone else give the orders. Wayne moaned as he leaned back and held his bleeding nose, red blood stains on his white shirt.

'Do you know how much this shirt cost?'

'Do you know how much it's going to cost if you don't shut the fuck up?'

Wayne shut up. Ryan picked up the bin and handed it to another of the men. He waited until the man filled the bin with the mobiles and key fobs, took it and faced the table:

'I'm going to give you a choice. You just have to make the right one.'

Ryan took out the letter Southern Gas and Electric had sent to Laura. He tossed it over to Sir Howard:

'This woman has two sons. Yesterday she was evicted. It wouldn't have mattered as she was just about to be cut off by you.'

Sir Howard looked up from the letter, unruffled:

'Presumably she didn't make her payments.'

'That's right, but not through lack of hard work. So here's what you're going to do. You're going to get on the phone to accounts and reimburse her for all her bills last year.'

Sir Howard still wasn't taking it seriously enough.

'Maybe you would like me to credit her account too, add ten thousand for inconvenience caused.'

'I don't know, ten thousand is small change for you guys. I think a hundred thousand would be more appropriate.'

Sir Howard let out a small laugh:

'A hundred thousand?'

'You're right, still too low, what with the bonuses you get. Lets say a hundred and fifty and we'll call it quits.'

Sir Howard shook his head and said:

'Okay, the joke's over.'

Ryan raised the detonator and his voice:

'Do it now!'

Sir Howard looked into Ryan's eyes and then looked away. Up until that second, he'd still somehow believed he could control the situation. But now he knew. He knew that Ryan had killed Ed and he knew that Ryan was capable of pressing the detonator and killing them all right there and then. He got on the phone to accounts. The room was silent as he explained it away to the person at the other end of the line. Sir Howard, feeling Ryan's glare on the back of his neck, started to sweat.

Once the call was over, Ryan yanked the phone out of Sir Howard's hand and smacked it into his face. As Sir Howard reeled in pain, Ryan said:

'That's for calling me a disgrace.'

The rest of the men in the room sat rigidly staring at Ryan, slack jawed and afraid to move a muscle. Ryan looked at each in turn, a smile tugging at the corner of his mouth. He made to press the detonator and suddenly shouted:

'Boom!'

Sir Howard, Wayne and the rest of the executives desperately tried to hide under the table. Ryan looked with disdain at Sir Howard:

'As you once said to me, have you no self respect?'

Ryan snatched up the bin of mobiles and key fobs and said:

'Don't call for help for ten minutes, or you might regret it.'

Taking one of the key fobs, Ryan backed out of the office and locked the door. Setting off the fire alarm on the wall, Ryan made for the fire exit across the offices. He guessed that the men in the board room were right now scrambling to grab the PE4 from the table and throw it out of the window. But they'd miss the block he'd stuck to the door handle. As Ryan descended the metal fire stairs, he saw the office workers pile out of the ground floor. If he was honest with himself, Ryan had always known he was going to kill the entire board. He pressed the remote detonator.

People instinctively ducked as the PE4 exploded, the windows shattered at the front of the building. The sound of the explosion reverberated through the air like a taut guitar string and the offices shook sullenly. In shock, nobody knew whether to huddle in the allocated fire escape stations or go and check what the hell had happened. Amid the confusion, Ryan crossed the road. He didn't look at the glass and blood strewn across the tarmac.

Ryan collected his rucksack from the fire escape at the back of the empty offices. He leaned across to the top of the fence, swung himself over and scaled down toward the long grass. As he walked by the stream, he heard the sirens.

23

To the consternation of DCI Chisholm, the meeting had been convened in Bath Police station. Not only had a case in his own backyard been taken from him, but his desk was now surrounded by two MI5 officers and a bloody Welshman.

Evan was there last, having come from out of town. The night before, MI5 had traced Ryan's hired Ford Focus. Checking CCTV from the motorway services, they spotted the car as it drove past the petrol station and down the service road. Evan decided to stay in the service station's Welcome Inn hotel as it would be cheaper than anywhere in Bath. It seemed as if the case was falling into the hands of MI5, so he wouldn't be getting any expenses for the trip. The overnight stay and petrol costs would all be his. He thought ruefully that Ryan's antics were starting to cost him.

Not that it was certain whose case it in fact was. The lead MI5 officer Angela Stephenson got off her mobile and turned to the others, fixing both Evan and Chisholm with a steely gaze:

'Might end up being between you two to liaise – maybe you can form some new cross border relations.'

Evan saw a slight smile on Angela's face before she got serious again:

'If Ryan has simply got revenge on the two people he thinks are personally responsible for him losing his business, it's a police case and down to you to catch up with him.'

Chisholm was as grumpy as he had been on the phone with Evan the day before:

'If we can ever find him. He's for sure not in my area anymore. Maybe he's gone back to bloody Wales.'

Evan knew the comment was aimed at him, but didn't rise to it. He was trying to work out Ryan's moves. It was true, he'd vanished. Sniffer dogs had been brought in, but by the time they arrived at least twelve hours had elapsed since Ryan had been at the Manor House. The trace was faint and it was soon too dark to pursue.

Evan didn't buy that Ryan had killed Huw and Edward purely out of personal revenge. He wasn't going to say that he knew Ryan. He obviously no longer did. But he didn't see Ryan committing two acts of murder then disappearing. Both had been well planned. And Ryan was someone who kept going until his mission had been accomplished.

Reaching for a piece of paper on Chisholm's desk, Evan took out a pen and quickly sketched a map of Britain. The other three watched with bemusement. Evan was tempted to smile as he recalled his 'small town' and 'big city' map. This time he drew a small circle where Swansea was and wrote 'Huw Hughes, bank manager'. Where Bath was located, he drew a larger circle and wrote 'Edward Cameron, bank CEO.' He spun the paper around for the others to see.

'He's working up a chain. He starts with the manager of the bank that put him out of business. He moves on to the CEO, a guy who gave himself a million pound bonus while liquidating companies in debt. Ryan could have taken that money. Instead, he blew it up with Edward Cameron like he's saying this is what you deserve. I think basically Ryan has thought, fuck it, he's had enough of the hypocrisy.'

Chisholm snorted:

'You joining the anti-banker movement now, Taff?'

'Just putting myself in Ryan's shoes. To be honest, I'm surprised there hasn't been more anger before. The Occupy London sit in and that kind of thing have all been pretty tame so far.'

Angela said:

'What about the London riots the last few summers? I know it's a bit far along the M4 from you, but we had half the city burnt down, it was pretty fractious.'

'So you're saying the riots were people rising up in anger?'

'Perhaps, though it was misplaced as they mostly just hurt local businesses. But it's something we've had to deal with.'

'We never got called down. But during the Olympics, we hardly had any police left in Wales because they were all seconded to London. And there's the hypocrisy again. You have people burning down their own streets and it's low priority. But you have a possible terrorist threat to a prestigious event and the whole nation's police forces are mobilized and called into action.'

'Okay, so you're saying all this anger has built up and Ryan has a list of people responsible that he's planning to target.'

Evan nodded. He was trying to work Angela out. She was sharp in every sense of the word. Chisholm was shaking his head:

'Great, we've got one Welsh madman killing bankers and a revolutionary Welsh detective on his trail.'

To Evan's surprise, Angela responded first:

'Which might not be a bad thing. He's certainly given us more of a lead to go on than anything you've done to date.'

That shut Chisholm up. Evan couldn't quite work out where Angela stood, but he was getting to admire her more all the time. Evan summed up his thoughts:

'Like I said, I'm just trying to get into Ryan's mindset. If I'm right about him, the question is who's next on his list?'

Chisholm, Angela and the male MI5 officer mulled this over. The male officer spoke first:

'Cameron was pretty much the top guy. There are other execs, but they are all pretty much on a par.'

Evan nodded:

'But who bailed out the bank?'

Angela sighed:

'Meaning it's the Government next, in particular the Chancellor.'

Evan shrugged:

'That's my guess. Ryan's a guy who doesn't stop until he's done what he set out to achieve.'

Angela made a quick call then informed the three men around her:

'We've upped security around the Chancellor. He's in London now but due in his constituency tonight. We'll head there, see about prevention.'

Angela looked directly at Evan:

'If you want to tag along, your input could be useful. You know Ryan better than me.'

"Tag along", thought Evan. He'd bloody pointed them in the right direction. On the other hand, he understood he was being granted access to a case that wasn't really his anymore. He nodded his acquiescence and made a mental note to call both his wife and the station back in Swansea. He also thought about Angela's second sentence. Yes, he knew Ryan well, but Angela's 'me' was more personal than 'us'. It was the second time he'd detected a hint from Angela that she somehow knew Ryan.

Before Evan could pose any suitable question, Angela had turned her attention to Chisholm:

'We need a photo fit of Ryan circulated, like yesterday, for police eyes only. I'll alert our guys but any police in the southern counties need to be aware of him. At this moment it doesn't look like the general public are in any danger so I don't want to cause unnecessary panic or let Ryan know we're on to him.'

Chisholm gave an ironic salute:

'You're the boss.'

Angela saluted him back:

'Try not to forget it.'

In his unmarked Escort, Evan followed the MI5 officers in their black-windowed Audi. The chancellor's home constituency was in Surrey so it meant driving along the M4 towards London before heading south on the M25. Only the day before Evan had been up and down the exact same stretch of motorway. They were halfway there when Evan turned up the news on the radio.

An explosion had occurred at the headquarters of Southern Gas and Electric, killing five members of the board. Police were treating it as suspicious.

In front of Evan, the MI5 car suddenly turned off at the upcoming junction. As Evan went after them, his mobile sounded, Angela on the other end:

'We've had news of an attack in Reading.'

'I just heard the news on the radio.'

'Intel we just received, it sounds very similar to the others. We're heading back there.'

The mobile cut off. Evan drove after the Audi as it did a whole circuit of the roundabout and went back onto the M4 in the opposite direction. They'd just passed the Reading junction so needed to backtrack.

It was past eleven by the time they entered the business area. Evan noticed that while modern office blocks symmetrically lined the way, less than half were in use, full parking bays oddly dotted alongside. The scene was quite surreal. In this urban office world, a block was cordoned off, the top floor windows of Southern Gas and Electric blown out. A heavy emergency service presence blocked any view of the dead bodies.

There wasn't much left for the fire or ambulance services to do. The fire from the explosion had been put out. And people were either alive or dead, with no in-between injuries requiring hospitalisation.

Evan followed on the tails of the MI5 officers who cut a swathe through the melee. Unlike the Bath DCI, the Reading equivalent was happy for MI5 to be on the scene, amazed they were there so quickly. Reading had its share of street crime, but a bomb killing the whole board of a gas company was not usual. So if MI5 had a say in the matter, they were welcome to it.

The Reading DCI had a couple of leads to hand over. There was a Sudanese security guard who'd been picked up and was down at the station. And there was also a man seen by the receptionist and not accounted for.

'Apparently he went to use the toilet. He wasn't with all the office workers and the bodies have all been identified. He's not one of them.'

The male MI5 officer asked:

'Got a name?'

'He left a business card, but it's on the receptionist's desk and we can't go into the building until the fire service gives us the go ahead.'

'What about a description?'

'Tall, late forties maybe.'

Angela stepped in:

'Where's the receptionist?'

The Reading DCI pointed to a group of people huddled in a car park a block up the road.

After talking with the receptionist, Evan and the MI5 officers were pretty sure it was Ryan. Once they were allowed into the offices, they had no doubt. Ryan's business card was found on the floor by reception. And footage from the CCTV monitor in the small security room clearly showed Ryan entering the building.

The MI5 officers got on their mobiles and urgently mobilised a manhunt. Evan left them to it. Crossing over to the empty offices opposite, he walked around to the wire fence at the back. Something had caught his eye. With his face pressed against the mesh, he saw it was sunlight glinting on a stream that meandered through the long grass.

Evan leant with his back against the fence. He longed for a cigarette. With his head tilted up towards the sun, he noticed that a window had been smashed on the second floor of the vacant offices. He climbed the metal fire steps and studied it. He guessed Ryan had been inside, but suspected there'd be no traces left to indicate where Ryan had gone next. Turning to look over the top of the fence, Evan pined for the times when he and Ryan had run cross country as kids.

Evan was jolted by his mobile ringing. He answered and heard Angela's voice echo. They were having a quick debriefing in the offices opposite Southern Gas and Electric. Instead of going back down the fire escape and around to the front, Evan climbed in through the broken window. He found the two MI5 officers and the Reading DCI downstairs. They raised their eyebrows at his entrance, but didn't say anything.

Angela explained that a manhunt was now under way for Ryan Morgan, including a helicopter that had just left London. Evan checked his watch. It was almost two. Ryan had half a day on them. He would be out of sight. Evan listened as Angela further outlined the case.

It seemed that Ryan was single-handedly committing acts of terrorism across the country so he was now solely MI5's responsibility. His photo fit would be made public. He was a danger to society and needed apprehending. Angela looked Evan's way, nodding acknowledgment as she said:

'As we know, Ryan is ex army, bomb disposal in fact, so he knows how to kill and how to evade capture.'

She took a breath before finishing off:

'At this stage, no connection is to be made with the other murders. We don't want any copycats, people getting ideas to go and start killing various CEOs, bankers, and politicians.'

Evan piped up:

'It won't be long before some journalist makes the link.'

'Sure, but it gives us a bit more time to catch him before the media makes that link.'

Angela signalled it was the end of their impromptu meeting. The MI5 officer and the Reading DCI left the building first. Angela nodded at Evan:

'Guess Ryan's plan wasn't exactly as you thought.'

'Guess not.'

In fairness to Angela, she didn't rub it in:

'Appreciate your help. We'll be in contact if we need more Intel on him. You're the person who knows him best.'

'I thought I did.'

'You can never really know anyone.'

'You sound like you're talking from experience.'

'I'm an experienced lady, though maybe not such a lady.'

Evan smiled, paused before he said:

'Ryan's a good guy – or he was.'

'I believe you. And I don't want to see him hurt anymore than you do. But he has to be stopped.'

'I know.'

Evan looked closely at Angela, now absolutely sure that she knew Ryan.

After Evan had driven off, Angela had a few moments of respite before the search team arrived. She wasn't very hopeful of finding Ryan in the vicinity. With his skills, he'd be long gone. Evan had told her all he knew about Ryan but she hadn't let on that she knew Ryan from her time in the army.

When Evan first said his name in the woods, she'd felt a shiver run through her. It was hard to believe that it was the same man she'd nearly had an affair with twenty years earlier. And it was even harder to believe that Ryan was on some cross-country killing spree. Was this the same man she'd known?

As a twenty-year-old cadet officer, Angela was destined for rapid promotion. She was as athletic as the best of the men and certainly brighter than most of them. As a woman in the army, she had to get the balance right – banter as well as the guys and show you could match their stamina while at the same time still be a woman men desired. This led to the next balancing act – sleeping around wasn't going to get you a good rep, but not having sex with anyone was also going to give you a hard time.

Angela had been close with one guy. They never had sex, but she gave him the occasional hand job to keep him happy. She didn't get much in return. But then there was her fellow female cadet Sarah for that. Every now and then, they found time to sexually satisfy each other. They never mentioned it and made sure no-one knew about it, both of them sure they weren't lesbian and it was purely sexual release without the hassle of dealing with a man.

Angela could handle herself, but one time in Sandhurst she'd let two fellow cadets get her alone out in the scrubland used for explosives practice. It had started as a game with one of the guys challenging her to a judo fight. But when the other guy joined in and they had her pinned down, she realised what was going to happen next. They'd managed to undo her belt and tug down her fatigues when Ryan appeared from behind a shrub.

The two cadets immediately jumped up, trying to make out it had all been a bit of fun. Appearing to be ignorant of what had gone on, Ryan simply warned them about messing about on land that contained explosives. At first, Angela was furious. A senior officer was turning a blind eye to two cadets nearly raping her. But when Ryan casually asked if Angela wanted a lift in his jeep, she understood what he was doing. She hadn't actually been raped. If she made any accusation, she was hardly going to last long in the army. Ryan had saved her from the ordeal and was giving her a way to save face. So she got in the jeep as if nothing had happened.

She was never bothered by male cadets again. They'd seen that she would both put up a fight and wasn't a grass so they respected her. Besides, they knew that Ryan would make them pay if they did it again.

Angela and Ryan would sometimes meet in the gym or mess hall. It was a platonic relationship, she told herself. He was ten years older and had a wife. Still, she couldn't help being a little in love with him.

Everyone knew the stories of Ryan's time in Kuwait, like how he'd run through the track dotted with mines to catch the insurgent who had put them there. Unlike most men he never boasted about it, which just further built up the myth around him.

And then there was the incident with Lieutenant General Edward Cameron. During her time in Sandhurst, it was well known that Cameron had fucked up in making the unit go through insurgent territory. But while others complained bitterly about this, Ryan remained silent on the matter. He had done his job and that was what was important.

Angela saw now that Ryan's resentment towards Cameron must have built up over the years. She wondered how much Ryan knew. From her position in MI5, she'd seen evidence of Cameron's deals. Without doubt he'd been involved in selling arms to Iraq. But it wasn't her area and he'd been acquitted. She also knew Cameron's bank had been involved in insider trading. But again, this wasn't her field. She didn't condone Ryan killing Edward Cameron, but she could understand his actions.

Angela thought about the last time she had met Ryan one to one. She'd asked him to demonstrate the de-wiring of an explosive. After he'd shown her, she'd stood close to him. Looking at her, he'd frowned. Unable to stop herself, she quickly kissed his lips. Ryan had frozen and that was it. But she could tell he'd liked it, she certainly had. They hadn't even had sex and she'd had several men since, yet she could never forget that kiss.

They never met as one to one after that. Ryan's wife got pregnant and he left the army. Angela did her stint then moved to MI5. She loved her job and had been immersed in it for the last ten years. She'd never heard from Ryan once he left the army, but she had kept track of his life.

Angela knew it was an abuse of power. The public really didn't know how much could be detected. It had taken a good few years to catch up with the internet revolution, but now they were able to monitor pretty much every email and phone call. There had been plenty of meetings about how much monitoring should be allowed and declared. They'd ended up with carte blanche, which Angela knew was about to be exposed by the media.

In her opinion, the monitoring was essential in order to prevent terrorist attacks. But she was also conflicted, believing that every human had a right to privacy. With her occasional check on Ryan's life, she was a prime example of the contradiction. It wasn't as if she was obsessed or even had the time to be. She hardly managed her own social life and hadn't been on her private Facebook account for ages.

She tried to think now if she had seen anything in Ryan's life that suggested he might start killing people. Last time she'd checked, Ryan was happily married with a son at University. She knew the son went on demonstrations, but he was young and Angela didn't think he posed any threat to anyone. Angela was genuinely happy for Ryan, though she felt he could have done more with his life than run a small security systems business.

Angela told herself that she checked on Ryan because she always felt she owed him. Deep down, she knew it was because she'd also loved him. Now, no matter what she had with Ryan in the past, her job was to catch him.

Evan pulled up at the roundabout lights. He watched traffic pour off and onto the motorway. In a minute, his would be one of the many cars zooming along the M4 as he headed back to Swansea. He wondered about Ryan. What had flicked his old friend's switch? He'd lost his business, his home and his wife. That was what. Wouldn't anyone flip? Evan tried to think what would happen if he lost his job in the police, his home was taken from him and Julie left him. Of course he'd fucking lose it.

There but for the grace of God go I, thought Evan. Not that he believed in God. But he knew the balance of your life working out or not was fragile. It took only one drunken fight or affair for your life to be irreparably damaged. And that applied to those in the force as much to those who streamed into the station every Friday night after a session on Wind Street.

A blast of a car horn brought Evan back to his senses. The lights had changed. He put the Escort in gear and drove off. Taking the M4 West exit, he wondered if he was getting old. He'd been offered early retirement the year before and had refused. It was all part of the cutbacks. Every year there was less money, less police on the street, less cases they could solve. Yet as times got tougher there would be more crime to deal with. Did those in power actually care?

Throughout the country, it was the police who saw how people were turning to crime. Evan didn't think there was an excuse for it, but he understood the socio-economic circumstances which perhaps caused it, something the government didn't seem to understand.

Evan loved his job and knew he'd be lost without

it. But who exactly was he protecting? As he'd said to Angela, was it more important to possibly protect a few dignitaries at the Olympics than prevent people burning down each other's livelihoods in the riots? Evan had never been a revolutionary. He was police through and through. His job was to keep order. But he was seriously beginning to question his role. Whatever Ryan's aims were, did he have a legitimate point in getting rid of those at the top? The whole system seemed close to breaking point and yet the politicians and fat cats continued sticking their snouts into the trough as if they had a God-given right to shit on everyone else.

24

Ryan stood on the slip road in the hope of hitching a lift. He knew it was risky but he needed to get away from Reading quickly. After the carnage he'd inflicted, a manhunt would soon be closing in on him. If they hadn't connected the dots before, they would now. He'd left his business card and was on camera as he'd entered Southern Gas and Electric. He was betting that it would take a few hours before his name and description went out. One lift to get him away from the area was all he needed.

Several cars passed by. For the first time, doubts crept into Ryan's mind. He was still sure about his overall mission, but had he made the right choice in taking the Reading detour? And had he needed to kill the whole board? As he stood with his thumb out, he felt alone. He couldn't remember ever feeling like that in his life. He didn't think about Sandra but about Gerard. He'd like to see his son before it was all over, but he doubted it would be possible.

When Gerard was a kid, Ryan had been so close to him. It was a pity they'd drifted apart now that his son was more or less an adult. At least he'd told Gerard face to face how proud of him he was, Sandra having told him he didn't show it.

Ryan remembered the one time he'd nearly been unfaithful. In Sandhurst there'd been a cadet ten years younger than him - Angela, that was her name. After preventing two male cadets raping her, he'd always felt protective – an older brother to her rather than his own sister. She'd probably not needed it as she was a tough, bright young woman in her own right.

He'd deliberately blanked any other feelings towards her. But then Angela had kissed him out in the shrubs. It was the same spine-tingling feeling he'd had when he'd first kissed Sandra as a teenager out camping. Feeling guilty, he'd made love with Sandra that night without protection. A month later, they found out she was pregnant.

That one day had mapped out his life for the next twenty years. Instead of staying in the army, he'd gone back to Swansea to set up family, home and business. Ryan wondered what Angela had gone on to do. From the occasional correspondence he'd had with guys like Jack Jones, he knew she'd left the army. The word was that she had joined MI5. Whatever she was doing, he was sure she'd be fantastic at it. Until now, he'd never allowed himself to wonder what would have happened if they'd had an affair.

He guessed Sandra would have left him and therefore Gerard wouldn't have been born. He would have stayed in the army and been called out to Afghanistan. Maybe he'd be dead by now.

As Ryan's thoughts got more morose, a van with 'Keyhan's Kebabs' on the side pulled over. A Kurdish guy in his twenties wound down the window:

'London?'

Relieved that his thoughts had been interrupted, Ryan got in. The driver told him he never normally picked people up, not that you saw many hitch-hikers in the UK, but Ryan looked like a good man. The guy slipped into the stream of motorway traffic and asked Ryan what his situation was – it seemed strange, a man his age in a shirt but with a rucksack and hitching a lift. Ryan gave an answer as near the truth as possible:

'Heading to the big City. Apparently that's where the money is.'

The driver nodded:

'But you know London, it's not paved with gold, my friend. Times are tough everywhere. Me, I just set up this business, doing all work myself. Have to see how it goes.'

The man patted his steering wheel before putting his hand out to Ryan:

'I am Keyhan.'

Ryan shook his hand and listened as Keyhan told his life story:

'In Turkey, there is nothing for my family. Six brothers, none of them with work. I studied law at University but I am Kurdish, so there is nothing for me there. I been to the prison three times, just because I am Kurdish. Here in UK, nobody cares where you are from. The life, it's not easy, but you can find work if you really want. Now I focus on the kebabs. Luckily, people always need to eat. Of course you can't only live on kebabs...'

'Guess you also need something to drink.'

'That too my friend, that too. And money, that is very important for the life.'

'But money can't buy you love, apparently.'

'Of course, don't forget a good woman, every man needs that.'

'So what have we got - kebabs, something to drink, money and a good woman, that about right?'

'That's it – the essential ingredients for the good life.'

Ryan and Keyhan both smiled, Keyan going on to tell Ryan about what actual ingredients were really needed for a good kebab. Ryan drifted off, just catching bits of what Keyhan told him. Apparently you could buy cheap pitta bread in bulk in Reading, which is why Keyhan was coming from there. His kebab shop was in South London, the same area as Ryan's son lived, but Ryan didn't mention that. Reaching the M25, Ryan got Keyhan to drop him off at the exit, Keyhan wishing him good luck and promising a free kebab if Ryan ever made it to Elephant and Castle.

Ryan made it to the leafy Surrey village of Parkgate by mid-afternoon. He'd already done his research so he knew where the Chancellor lived and that he was due to be there for some PR stunt the next morning, which presumably meant he'd be down that night.

Ryan had gathered the information at the same time as he'd looked into Edward Cameron's life. He'd even printed out an article to re-read nearer the time.

A three storey Victorian terrace, the chancellor's house wasn't much bigger than Ryan's old Mumbles home. The difference was that the Chancellor had probably paid ten times as much to live in Surrey rather than Swansea. Several houses along the row were for sale. If they'd been bought at the height of the housing boom, the owners were probably in negative equity now that prices had plummeted. As Ryan knew so well, if they'd lost jobs they wouldn't be able to afford the mortgage and even if they sold the house they would still be in debt. It was lose, lose.

The long back gardens backed onto the village common, a small lake in the middle with ducks gliding along. At tables outside a café, mums in sunglasses chatted over cappuccinos while their children ran in the play area. For some, wealth and relaxation still prevailed.

Checking nobody was looking, Ryan casually went up to the chancellor's garden gate. On it was a sign, 'Beware of the Duck', with a photo of a Muscovy duck. Ryan opened the gate and instantly hid behind a tool shed. In the middle of the garden he'd spotted a small pond. Looking through the tool shed window, he now saw the Muscovy duck flap out of the water. Quacking loudly, it waddled in Ryan's direction. Ryan didn't have any qualms about killing a duck if necessary, but he was saved from doing so when the back door of the house opened. A young Thai guy in nothing but tight-fitting swimwear and an apron raised a fist as he shouted at the duck:

'You be quiet or you go in curry!'

The duck turned on the guy and hissed through its beaked nostrils. The young man went back inside. The duck seemed to forget about Ryan and waddled back into the water.

Ryan took off his rucksack and propped it against the shed. He noticed that the tools inside were immaculately clean. And looking around the garden, he saw plenty of flowers but no vegetables. While the Chancellor suggested other people grow their own food, he clearly didn't. It even seemed that he had a housekeeper to cook the food.

From his rucksack, Ryan took out the miniature CCTV camera he'd kept as a souvenir from his business. The latest device, it was remotely operated. Ryan didn't know how his conversation with the Chancellor would pan out, but he was sure it would be worth recording. Coming out from behind the shed, Ryan strode to the back of the house. He didn't glance at the pond, but heard the duck splashing out of it, a cacophony of quacks as it closed on his heels. With the duck so loud, Ryan opened the back door without being heard, shutting it behind him just as the duck ran into the bottom glass panel.

Ryan quickly crouched behind an armchair. Sure enough, the Thai guy came rushing into the room. This time he was brandishing a sharp chef's knife. The guy glared at the duck through the glass panelled door:

'I warn you!'

After a short stare-off, the duck waddled away. Triumphant, the Thai guy went back to the kitchen, firmly shutting the partitioning door. Ryan rose from behind the armchair. He was glad he hadn't had to face the guy. He wasn't sure he would beat a crazy knife-wielding Thai chef.

Seeing he was in a study-cum-lounge, Ryan felt it was as good a place as any to talk with the Chancellor. He positioned the miniature CCTV camera on a bookshelf and found himself a more comfortable position between the chaise-longue and wall. Out of sight from anyone entering the room, he also had leg space to stretch in. While he was waiting for the Chancellor to arrive, Ryan decided to re-read the article about him. Taking the pages out of his back pocket, he unfolded them and looked at the photo.

George Oswald had a small arsehole of a mouth, a doughy complexion and the onset of a double chin. Only forty two, George was young for his position, but had been involved in politics since being a Tory Boy at the age of fourteen. A descendant of English aristocracy, the Chancellor had continued to uphold the family traditions. After attending Eton and Oxford, he'd married a baroness and had a son who was at a private boarding school. George was a millionaire just from inheritance, had several homes and annually attended the Bilderberg Conference of the influential rich elite.

That was in the article's introduction. The journalist then got started on the interview, asking

George about the expenses scandal. He'd been caught out claiming twenty three pounds and seventy five pence for duck food. On paper, the Chancellor came across as pompously arrogant as he did on TV:

'I don't check every receipt my secretary puts in for. But look, I pledge now with you as a witness that I will personally reimburse the public purse. Not only that, but from my own pocket I will feed every duck in my local park.'

After the article, the press had of course jumped on the idea, which is why the Chancellor was coming down to his constituency for the weekend.

Later in the interview, the journalist questioned the Chancellor about the price of council houses being sold off. It was for example, very difficult for teachers to live in London. George dismissed the question:

'Look, two teachers on forty five grand a year each can easily afford the mortgage. I don't see what all the fuss is about.'

It might be different for private school teachers, thought Ryan, but he didn't know any teacher who earned forty five grand. It was more like half that. The Chancellor simply didn't have a clue, or maybe chose not to.

Having had the first two issues dismissed, the journalist tried a third avenue:

'The new liquidity support scheme you are proposing will see £100 billion injected into private banks if they require it. In contrast, your latest spending review has seen £10 billion in cuts to the public sector. Is there not a contradiction here?'

'The liquidity support scheme is there to preserve confidence in the financial system, to protect the British High Street and avoid the crisis on our doorstep. Together with the spending review, it will stimulate the economy.'

Adept at being deliberately vague, the Chancellor simply wasn't going to give anything away. At the end of the interview, the journalist asked the chancellor if he had any tips on how people could save money in this time of austerity. As described in the article, George Oswald put down his jam scone and wiped his mouth with a napkin before declaring:

'I'll give you a personal example. I could have caught a taxi here. But I thought no, I'll cycle. People need to use their initiative.'

Ryan didn't know London well, but he didn't need a map to know that the Chancellor's Downing Street office was a ten minute walk from the Ritz on Piccadilly where the interview was taking place. First, why would anyone take a taxi that short distance? Second, it didn't occur to the baby-faced chancellor that he was eating in a hotel restaurant that most people would never go to in their lives as it was exclusively for the rich. The man was either an imbecile or a bare-faced hypocrite.

Ryan refolded the article, pocketed it and waited to meet the chancellor.

25

Sitting across from his wife at the dining table, the Chancellor George Oswald studied her with cold detachment as she said:

'Such a pity you can't make it – should be quite a gathering. That Dubai prince will be there for one.'

Of course he would prefer to be in Monaco rather than his bloody Surrey constituency, thought the chancellor, but he'd also rather be there without Beatrice and the kids. She was off to get them from boarders any moment, making a long weekend of it. She loved showing off her royal connections to the children. She probably dreamed of copulating with the Prince, but she was realistic enough to know that, with his wealth, he could pay for much younger, prettier models. And the Chancellor's wife was hardly a model as it was.

The Chancellor dabbed the croissant crumbs off his lips with a napkin.

'Duty calls.'

'You know, it really mystifies me that you ever took up this position. It's so not you.'

What was him? Preferring nubile young men to her? He was hardly going to tell her that. But she had a point. How had he become Chancellor?

He could have lived off his father's wealth, or indeed his wife's, but what would he do with his days? He'd never been good at polo or other such hobbies. He liked to be involved, needed to be needed.

After Eton, he'd gone to Oxford because that was what was expected. His father had arranged for him to attend the Bilderberg Conference, so he did that too. It was there that Donald had collared him, instilled the idea of becoming Chancellor. George was well aware he was being used, but thought he could also hold his own in office - prove his worth to his father, to Donald and everyone else.

Turned out to be bloody harder than he imagined, always having to compromise and bend over for this person or that. All for very little gratitude, not to mention the constant and hysterical media mockery. Nobody seemed to understand that it wasn't him pulling the strings. Hard to tell who was anymore, but there were certainly people more powerful than him.

Edward Cameron had thought his bank had been bailed out because of family ties and Oxford loyalty. Poor old chap hadn't realised George had been instructed to do it. Banks had to be kept running so people could keep making money. News of Ed's death had been pretty shocking. Perhaps it had been an accident, but it was also entirely plausible that the misdemeanours of South West National had instigated a thoroughly more stern course of action, as it had lost important people money. The Russians or the Chinese could be pretty bloody ruthless. George shuddered at the thought. For all his wealth and influence, those types of people didn't give a damn for social standing. They'd slit your throat, or drop plutonium in your tea at the drop of a hat. Bloody foreigners, no respect for their betters, didn't even think they had any betters. God forbid the British underclass ever took a page out of their book, then the game would surely be up.

Beatrice was still going on:

'Not as if anyone appreciates the work you do.'

George sneered back:

'So lovely to have a wife who has confidence in one's abilities.'

'You know I appreciate you darling, but that budget of yours took a bit of a battering. Everyone is talking about how you dropped the ball. I know you're not much of a sportsman, or politician, or much of anything really, but really darling, what were you thinking? You're normally so very good at pinning it on the other chap, was there no one in cabinet you could hang it on? You need to get a grip George, Daddy would be mortified.'

'There was absolutely nothing wrong with my budget. The media simply want to make me look bad. People have been living off the Government for far too long. What people don't realise is those cuts are actually helping them get off their lager sodden and nicotine drenched lazy arses.'

George's wife smiled:

'I do love it when you talk common, keep up the good fight, as long as it doesn't affect us and our dearest friends, screw the lot of them....'

She blew him a kiss and departed. George finished his breakfast and left for work.

He was prevented from walking to his parliamentary office by a security guy, who quietly informed George that Edward's death was not only being treated as murder, but that it was possible the Chancellor was on a hit list. George found this preposterous, but let himself be driven down the road as he was appraised of the facts and the course of the current investigation.

Apparently some Welshman who had lost his business, and probably his mind to boot, blamed the bank that liquidated the company. George failed to see what he had to do with it, despite the fact he had bailed out all the banks using taxpayer's money and protected the bankers from any legal proceedings to hold them to account. It was all a storm in a teacup and would no doubt blow over in no time at all. In any case, the man was hardly likely to penetrate Parliament security.

He'd only sat at his desk for a matter of seconds before the phone rang. His secretary informed him that Andrey from City Bank was on the line. George took the call and Andrey's Russian inflection crackled irritably in the earpiece:

'Just calling to see how things are moving along.'

Nothing was ever spelt out with Andrey, all very cloak and dagger. But then as George knew, the lines probably were bugged, so he answered in kind:

'The matter is being dealt with.'

'Good, by Monday please.'

The line went dead.

There'd been no threat in Andrey's voice, but there didn't need to be. George knew what needed doing. Until now, he'd just doled out money to banks on a one to one basis. With Andrey representing a whole consortium, the new liquidity scheme would ensure that not only City Bank but every bank in the city would have an emergency escape route. Even he thought that was a bit much to get away with, but it wasn't as if he had much choice. They had him by the balls.

George hauled in his senior adviser, bawled the man out before he even had a chance to sit:

'Is that bloody scheme drawn up yet?'

'Almost, we're just putting in the finer...'

George slammed the desk:

'I want it in front of me in an hour.'

His advisor scuttled out. George looked at the packet of duck food on his desk, left by his secretary. He still hadn't paid for it out of his own pocket. So who was having the last laugh?

The phone rang again. This time it was John Deacon, the head of MI5, calling personally. There'd been an explosion in Reading, killing the whole board of Southern Gas and Electric. While the news was of course shocking, George didn't know anybody on the board there. The Government certainly hadn't helped the company, in fact he knew it was about to receive a record penalty for misleading customers. He'd wangled a copy of the report and given it to Ed, at his bequest as apparently he needed it for a friend. But nobody apart from Edward knew that and he was dead. Keeping quiet about the report, the Chancellor told Deacon he couldn't see a connection to himself. There were far more pressing matters to be dealt with.

Deacon agreed that it now appeared unlikely the chancellor was a target, but tight security would still be in place. George shook his head in disbelief as he stared out of the window at the Thames. Some mad Welshman was going around blowing up CEOs. What was the world coming to?

Across the river from parliament, down in Elephant and Castle, Aitch cut through the charcoaled shopping centre. The summer before it had been burnt and looted. Nearly a year on, the Nike trainers and hoody that Aitch wore were from that smash and grab.

Aitch's actual name was Achibe, his mum not wanting him to forget his Nigerian roots. But it wasn't cool in school. For a start nobody could say it properly, so it had been abbreviated and ended up as a single letter, H. That had set a trend. His backup man Osagie was known as OG and his sidekick was called TJ, Aitch not even able to remember what the two letters stood for.

Aitch's mum Grace had her food stall in the hotchpotch market between the burnt out shopping centre and underpass, where she'd been cooking the same spicy bean dishes for twenty years.

Aitch liked his food spicy, but preferred Nandos chicken. Go in and get sat down at a table by some hot talent, get your free coke refills as you looked for any single girls. His mum's place, you had to stand in the cold while you got served, wasn't no place to sit.

It was amazing that her stall was still standing after all these years. Aitch guessed the cafes, restaurants and food stalls hadn't been torched or looted because people needed to eat. He didn't stop as he'd already had an earful from his mum that morning. All the time she'd lived in Britain and she still spoke Pidgin English:

'You go to jobcentre yet?'

'Just chillin' mum.'

He knew his own English wasn't BBC, was cadged from movies, music and the street. But least him and his mates had made the language their own.

'And how you hope find a job 'just chillin''?

'Aint no jobs out there.'

Wasn't no lie. There were no jobs out there. None unless you included cleaning toilets. And there was no way you'd catch him doing that. Sure there were new laws, trying to make you accept any old shit but that didn't make sense as you'd end up with less money than if you got jobseekers allowance. What you had to do was play the system, sign up for some back to work scheme, shit like that.

Aitch knew what was coming next. Sure enough, his mum shook her head:

'I come to this country with nothing. You need to work hard you want to achieve something. You got to do something with your life.'

Like his two older sisters had, no doubt, thought Aitch. One was nineteen, already had two kids, both from different dads, neither man around while she lived off benefits. The other, last known address was Kings Cross. With Aitch keeping his thoughts to himself, his mum got in one more shot:

'You need new trainers.'

Aitch looked down at his scuffed Nikes while his mum plodded out of the council flat, down to her stall. She'd known where he'd got his Nikes from, but hadn't come out and said it. Instead she'd stopped giving him handouts, said from now on he had to pay his own way in life.

In a way, his mum was right. His Nikes were worn out from a year's wearing. There wasn't any shopping centre left to rob, so he needed cash if he wanted new ones. Instead of feeling the gloom, he was going to spread some doom.

There were no shops left to loot, but the riots had given Aitch a new idea – make some of the local food places pay up or burn them down. You couldn't do it with a place like Nandos because it was a multi-national, would simply close down and move elsewhere. But the Kurdish Kebab place that had just set up could be shaken down. Was just one Kurd who ran it, another one or two helping out.

Meeting OG and TJ by Nandos, Aitch exchanged hand clasps, outlined his plan. The other two unsure, TJ asked:

'We just go in there?'

'Fuck yea. They is new to the area, don't know shit. We tell them we in charge, that's what they believe.'

'What if they don't?'

Aitch thumbed at Osagie:

'We make them. You think some skinny Kurd gonna mess with OG?'

Aitch led the way, the other two stepping up to be by his side as they swaggered along the underpass, came up on the other side of the road.

Keyhan's Kebabs was just opening, the guy flipping the door sign to show it was open. Aitch cowboy-walked into the place, OG and TJ falling in behind him.

Keyhan gave them a broken toothed smile:

'What I get you guys?'

'More like what you gonna give us. You Keyhan, this your place?'

Keyhan smiled proudly:

'I am Keyhan, this is mine – Keyhan's Kebabs.'

'I'm gonna call you kebab man. Now see here kebab man, you is new to the area, don't know how things work around here.'

Keyhan tried to keep his smile:

'We are new, but not look for any problems. We are friendly with everyone. I see you around. Your mum has the stall in the market yes?'

Keyhan's attempt at appeasement had the opposite effect on Aitch:

'What the fuck you speaking about my mum for? You spying on me?'

Keyhan raised his hands in peace:

'No man, is nothing like that. I just look around to see what other food is selling in the area. There is no kebabs so I think is good place to set up.'

'But you set up without asking. You want to stay open, you gonna have to start paying.'

'I no understand.'

'Okay, let me make you understand.'

Aitch pointed out of the window at the burnt-down shopping centre:

'That there is our signature. You don't want that to happen to you, you pay up.'

Keyhan swallowed:

'Come on man, I'm just trying to run a business, no harm to anyone. How about I give you free lunch, then we all be friends?'

Aitch glanced over his shoulder at the other two:

'You want to try some of this Kurdish shit for free?'

OG screwed up his face:

'I'm more liking Nandos.'

TJ shrugged:

'Me too.'

Aitch turned back to Keyhan, lashed out a hand, swept a bowl of chillies off the counter, the chilli juice splattering Keyhan's legs. Keyhan remained still. Aitch stared him down:

'We is back tonight. You want to stay open, you pay ten percent of what's in the till. And every Friday night after that. You understand now?'

Keyhan nodded. Aitch turned, gave a nod to OG and TJ. He rolled his shoulders and led them out of the kebab shop.

26

Ryan smelt the aroma of Thai curry wafting under the door. He checked his watch. It was six thirty. He didn't know what time the chancellor was due back, but presumably he'd be in time for dinner. Right on cue, Ryan heard the front door open and the chancellor's booming voice:

'All this security is completely unnecessary if you ask me.'

Another voice said:

'Just doing my job sir.'

Tensing, Ryan guessed the voice belonged to some security guy. The Chancellor reluctantly gave in:

'Very well, go ahead. Don't worry about the housekeeper. I don't think he's planning to kill me, unless he's put too much curry powder in my dinner.'

Ryan heard footsteps on the stairs. With the security guy out of hearing, the Chancellor whispered to the Thai housekeeper:

'I hope you cleaned up the bedroom.'

The footsteps came thudding back down the stairs so that Ryan couldn't hear the Thai housekeeper's reply. The study door opened. Ryan coiled, ready to spring if he needed to. The door shut and Ryan relaxed. He heard the security guy say:

'All clear sir. Is there a room you'd prefer me to be located in?'

The Chancellor complained:

'Now look, I don't mean to be rude but I've had a bloody hard week and right now I require a bit of privacy. So why don't you go and sit in your car and I'll have some curry brought out to you later. If this crazed maniac happens to turn up while you're eating, I'll show him my old judo moves.'

'Afraid I've been asked to keep a close watch sir.'

'I assure you it will be okay, Who's your supervisor, Deacon?'

'Yes sir.'

'Get him on the phone for me.'

A phone conversation later the security guy went out to keep watch from his car. As soon as the front door was shut, the Chancellor exhaled loudly:

'One damn thing after another.'

The Chancellor softened his tone:

'But I have some good news for you, my handsome chef. After much twisting of arms I've got your docs processed. You'll be a British citizen in the next month.'

The housekeeper squealed in delight:

'You are genius.'

'Come and show Georgie Porgie how much you

appreciate his efforts.'

Ryan endured the Chancellor's moans, culminating in:

'God I needed that. Dinner in an hour? I'll be in the study. Don't disturb me.'

The Chancellor entered the study, Ryan hearing him zip up his trousers as he did so. Closing the door, the chancellor put a briefcase on his desk and picked up the phone next to it. He paced the room as he waited. When someone finally answered, the Chancellor let out a stream of impatience:

'Donald, at last... Where am I? At home in my bloody constituency. Doing that bloody stupid duck feeding stunt... Of course I'm not paying for it personally. Made sure it came out of the bitch's wages... I'm sure she does have nice tits, but it's not really my thing. If she weren't giving the PM a blow job once a week she'd be out of a job, I can tell you.'

The Chancellor took a breath before resuming:

'Twenty three bloody pounds - it literally is duck feed. Joe Public doesn't have a clue. I've spent the whole week arranging the liquidity support scheme... I know, but they've got me by the balls... Yes, I like them squeezed, but not that much.'

In his hiding place, Ryan thought the phone conversation was worth recording. Using the remote control, he turned on the miniature CCTV camera he'd placed on the bookshelf. Turning his attention back to the phone call, Ryan heard the Chancellor say:

'If the treasury had an actual vault of money, not

only would it be empty but there would be a bloody huge hole at the bottom of it, rusty from being there for so long. Any backup funds have long been sucked out of the Government's arsehole... I don't care if I'm mixing my metaphors. What I care about is how we can get that money.'

The Chancellor sighed:

'Yes, I'm sure the line is safe. I did a deal with MI5. They got a bigger budget in return for ensuring that I had one private line debugged. It's in writing. Besides, they're too busy trying to track down that nutter who's killing off CEOs. Any luck and he'll do in the CEO of City Bank next. That would make the problem go away... It was a joke, Donald...'

The Chancellor clicked open his briefcase:

'I have the papers right in front of me. We'll get it put through Monday morning.'

The Chancellor paused before trying to sound nonchalant:

'A hundred billion.'

The Chancellor waited, then smiled:

'You can? You know I'll be forever grateful... Not that grateful, you dirty bastard. Okay, until next time in Dubai, goodbye.'

The Chancellor clicked off the phone and exhaled in satisfaction. He quickly made another call, leaving a message:

'Darling, guess you must be on the plane. Such a pity I couldn't join you and the kids, but you know this wretched duck feeding stunt must be done. Call me when you land.'

Behind the chaise-longue, Ryan frowned. He'd been a businessman but in a very concrete way, getting paid for work he carried out. He'd never really understood the abstract financial world of hedge funds and the like. But he knew that a hundred billion pounds wasn't duck feed. Piecing together the Chancellor's phone call and the newspaper article on him, Ryan could just about work things out. The Chancellor's liquidity support scheme was purely for the benefit of the banks, was being put in place out of pressure from the banks and was being paid for by another bank. Ryan was now absolutely sure that George Oswald was a despicable hypocrite who deserved his fate.

Ryan saw that the chain of people he'd lined up to take a fall were in fact quite minor. Even the chancellor relied on someone else to provide money, like this Donald, whoever he was. Ryan seemed to remember from his research that the CEO of Goldman Sachs was called Donald. Maybe it was him. In turn, Donald was probably mixed up in a web of high finance dealings around the globe. Ryan couldn't take them all down. But he could make a stand.

Edging to the end of the chaise-longue, Ryan watched George skip over to the glass panelled back door. Turning his head one way then another as he mirrored the Muscovy duck on the other side, George cooed at his pet:

'Don't worry, I won't let him put you in a curry.'

The Chancellor closed the curtains, waltzed over to the sound system and put on a CD. As Handel loudly reverberated around the room, the Chancellor picked up a symphony conductor's baton. He sang out with the violins:

'Georgie Porgie, you are so naughty…'

The chancellor undid his belt, dropped his trousers to his ankles and bent over. He wiggled his pale arse in the air and readied the conductor's baton. As the music crescendoed, George Oswald whipped his buttocks with it.

Ryan looked over at the miniature CCTV camera on the bookshelf. He was so glad this was all being recorded. Having seen enough, Ryan emerged from behind the chaise-longue. The Chancellor looked startled as he saw Ryan stride towards him. With his trousers still around his ankles and the conductor's baton in his hand, the chancellor put his hands up in a mock judo position. Ryan kicked him in the balls. As the Chancellor doubled over, Ryan smashed his fist into the chancellor's face. The Chancellor fell into a motionless heap. Ryan looked down at the chancellor and said:

'I think you need to work on those judo moves, George.'

With the Chancellor still out of it, Ryan yanked him over to a chair and tied him there by his clothes. From the chancellor's desk, Ryan took the liquidity support scheme papers. He crumpled one of the sheets into a ball, held the chancellor's head back by his hair and stuffed the ball of paper into his mouth.

The loud music would cover up a normal conversation, but Ryan didn't want the Chancellor screaming his mouth off and alerting security.

Regaining his senses, the Chancellor gawped at Ryan in horror. Ryan smiled:

'Hi, I'm the nutter that's killing off CEOs, although it's a bit more specific than that.'

The Chancellor desperately tried to speak around the ball of paper in his mouth. Ryan instantly put up a warning hand:

'Don't speak with your mouth full. Didn't they teach you that at Eton?'

The Chancellor didn't answer. Ryan pointed to the miniature CCTV camera on the bookshelf:

'That camera is all that's left of my business. Wireless and remotely operated, it stores the footage in a microchip. A brilliant little device.'

The Chancellor looked wide-eyed from Ryan to the camera and back again. Ryan confirmed the Chancellor's thoughts:

'Yes, your phone call and buttock whipping antics have all been recorded.'

Ryan screwed up the remaining sheets of paper that made up the liquidity support scheme and said:

'Basically it's like this. My business was liquidated by South West National. Because of this I lost my home and my wife. Admittedly I can't blame the bank for her leaving me, but I did kill the bank manager she ran off with. Now he claimed he was just doing his job, so I went to the bank CEO, Edward Cameron. I think you know him, I killed him too. He didn't show much remorse, so I thought I'd go to you, find out why the bank got bailed out but I got liquidated.

'The board of Southern Gas and Electric was just a

detour. You see on the way here I saw first hand how other people have been fucked over by the banks, the energy companies and the government. You've all been at it, rigging prices so you can rip us off and line your own pockets.

'So now I'm here. And I want to get this straight. While my business was liquidated for being in debt for a few thousand, you bailed out South West National to a tune of forty billion. Your new scheme, if I understand correctly, is giving a further one hundred billion to the banks.'

Ryan took the newspaper article out of his pocket, unfolded it and found the line he was looking for.

'According to you the reason for this new scheme is, and I quote, "to provide confidence in the financial system" and "to stimulate the economy". Personally, I think you're just fucking the whole country over. So man to man, answer me honestly. Are you ripping us off?'

The Chancellor tried to open his mouth again. With one swift movement, Ryan grabbed a ball of paper and stuffed it into the chancellor's mouth. As the chancellor gagged, Ryan explained:

'Every time you try to lie, you'll eat your words. It's a yes or no answer. I've heard you talk on TV, read your newspaper interviews. I'm here in person and I don't need any more bullshit. So just nod or shake your head. Are you ripping us off?'

The Chancellor gulped, the paper balls in his mouth making it difficult to breath. Ryan stared at him. The Chancellor nodded. Ryan asked for confirmation:

'So basically you're just lining each others' pockets?'

The Chancellor looked desperately at Ryan, who made the question clear:

'Yes or no?'

The Chancellor slowly nodded. Ryan looked thoughtful and said:

'A final question that the public might like an answer to. Can you confirm that you fuck your male chef?'

With tears in his eyes, the Chancellor gave the slightest nod. Ryan nodded back:

'Finally some truth out of you.'

Ryan sighed:

'But I'm still going to kill you.'

The Chancellor's eyes grew wide as Ryan forced another ball of paper into his mouth. Ryan then pinched his nostrils closed. The Chancellor gasped for breath and Ryan stuffed in a final ball of paper, clasping his mouth firmly shut. The Chancellor struggled in the chair, but Ryan held him tight in an armlock while blocking his breathing. With his last breath quickly exhausted, the Chancellor silently choked and slumped forward.

Ryan checked that the Chancellor had no pulse. He listened and heard pans rattle in the kitchen. He looked out of the back door and saw the duck was moping in the pond, head tucked in as if it knew what had happened to old baby-faced George. Ryan took the CCTV camera from the bookshelf, stepped outside and walked quickly past the pond without the duck so much as giving him a hiss. He collected his rucksack and left the garden.

The Chancellor would be found within an hour so he had to move fast. If security services had worked out he was going to get to the chancellor, had they foreseen his final action? Ryan had a feeling Evan was on to him. Maybe he'd see his old friend before the end.

27

Evan spent three hours stuck in unmoving traffic between Bristol and the Second Severn Crossing. He didn't find out until later, but an articulated truck full of plucked ducks had jack-knifed and ended up on its side across all three motorway lanes. Nobody was badly hurt and the ducks were already dead as they were on their way to various Chinese restaurants in South Wales, but it still took ages for it to be cleared up.

Without even a bottle of water, Evan sweltered inside his unmarked Ford Escort. He wished it was like in American movies and he could just place a magnetic siren on the car roof and whiz by on the hard shoulder. But even if he'd had a siren, he was jammed in the middle lane. There was no point in seeing if he could be of any assistance as the three lanes of non moving vehicles stretched for miles. So instead, he got out of the car to stretch his legs.

A few of the other drivers were out and smoking.

Evan looked away as otherwise he would succumb and cadge a cigarette. His mobile sounded and he checked the caller ID. It was Ryan's son. Evan took the call in the car. He hadn't got around to informing Gerard or Sandra that Ryan's face would be on national news. After telling Gerard that, yes, Ryan was wanted for the murder of the whole board of Southern Gas and Electric, Evan closed his eyes. He rubbed his head to try and get rid of the pain.

Not only was he stuck in a traffic jam while his old school friend was trekking cross country to commit multiple murders, Evan had just had to explain things to Ryan's son. Gerard had needed time to digest the news, which was understandable. Evan hadn't said that Ryan was also wanted for Huw and Edward Cameron's murders, but Gerard would soon work that out. Nor had Evan explained his own mixed feelings about what Ryan was doing. Evan was tired and wanted to call his wife but was afraid he'd take his irritation out on her by mistake.

Hearing the sound of engines, Evan opened his eyes and saw traffic starting to move, though in the slow lane only. Manoeuvring across, Evan managed to edge into the slow flow. He couldn't bear continuing at the snail pace so took the turning off as soon as it appeared. Even if it was a longer way around, he'd go via the original Severn Bridge.

Just before the bridge, Evan pulled into the service station. He was out of the traffic but needed to recoup before driving back to Swansea and his wife.

The coffee was overpriced and under flavoured, but

Evan didn't care. Sitting with a view of the bridge that stretched over the estuary, he felt his calm return. When he was young, there'd only been the one bridge. Anytime there was a high wind, it would be closed. Of course you could drive around by Gloucester, but he'd liked the idea that Wales didn't always have to be connected to England.

Evan suddenly shivered, remembering a time when he and Ryan were kids. On a cross-country practice run, they'd gone along the disused rail track that ran through the woods in west Swansea. Stopping to get their breath, they'd leant over the edge of an old bridge. On the single lane road below, just the occasional car passed. Evan couldn't remember whose idea it had been to drop tiny stones onto the roof of the next car, but they'd both done it. The car braked sharply. The driver's door flung open and a guy furiously jumped out. Spying Ryan and Evan on the bridge, the man ran up the slope to remonstrate with them.

Ryan and Evan pelted it. But Evan had hesitated a second so was a bit behind his friend. Glancing over his shoulder, he saw the man gaining ground. In turn, Ryan looked over his shoulder and urged Evan to keep going. But Evan faltered and let the man catch him. The good friend that he was, Ryan had gone back.

After giving the boys a scolding and taking their addresses, the man went back to his car. Ryan had lied about his address but Evan had been too honest to give a false one. In any case, the man never carried out the threat to inform their parents.

As he drank the weak coffee, Evan wondered if

the childhood event was significant. Did it show even back then that Evan was marked for a career in law enforcement whereas Ryan would end up as a murderer? No, he thought, it probably just showed that Ryan had always been faster.

No longer irritated, Evan was now looking forward to going home rather than feeling desperate to be there. Not just to see his wife, but even his layabout son. After dropping out of University, Evan's son had never looked back. A grown man child of twenty four, he had recently moved back into the house. One day, his son claimed, his band would make it big. But until then he was living off his parents.

Evan thought Julie spoiled their son, but he'd never made it a huge issue with her. After they'd fallen in love at the police academy in Newport, she'd given up her career to raise the kids. Out of respect for Julie's decision, Evan let her be in charge when it came to family issues.

Their daughter couldn't have been more different. Hard-working, conscientious and successful at whatever she did, she could have had any career. She chose teaching. With her grades, she had the pick of any school in the UK, let alone Swansea, and she'd chosen to work in the most deprived. Evan felt pride that she'd gone to work in the same Townhill primary school he'd been to. As a teacher, she was never likely to earn much, but she didn't care. And at least teaching was a fairly secure job, thought Evan.

Ready to head back, Evan got out his mobile. He'd call Julie to say he was on his way. Maybe she could arrange a family Sunday lunch for the next day.

Before he could make the call, his mobile rang. He saw it was Angela. Maybe they'd caught Ryan, he thought. Angela's first words dismissed the idea:

'Ryan got to the Chancellor.'

'Ryan killed him?'

'He choked the Chancellor to death in his own home while security was in the car outside. By the time the Chancellor was found, Ryan was long gone.'

Evan took a deep breath. He didn't want to say he'd been right, but bloody hell, he had been. Instead, he said:

'Fucking hell, it's like he's turned into Jason Bourne.'

'Ryan was always capable of doing more than he did with his life. Now he's putting all those old army skills to use, unfortunately not to the right use.'

Evan thought about what Angela had just said. It was the first time she had explicitly admitted she knew Ryan from his army days. He didn't ask her about that, but said:

'Maybe it is the right use. He's not killing civilians but a few specific rich people who took from the poor.'

'So now you're saying he's more like Robin Hood than Jason Bourne?'

Evan laughed. He was taking to Angela more all the time. She quickly got serious again:

'Look, I'm not going to get into whether what he's doing is right or wrong, but we have to stop him. I want to set up a televised appeal using Ryan's family, try and get to him on a personal level.'

'You think that will work?'

'I don't know, but he's got to be stopped and we need to try everything possible. We've got a manhunt going on now in Surrey but he's slipped the net again.'

'I can't see his wife making any difference. Her leaving him was one of the fuses that blew.'

'What about the son?'

'He's in London.'

'Can you get there tonight?'

Evan went silent. Angela hadn't acknowledged he'd been right and didn't care how far away he was. But that was because she was focused on the job. As he should be. Ryan had to be stopped. And Angela was giving him a way back in. He shouldn't have given up so easily anyway, should have followed his initial instincts about Huw's murder. He said:

'I'll get to him in a couple of hours.'

'Good. I'll set up a press conference for first thing. Convey that we need a personal appeal for Ryan to come in. Even if it doesn't work, it might jolt him into making a mistake.'

Evan doubted it would, but he didn't say so. Before she clicked off, Angela said:

'And if you think you know Ryan's next move, tell me.'

It wasn't a direct acknowledgment that he'd been right, but it was some kind of admission. He dug out the UK map he'd sketched from his pocket and unfolded it on the table. He looked at the three circles he'd marked – Huw in Swansea, Edward Cameron in Bath and the chancellor in Surrey. He added a circle where Reading was and wrote 'Southern Gas and Electric'. He wasn't sure how Reading fitted into the chain, but it was still on route. Evan drew between the dots. Ryan was slightly zigzagging but he was surely going from Swansea to London.

It was near midnight by the time Evan reached Gerard's flat in Elephant and Castle. He'd called to say he was on the way, let Julie know he would be away another night and then driven back along the M4 once more.

Sat across from Gerard on a sunken second hand sofa, Evan was exhausted. The place was a typical student flat share, the other tenants out for the night celebrating the end of their courses. In his time, Evan had often knocked on doors to deliver news of deaths or arrests. But it was a bit different informing someone that their dad was a multiple murderer, especially when Evan had known Gerard since he was a baby. He was giving Gerard time for it to sink in.

Looking up, Gerard seemed to come to terms with it:

'I thought dad had it under control. When I saw him, I could see he was slightly different from usual but he was still so rock solid. I knew mum leaving him hurt more than he showed, but I didn't think he would actually kill him.'

Evan waited for Gerard to continue. He was in no hurry to get back to the question of whether Gerard would do the TV appeal. He just couldn't see it having any effect. He was more interested in anything Gerard might say that would lead to some clue as to Ryan's next target. A final destination, Evan felt sure. Gerard seemed to be thinking along the same lines:

'When he said goodbye to me, it was like it was the last time. I though it was just him being awkward.'

Evan sat back in the uncomfortable sofa. He'd been cramped in the car most of the day, but he was too tired to raise himself up. Gerard shook his head in thought:

'I knew the explosions in Bath and Reading were linked.'

Like any decent journalist, Gerard had made the connection.

'With Huw, I could see it as revenge. But that bank CEO, the Gas company execs and now the Chancellor – it's like he's deliberately targeting the wealthy elite who exploit the rest of us.'

Evan didn't respond. His mobile bleeped with a text from Angela, asking if Gerard had agreed to do the appeal. Evan passed on the message. Gerard looked solemn as he said he would. Evan relayed the answer. He looked tiredly at Gerard:

'Okay if I kip on the sofa tonight?'

For the first time, Gerard lightened up as he went to get a pillow and blanket. Internally, Evan shook his head. Instead of being in bed with his wife, his own son across the hallway, he was sleeping on the sofa in Ryan's son's flat – the son of a man wanted for eight murders.

From his position at the mouth of the underpass,

Ryan looked sadly up at the window of Gerard's flat. It had been wrong to try and see his son. Scouting the area first in case police were waiting, Ryan had ducked down a side street when he saw Evan get out of a Ford Escort. Had Evan worked out that Ryan would want to see his son before it was all over? It probably wasn't that difficult an assumption to make.

Needing to hurry from Surrey, Ryan had stolen an old Nissan Micra. Out of place in the wealthy area where the Chancellor lived, the car must have belonged to an au pair or cleaner. Ryan was sorry to take it but the other cars available all had alarms fitted.

As a youth in Townhill, everyone had practised hotwiring. It was nearly forty years since he'd last done it, but the Micra started without a problem. He dumped the car as soon as he reached the outskirts of south London, not knowing how soon the theft would be reported and the police would be on his trail.

Ryan had actually only been to London a few times in his life, most of them in the last few years as he helped set up Gerard at Uni. It was easy to forget just how much London magnified the state of the nation. The few houses with 'For Sale' signs in Surrey were nothing in comparison to street after street with houses for sale in Croydon.

As Ryan made his way on foot to Elephant and Castle, he saw that the problems in Swansea were ten times worse here. It had always been a run-down area, but Ryan hadn't noticed it was this bad before.

Things had deteriorated in the six months since he'd last been here. Gerard had never said anything. Or maybe Ryan had been too preoccupied to ask.

It wasn't just the odd store boarded up, but a whole shopping centre. Half of it had been burnt down. And the blocks of flats that were still standing looked like they shouldn't be.

Ryan saw Keyhan's Kebabs. The guy had said his place was in Elephant and Castle. Outside the shop, a gang of Kurdish guys stared with hate-filled eyes across the road. Ryan followed their sight line. Above one end of the underpass, several young black men loitered with intent.

The anger seemed to come off the two groups in heat waves. No doubt jobless and without money, they all still sported various brand name jeans and trainers. They'd grown up with everything in view – iPhones, Sky TV, Wii's – but how could any of them afford it if they didn't have work? Simple, steal it. And meanwhile vent your fury on your fellow non-workers.

The world was fucked. And it had been fucked by the rich elite who didn't give a fuck about anyone else. Ryan had encountered the hypocrisy all along his journey, first with Edward Cameron and then the board at Southern Gas and Electric. The final confirmation had been with the chancellor. The banks, energy companies and the government had looked after themselves and that was all.

Ryan wanted to go over and shake the youths, make them see they were fighting the wrong people.

But he knew if he tried, they'd think he was crazy. They'd probably turn their aggression on him and kick the mad old bastard to death. He wasn't afraid of dying, he'd been right to the edge already a few times in his life, back in Kuwait. But he wasn't quite ready to die just yet.

Ryan had the CCTV microchip of the Chancellor admitting he'd ripped off the country and wanted to leave it with Gerard, but he would have to post it. Knowing there was no hope of seeing his son, Ryan traipsed towards the City. He could see the tops of the tall glass buildings from Elephant and Castle. And as he crossed the Thames via Southwark Bridge, the square mile of glass banks loomed into full view. It wasn't a castle, but Ryan knew it would be just as difficult to penetrate. The area probably had more CCTV cameras than any other part of the country.

But the City had its weaknesses. Ryan's research had shown him that there were plenty of unoccupied buildings. Some Banks had gone bankrupt too. Unlike at the vacant offices in Reading, he was sure security would still be in operation so he would need to bypass it.

This is where the Occupy Movement could help him. There was only a ragtag bunch of tents that remained encamped, but it provided enough camouflage. With his hood up, Ryan crossed over to avoid the patrolling constable. Taking his rucksack off, Ryan made as if he was settling for the night on the ground by one of the tents.

From his prone position, he scanned the

surrounding banks until he spotted the one he wanted. Northern Bank hadn't been saved by the Government, presumably because the execs had no connections. However, the small red light still flashed above the alarm box so security was still fitted. Ryan took a screwdriver and wire cutters from his rucksack. He waited until the police officer moved along the street, then made his move.

He unsteadily got to his feet and staggered to the side of the bank. If anyone was watching, it would look like he was having a drunken piss. He quickly checked over his shoulder, then sprang into action, pulling himself up onto the entrance wall. Directly under the CCTV camera, he stuck black masking tape over the lens. He was guessing, but the disused bank probably didn't have a live link up. The camera was just for footage to use after a criminal act had occurred.

Ryan nimbly unscrewed the alarm box. Clasping the screwdriver in his mouth, he held the box cover with one hand and took the wire cutters from his belt with the other. A drop of sweat dripped into his eye. He blinked it away and cut through the wires. He heard the footsteps of the plodding constable echo through the nearby empty City streets. Quickly putting the cover back in place, Ryan dropped down to the ground and made it back to his supposed sleeping pad just as the policeman turned the corner.

After half an hour, the policeman went on his next walk around the block. Ryan grabbed his rucksack and jogged to the bank entrance. Working on the door, he soon had it open. He strode inside, moved past the potted plastic plants in the deserted reception and headed up the stairs. With the place to himself, he'd be using the top floor - his very own penthouse suite to provide a view of the City he'd soon have crashing down.

28

South of the river from the City, Keyhan served a kebab to another customer. He tried to dismiss the payment but the guy insisted before joining the group outside. Between serving customers, Keyhan had been on his mobile all day, mobilising backup.

After the three black youths had threatened him, he'd silently cleaned up the mess. In Turkey, he'd been castigated for being Kurdish. He'd been arrested and beaten several times simply because of his nationality. He'd sought refuge in Great Britain, realised it wasn't so great as he waited two years before gaining his status. He'd lived on nothing and didn't want to live off the government. After years of hardship, he'd set up his shop and three kids thought they could ruin it?

He was so incensed, he'd called every friend he had and made it a race issue that affected all of them. Word had spread and now twenty Kurdish guys milled around outside the kebab shop.

Across the road, Aitch and his two mates saw the

group of Kurds getting bigger. OG just watched, silent as ever. It was TJ who was the worrier:

'They is up to something.'

'Yea I see.'

'Maybe it aint gonna work H.'

'They can't have protection every day.'

'More worried about our protection.'

'They aint gonna do nothing, is just show.'

'What if they start?'

Aitch gestured at Nandos, the place packed inside, several men smoking outside:

'Look around. Those Kurds come over here and start something, gonna be a hundred black guys to deal with.'

'Well, it looks like they moving now H.'

Aitch hadn't expected this. But he still acted nonchalant. If the Kurds came over looking to fight, all they had to do was slip into Nandos. First, the Kurds weren't going to start fighting in there with all the witnesses and CCTV. Second, if they were stupid enough to do that they'd be faced with a hundred black men. Okay, most of them weren't anything to Aitch, but for sure they weren't just going to look on while three black kids got attacked by a load of Kurds.

Outside Keyhan's, the group of men finished off their kebabs. Wiping their mouths, they chucked the wrappings in the plastic bin. All nodding to each other, they set off down the underpass.

Aitch, TJ and OG braced themselves, eyes on the underpass exit by Nandos. With no-one appearing after several minutes, Aitch tried to dismiss it:

'See, is nothing, probably just some Kurd night out.'

TJ was still on edge:

'You hear that?'

Mingled with the sound of traffic, glass was being smashed. The three of them cocked their heads, heard that the noise was coming from the market stalls. Not waiting for the other two, Aitch dashed over to the railings.

The Kurds were destroying his mum's stall, had already broken in, the cooking equipment being smashed to bits. Uncontrollable tears filled Aitch's eyes as he ran down the slope. He didn't care that he was outnumbered because he knew that no matter if he got beat to shit, his mum's livelihood had just been ruined.

Out of London, west along the M4, Laura washed up while her sons slept. Earlier in the day, she'd watched her sons happily playing in the old farmhouse grounds. All kids needed was a place to run around in and sticks to use as toys.

She'd woken in fright that morning, finding her oldest gone. She immediately picked up her youngest, ran downstairs and out of the farmhouse. To her relief, the oldest was poking around the remains of the fire from the night before. The man who'd made the fire had gone. She didn't even know his name. But he'd shown her that good people still existed. And he'd given her hope.

They could use the farmhouse as a base while they

got back on their feet. There were enough cans of beans and tacos so they wouldn't starve. They had running water. They'd go into town tomorrow, find a citizens advice bureau, go from there. Surely the authorities couldn't just let her family be homeless.

Standing at the sink as she washed up, she froze on hearing a voice behind her:

'Thought you could hole up here did you?'

Laura turned and saw one of the bailiffs from the day before, the skinhead who'd shoved her to the ground. She saw the mean look in his eyes, remembered her ex husband having the same look. She knew there and then that the bailiff was planning to rape and beat her while her kids slept upstairs. She didn't scream out, not wanting her boys to see whatever happened. Just as she didn't glance at the knife on the draining board, but as soon as he took a step closer, she'd grab it and fight for her life.

Further along the M4 corridor, over the bridge into Wales and on to Swansea, Kristine sat on the edge of her bed, her mobile gripped in her hand. The door of the room was unlocked and the window had no bars but she might as well be imprisoned.

It had turned out that the room wasn't exactly rent free, but was in exchange for working behind the bar. When she'd asked for her pay after the bar had closed that night, Richard had feigned surprise, said didn't she have the room?

Taken aback, Kristine had asked how she was supposed to live. As if he was giving charity, Richard had given her just enough for basic food and toiletries. She'd almost walked there and then, but had to take stock.

The money she'd saved from working at Morgan's had run out. With no payment from her bar work she had literally nothing, no way of renting another flat. What was she going to do, take Richard to court? Even if he was made to pay up, it would take ages. Where would she live until then?

Richard had turned out to be a complete bastard. And Ryan, what had happened to him? Kristine couldn't believe it when she saw the news. Was he really responsible for killing all those people? She thought she was good at reading people but she didn't know anyone.

She looked at her mobile. She had to call her parents in Latvia. It was time to go home.

Six in the morning, Owen left his house and traipsed to Wind Street. With the revellers gone home, he was in to clean up their mess.

Rubber gloves donned, Owen wiped up the piss and puke from a few hours earlier. He was nearly forty years old and this was how he supported his wife and kids.

The job didn't even really provide financial support as they had less to live on than if he'd been signing on, with all the benefits that entailed. But if he hadn't accepted the job, the benefits would have been cut, so what choice did he have?

Owen wanted someone to blame. Ryan had been

first on the list, but it had initially seemed as if the bastard had moved – Owen had gone over to Mumbles one day and seen the house up for sale. Then Ryan's name and face had appeared on national news - Ryan had lost the plot and started blowing people up. Owen didn't know how he felt about that. In a way he understood Ryan's rage.

The next person on Owen's list was the patronising job centre officer. He'd like to throttle the fucker, pictured himself beating the prick to a pulp. But then he also envisaged the security guy, police arriving and prison. And then what good would he be to his family?

And then, for one dark second, Owen thought life would be easier if he didn't have a family to look after.

He squirted out more bleach and scrubbed harder, ridding himself of toxic thoughts. His eyes were watery, but he told himself it was the chemicals.

Crushed between the toilet and wall, Johnny slowly regained consciousness. His head hurt, but not from a hangover. He tried to move his right arm, but it had gone numb under his body. He shifted onto his side, massaged his right arm with his left to get the blood circulating. Then he felt the back of his head. There was a lump.

With a frown, he realised where he was. A toilet. One he recognised. Morgan's Security Systems. It started to come back to him. He'd broken in, fallen. How long had he been out cold for? Long enough for the alcohol to wear off, to be replaced by hunger and thirst.

Had anyone missed him? Unlikely. He could have been there for weeks and no-one would care. Moroseness took over. Maybe he should just lie there and die. What was there to live for?

A strip of morning sunlight reflected off a shard of glass in the window frame, the glass smashed from where he'd broken in. He was so thirsty. Self preservation kicked in. He was in a toilet, therefore there was a sink and water.

He struggled to his feet in unsteady jerks, first onto his knees while he leaned on the toilet, then to a standing position with the sink providing support.

He turned on the tap and drank in huge gulps, water dripping down his chin. His thirst quenched, he threw water over his face, some of the water splashing onto the toilet and floor.

He was alive, that was a start. Yes, life was shit, but he had to try and do something with it. What was it Ryan had said to him – don't give up.

He'd go home, shower, get a CV together and go to the other companies. The doors of Morgan's were doubled glazed so he'd have to get out the same way he'd come in – through the broken window. He stood on the toilet lid, ready to lever himself through the window. But the lid was slippery from the water that had splashed onto it and his legs were wobbly from two days inaction.

Johnny crashed into the window frame and a shard of glass pierced his neck.

29

Ryan stretched his long limbs and looked out of the top floor windows. He squinted as the morning sunlight reflected off the glass buildings that surrounded him, bouncing off at all angles. There was hardly anybody in the streets below, the City empty. Banks, finance offices and the Stock Exchange didn't operate at weekends. The hi-tech, sci-fi designed buildings didn't include housing so the only occupants visible were in the tented remains of the Occupy Movement.

The encampment briefly hit Ryan with a flashback to the nomads in Kuwait. It would be nice to be riding with them now. He shook the thought away. He had to focus on accomplishing his mission. The City below and around him had to be taken down. Ideally, he would have operated from within somewhere like the Stock Exchange, but he knew gaining entry to such a place would have been extremely difficult. The security would without doubt include live police link up and actual guards. Even if he forced his way in, he'd have very little time to set up explosives. Plus, he wanted to avoid any civilian casualties.

His chosen building would cause enough damage to wake people up. He also had a few explosives to set out in other places. If possible, he wanted to get the area cleared of security guards and the tent dwellers. He was confident he could carry it all out. What he wondered was how people would perceive events. He hadn't put out any message and no doubt the media would spin it to show him as a crazed lunatic. He just hoped that someone would understand his actions. The CCTV footage of the chancellor admitting the truth would also show Ryan killing him so might work against his mission. He would get the microchip to Gerard and his son could decide.

In the press room, Gerard took his place behind the desk set up with microphones. In front of him, several cameramen got their equipment ready while technicians checked the sound levels. In the rows of foldable chairs, TV reporters and newspaper journalists prepped themselves. It was funny, thought Gerard, his life ambition was to be where they were, yet here he was on the other side of the microphones and cameras.

He'd hardly slept as he'd rewritten what he'd say several times. His dad had killed eight people. Apart from Huw, there was no personal reason for the other murders – the bank CEO, the gas company chief execs, the chancellor. What were the right words? A little guiltily, Gerard realised he was concerned about how he would came across. A prospective journalist had to be articulate. Fuck it, he thought, he wouldn't stick to a script. What the situation called for was for him to express his true feelings.

From a side entrance, Angela cast her eyes over the mass of media people. She wanted to be out in the field, tracking Ryan down, but had no choice, especially as she'd been summoned to an early morning meeting with the commander in chief. At that moment, she was still on the case, but Angela knew that she was about to take the flak for the chancellor's death. It was hardly her fault that, between them, the chancellor and commander in chief had authorised security to remain in the car outside, but there wasn't a lot she could do about that. If she made that particular phone conversation public, she'd never work again. On the other hand, it was a bargaining tool for keeping her job.

With the government on high risk alert, the PM had been given top notch security. Angela knew it was part of MI5's remit, but still felt slightly uneasy. This was not a case of a terrorist group killing British citizens, but a lone man deliberately targeting the elite. And she wasn't sure that the media had been right to make Ryan out to be a danger to the general public. However, showing doubt hadn't got her to where she was. The live appeal from Ryan's son would no doubt bring in prank calls and false leads, but if one tip-off proved good, it would be worth it.

Apart from anything, Angela wanted to find Ryan before any trigger happy colleague did. He had to be stopped, but he didn't have to be killed. She couldn't stop herself seeing Ryan as she remembered him. Ryan had saved lives in Kuwait. He'd stopped her being raped. And had even refused to have an affair. This was a man with moral sense.

She'd never been bitter that he didn't see her again after that kiss twenty years ago. In fact, she felt he'd done the right thing. It had helped her become who she was. She'd never found the right partner and it was too late to have kids but she was a lead MI5 officer who dedicated herself to protecting her country.

Was Ryan really a danger to national security? This question kept nagging at her. A switch had obviously been flicked in Ryan's mind to make him kill civilians. But she could see the logic to it. He wasn't killing random British citizens, he was taking down the rich elite. The bank CEOs, the gas company execs, the Chancellor - everyone knew they were ripping off the country to help themselves. By getting rid of them, was Ryan the real patriot?

Angela dismissed the question. First, they had to find Ryan. Then she could see about saving more lives, including Ryan's.

At the back of the room, Evan stood with a coffee. Distracted with his own thoughts, he didn't take in the proceedings. He hadn't vetted Gerard as he should have done as he didn't mind what Ryan's son said. It was highly unlikely that Ryan would be watching the TV appeal. And even if he did see it, Evan didn't believe it would affect Ryan one way or another.

What Evan was trying to work out was where Ryan

was now. After killing the chancellor, what was next? The PM maybe, but in fact the Prime Minister had less say on the banks being bailed out than the chancellor. So if Ryan was going to go further up the chain, he'd need to kill those in world-wide finance. Ryan was highly skilled, but he wasn't Jason Bourne. Evan couldn't see him escaping the country and going on an international killing spree. No, Evan felt sure that Ryan's final target was here in London.

Ryan waited until the day shift constable had rounded the corner before stepping out of the Northern Bank entrance. Across the street, the few people living in the Occupy tents were getting breakfast ready. With his hood up, Ryan jogged along the opposite side. Taking a turn, he stopped and bent down as if to do up his laces. In fact, he pressed a piece of PE4 into a crack in the pavement. He deftly moulded the substance into an arrow shape that aimed towards the Stock Exchange ahead of him. With the charge already inserted into the malleable plastic, his remote detonator would do the rest. It was a fair distance to the building, but he reckoned that it would take out the glass entrance.

He jogged at a good pace for a few streets until he came to a corner shop at the edge of the square mile. Next to Bank tube station, the shop had just opened. Pulling his hood down, Ryan entered the shop. Here, he wanted to be recognised. Ryan deliberately raised his face to the shop's CCTV camera.

Behind the counter, the old Pakistani shop owner

stared at Ryan as he bought a disposable mobile phone, an envelope and a stamp. Glancing at the newspapers on the rack, Ryan saw his name and photo on the front pages. The photo showed him post-race, his face red and tired-looking but exhilarated. Ryan guessed it was taken by the local Evening Post at the Run for Cancer. That day in Swansea Bay seemed a long time ago.

The shop owner glanced to the side and Ryan saw that the man had a small TV in the corner. The owner involuntarily stepped back as Ryan leaned over the counter to look. In the top right of the screen was the same photo of Ryan from the newspaper. At the bottom, a phone number to call scrolled across. And centre-screen, Gerard was talking to camera. Ryan looked the shop owner in the eyes:

'Can you turn it up?'

Not knowing what else to do, the shop owner did as he was asked. From the TV, Gerard's voice got louder:

'…Yes, he's killed. But who has he killed? The rich elite who have brought our country to ruin and keep the rest of us impoverished. A bank CEO who gave himself millions of pounds in bonuses while repossessing our homes. A board of energy execs who mislead us so they could make more money. The Chancellor who bailed out the banks, impoverishing the rest of us, deliberately allowing the wealthy to exploit the situation and reward themselves ever greater sums of money whilst we starved.'

Gerard looked directly to the camera:

'So, dad, if you're listening, I'm proud of you. And

to everyone else, it's time those responsible for the economic crisis settled their debts.'

Ryan cracked a smile. He turned back to the wide-eyed shop owner and nodded at the TV:

'You can call that number, tell them I'm here.'

With that, Ryan strode out of the shop, quickly posting the CCTV footage of the Chancellor to Gerard. Ryan set off at a jog and almost sprinted to the vacant bank. He wanted them to come, but he had to be in position first.

There was commotion in the press room. With little success, Angela and the other MI5 officer tried to cut the press conference short. The problem was that the various TV stations and newspapers were lapping it up. It wouldn't make any difference anyway, thought Angela. Gerard's words had already gone out live and besides, outside the press room, Gerard could say whatever he wanted – it was a free country. Her head was definitely on the block now. She should have vetted Gerard herself instead of letting Evan do it. She didn't have time to remonstrate with him as her mobile was already ringing.

The other MI5 officer took up the mantle and ploughed through the scrum of reporters to reach Evan:

'I thought you vetted him.'

Evan had started listening to Gerard halfway through, realising he'd gone way off script. He wasn't sure how to take Gerard's impassioned speech, but thought maybe it could be useful:

'Look, requesting Ryan to give himself up was never going to work. His son being proud might unsettle him, it might give him pause for thought, think about stopping what he's doing.'

The MI5 officer looked ready to punch Evan, who simply turned his gaze on the melee of reporters and journalists, all plugged into their various recording devices. Making her way through the crowd was Angela, her mobile glued to her ear.

Something clicked with Evan. What was it Ryan had said that time in Townhill when Evan had gone to warn him off Huw? He'd said something about people not appreciating the view because they were plugged into their Sky TV. He'd mentioned the nomads he'd seen in Kuwait, said maybe everyone needed to start from scratch and live with nothing.

Angela clicked off her mobile as she reached Evan and the MI5 officer. Just as she spoke to the MI5 officer, Evan knew where Ryan was, his eureka sentence uttered a split second after Angela's:

'We've had a sighting of him.'

'He's going to take down the City.'

Angela glanced at Evan:

'That's where he's just been seen. Pity you couldn't work it out a bit quicker.'

She turned back to the MI5 officer:

'Get a special forces team together.'

The MI5 officer nodded:

'I'm on it.'

He thumbed at Evan:

'But please don't let him near me.'

Angela exhaled:

'We need him. If it comes down to a stand off, he could be useful in a negotiation. He knows Ryan better than anyone.'

The MI5 officer gritted his teeth and got on his mobile. Angela led the way out of the building, Evan having to keep up. He said:

'Those boys are going to take him out.'

Angela kept walking as she spoke:

'Not if I can help it, but I'm going to need your help. And in the end, it's going to be up to Ryan.'

On the top floor of the vacant bank, Ryan checked that everything was ready. The door was wired with detonator cord and PE4 had been attached in several places around the building. In front of him, he had the wireless detonators, his newly bought mobile and binoculars. He picked up the binoculars and looked down at the City streets. He smiled sadly as he recognised a figure below, his friend having finally caught up with him.

Evan craned his neck to look up at the non-working bank. Around him, the army of Special Police were starting to swarm. The call from the shop had been verified and various CCTVs checked. Ryan had been tracked to the building that loomed above Evan. All he could see was light reflecting off the glass. Was Ryan up there? And if so, how was this cross country trek going to end?

30

Ryan felt alive and focused. His breathing was even and he was on the last stretch of the cross-country run. He felt wired, like the times when he'd had seconds left as he de-wired explosives in Kuwait. This time though he'd be setting them off. With his twenty-twenty vision heightened, every edge of the glass architecture in front of him was in sharp high definition.

Through his binoculars, Ryan saw the armed Special Police swarm through the City streets, ant-like between the sci-fi high-rises. He guessed they were taking precautions and making sure all exits were covered, but he wasn't going anywhere. And he was ready for their arrival.

Hyper-alert, Ryan heard the stealthy footfall outside the door. He didn't know for sure, but he envisaged a unit of five or six armed special police. The silence showed him they'd stopped and he knew what they were looking at as they worked out their course of action.

At the top of the stairwell, five special police had halted under the hand command from a sixth member of the unit at their head. In front of them, they saw the PE4 attached to the doorframe, detonator cord wired under the door. It was impossible to tell if it was possible to detach the explosive without setting it off. The guy at the front swirled a finger and the unit backed away down the stairs.

Ryan heard the footfalls recede. He trained his binoculars on the building opposite. The bank that the glass high-rise housed didn't operate on a Sunday, but someone had gained entry to it.

In the binocular sight, Ryan saw a sniper with his high-powered rifle aimed directly at him. Ryan didn't flinch. He'd expected this. If the sniper shot him, the detonator attached to his shirt would go off so his plan would at least be partly carried out. However, Ryan was hoping to avoid casualties. If possible, he wanted the police, tent dwellers and any security guards to be out of range. He reckoned the sniper wouldn't shoot with the situation so volatile. He would wait and for sure need orders to make the kill.

Sure enough, as Ryan adjusted the binoculars' sight slightly to the right, he saw a man and woman in sharp suits, presumably MI5 officers. The male officer nearest to the sniper looked ready to grab the sniper's weapon and pull the trigger himself.

But the male officer wasn't in charge. Next to him the female MI5 officer was more focused, on Ryan in fact, her eyes obscured by binoculars as she scoped him watching her. She had a palm up, a visual order for the sniper and other MI5 officer to hold fire. There was something familiar about the woman, but he wasn't sure what.

Behind the MI5 officers was another figure. Partially blocked by the officers and window frame, Ryan couldn't see the person's face but he recognised the crumpled suit. It was Evan.

Deliberately going slow-mo, Ryan gently swapped the binoculars for the disposable mobile. So that they could see his actions weren't preceding violence, Ryan slowly raised the mobile.

He wanted to make a final call.

The tension in the top floor office was unbearable, as was the heat. With the bank not officially open, no air con was on and the sunlight reflected brutally through the glass.

The sniper had his finger on the trigger, his sight on Ryan. It was a fair distance between the buildings, but with Ryan unmoving, he would get a hit. Through the rifle sight, the sniper could see Ryan had detonators at hand. So he wouldn't be firing until the order came through his earphone.

Nearest to the sniper, the MI5 officer was perfectly still, but inside he was livid with impatience. He knew they had to wait, be sure of how explosive the situation was – literally. But he wanted it to be over. Ryan had outwitted them at every stage on his cross-country killing spree. And his bloody Welsh DCI buddy had hardly helped track him down. The officer needed to release his fury.

Next to him, Angela was calmer. She could feel the various tensions, knew both the sniper and her officer wanted nothing more than to shoot Ryan. But she was doing her job. Of course, Ryan had to be stopped. At present, however, he wasn't putting any life in immediate danger. Morally he had to be apprehended rather than killed. Besides, her duty was to see the unit of special police safe. Ryan had the place rigged, so until the unit came out of the building, there was no way she was giving the order for Ryan to be shot. And more than anything, she wanted him to stay alive.

Behind Angela, Evan tried to gain a better view but it was partly obscured by the MI5 officers and window frame. The tension in the room was so highly-strung, he didn't dare take a step sideways for fear of setting off the sniper. Although he couldn't see clearly into the building opposite, Evan knew Ryan was in there. And he knew in his bones that someone was going to die, he just didn't know who. Inside his crumpled suit, sweat dripped down his body.

Evan's mobile rang.

He didn't jump, but froze to the spot. The other three in the room also didn't move a bone.

Evan took out his phone. He saw that it was a new number and was pretty sure he knew who was calling.

'Ryan?'

A fissure of a smile almost cracked across Ryan's face as he spoke into his mobile:

'I guess you caught up with me.'

Evan answered:

'Guess so.'

They were both silent for a second, each gauging how to proceed. Ryan had planned simply to tell Evan to vacate the building and clear the area. He guessed he was feeling more emotional, his friend's voice was getting to him. For his part, Evan knew that directly asking Ryan to stand down wasn't going to work. He wasn't an expert negotiator and didn't know what the protocol was. But what he did know was that Ryan had been his friend since they were kids.

'I was thinking about those cross-country runs we used to go on. You remember that time when we dropped stones on a car that drove under the old railway bridge?'

Ryan didn't respond, just frowned in consternation. Evan went on:

'The guy from the car ran after us so we scarpered, but I hesitated for a second and he caught up with me.'

Evan laughed nervously:

'You always were faster than me.'

Ryan's jaw throbbed. This wasn't the time for his memory to be jogged.

'I don't want casualties, Evan. You clear the area of yourselves, the Occupy group and any security guards, then there will just be rubble to clear up after.'

In the sweat-drenched office, Evan exhaled. His mobile was on loudspeaker so the others could hear everything. The sniper flexed his fingers, making sure they weren't trigger happy. The male MI5 officer swung a look to Angela, waiting for her command.

Angela lowered her binoculars, turned to Evan and gestured for his mobile:

'Let me try.'

Ryan was about to switch off his phone when he heard another voice:

'Ryan, this is Angela Stephens MI5, we were at Sandhurst together, do you remember me?'

Ryan shivered as he recognised her voice. He picked up his binoculars. It really was Angela. Nothing surprised Ryan any more. First his old friend, then the only woman he'd nearly had an affair with. It was like a man's dying moments in some film. Except this was real. He heard Angela's voice again:

'Ryan?'

Ryan quickly worked things out. MI5 was the right place for Angela to end up. He'd heard on the grapevine she'd got a job with them, so it had turned out to be true. He nodded:

'I'm here.'

'Ryan, we only knew each other for a short time, but I've always admired what you did in Kuwait and I've always been grateful for what you did for me. You saved me being raped once. Do you remember that?'

'I remember.'

'You're a good guy Ryan, and now I want to help you.'

Ryan shrugged:

'I'm not sure you can.'

'Ryan, there's a guy here ready to fire. I don't want you to be a casualty. I'm sure Gerard doesn't either.'

Ryan knew what she was doing, making it personal, first with their shared past and now with his son. He guessed it was well intentioned, but it wouldn't work.

'He'll survive.'

'What about his future? How's he going to get work after his dead dad is labelled a terrorist?'

Ryan swallowed:

'There aren't any jobs anyway. We've been fucked over for too long. That's why it's time to take a stand.'

'Look Ryan, maybe I agree with you. But there doesn't need to be any more casualties. We can sort this out, on the ground.'

Ryan looked down through the glass at the streets below. He knew Angela was doing what she had to, but his resolve was hardened.

'You need to clear the area.'

Ryan clicked off his mobile.

Angela handed Evan's mobile back to him while keeping her eyes on the building opposite, willing Ryan to step down. Her words hadn't had much effect. To try and save him, she'd shown her vulnerability to the other guys, letting them hear about the near rape. Maybe the Ryan she knew from her army days wasn't the same guy. Maybe she couldn't save him. The male MI5 officer shrugged:

'Guess that was the negotiation.'

Evan pocketed his phone:

'He's not going to back down. It's just whether buildings or people go down with him.'

The male MI5 officer turned to Angela:

'The unit's safe. We take him out?'

Evan turned to her too.

'And if Ryan's wired himself up?'

Angela exhaled. She had a split-second decision to make. The sniper didn't adjust his sight but his ear throbbed in anticipation.

Ryan picked up his binoculars. He'd stood motionless for long enough. They'd had enough time to either shoot him or move out. Looking across, he saw that the top floor of the building opposite was empty. Angela had done as he asked.

He roved his sight down to the ground. No-one remained by the Occupy tents. He trained the binoculars along the street. Gathered at the end were the special police and MI5 officers. Evan stood slightly apart from them.

Ryan put the binoculars down and stepped right to the glass. He was at the edge. He was still alive, but this was his last minute on earth. He thought about his son. Since seeing Gerard on TV, Ryan knew his son's drive would see him alright in life.

Sitting watching the Robert Ryan film together had been a good last thing to do as father and son. His situation made him think of the last scene in The Set Up. Cornered in an alley, Robert Ryan knew it was the end, but he also knew he'd done the right thing.

Ryan turned his thoughts to the time Evan had

reminded him of. They must have been about eleven. On one of their cross-country practice runs, they'd stopped at the bridge. He wasn't sure whose idea it was. In his mind, he saw the two boys simultaneously meet each others' eyes in mischief before dropping the stones.

They hadn't expected the car to brake or the man to run after them. They'd bolted, but when Ryan glanced over his shoulder he saw Evan about to give up. He urged his friend on, but Evan let the man catch him so Ryan went back to take his share of the blame.

Ryan smiled and pressed the detonators.

Cal Smyth's first novel is also available:

WRONG WAY AROUND

You're supposed to do the crime first, and then go on the run. They did it the other way around…Adrift in Tokyo, photographer Colin and hostess Linda hit it off – in a whirlwind of passion, they marry in Vegas and head to Mexico for a life of adventure. But when money runs low, they end up in London – grey skies and dead-end jobs turning their dreams sour. Until an incident with Linda's sleazy boss leads to a lucrative blackmail scam that reignites their passion. The couple embark on an exhilarating crime spree, but as it spirals out of control, will it consume their relationship?

A gripping contemporary thriller which explores the conventions of sex, violence and morality… With nods to Richard Stark, Elmore Leonard and Jim Thompson, Cal Smyth has written a relentless noir thriller that hooks you instantly.

www.iponymous.com

Read the first few thrilling pages now…

Prologue

Colin ignored the food on the breakfast tray as he snatched at the postcard that came with it. The postcard picture depicted a topless beauty reclining on a white sand beach, turquoise sea lapping onto the shore. Phuket was in italics at the top, looking like it was pronounced "Fuck it", which seemed appropriate. Colin flipped the card over.

There was no message, just Colin's name and prison address. It wasn't her handwriting, but he knew it was from Linda. This could prove that she was still alive and that he hadn't killed her. He had to speak to his lawyer.

In his excitement, he accidentally clattered over the tin tray. It brought him to his senses, dashing his sudden dream of freedom. Before he even called the guard, he knew it would be no use – she was too clever to leave fingerprints. Staring at the postcard, Colin pictured Linda far away on some Thai beach while he rotted in his cell. As his euphoria died, he wondered how it had come to this:

You're supposed to do the crime first, then go on the run – we did it the other way around. Maybe that's where we went wrong…

CHAPTER 1

They met in a bar in Shinjuku, Colin there with a group from Hello Tokyo, the magazine he'd just done a fashion shoot for, pretending to be happy. Truth was, he'd had his fill of Japan - it just wasn't his cup of green tea.

The bar was called London Calling, as retro as you could get. A screen silently showed clips from Blow Up, Peeping Tom and Performance – red double-deckers and black cabs sliding into view. A jukebox played The Clash, The Kinks and Saint Etienne – names of famous streets and bridges drifting into hearing.

The Japanese men loved the place because of the western hostesses that worked there. Especially once they'd had a few Kirin beers and their true lewdness came out.

The group's hostess sashayed over to them in a body-accentuating silk green dress, tray of snacks in one hand. Striking a pose, she swished her blonde hair off her face, which of course sent the Japanese men wild. Shinji, one of the magazine editors, leered:

'You are very b–e–a–utiful.'

The others all laughed at his deliberate English pronunciation. The blonde hostess smiled a fake smile as she placed bowls of shiny nut-shaped puffed rice on the low table, to go with the half-drunk beers. At first glance she looked like just another girl in the wannabe Monroe mould.

Colin looked at her face more closely, for photographic purposes he told himself. It was the flexibility of her face that was fascinating. She had a mouth that could laugh easily but also curl in hate.

He should have known then he was in trouble.

The hostess finished serving, turned and saw Colin looking at her. Not needing to put on a fake smile for the western customer, she met his look, both of them holding it before she turned and went on her way.

Shinji saw the exchange of looks, turned to Colin:

'You like her too huh? Leave some girls for us! You have already one waiting.'

Shinji gestured to the porcelain-faced model sitting impassively next to Colin, who he'd been shooting all day in Yoyogi Park, under the cherry blossom. Shinji turned back to the rest of his gang:

'You know why he gets so many girls?'

The others shook their heads in unison, letting Shinji answer his own question:

'Because he is Englishman and he has very big penis!'

The group burst out laughing, drinks spluttering from their mouths. The more beer they drank, the more roles reversed, thought Colin, the Japanese men getting louder as the English man sat back, observing.

Colin finished his beer, stood up:

'Guys, I'm off.'

'Oh no, only joke, stay for more beer."

'I'll send the hostess over on my way out.'

Shinji gestured to the model:

'But look, you leave her very sad.'

Without looking, Colin left the table. At the bar, the blonde hostess was filling up her tray with more beer to be served to another table. Colin paused by her:

'Pretty busy eh?'

'Uh huh.'

'Your fan club over there is ready for their next round.'

'You're not?'

'What, part of the fan club or ready for another beer?'

She carried on putting glasses of beer onto the tray as she answered:

'Either.'

'I'm going now, but I'll come back later. What time do you finish?'

'Why,' her Mancunian accent came out in full as she sarcastically said:

'You want to walk me home?'

Colin let that hang there for a few seconds, enjoying their banter:

'No, but I'll buy you a drink.'

The hostess started to walk off with the tray, then briefly paused, smiling over her shoulder:

'Midnight.'

Colin was waiting for her when she came out of the bar, leant against the wall and twisting an old train ticket in his fingers. He had steady hands, but if they weren't holding a camera, he didn't know what to do with them.

Over her dress, she had a lightweight wrap-around jacket with a wide belt. Colin was in his usual – jeans, T-shirt and hoody zip-up. He might have been a fashion photographer, but he didn't care about his own fashion. Years taking photos of other people's appearance had that effect – so much of it was a facade.

As the hostess walked on by, she could only half prevent a smile:

'So you're serious?'

'About what?'

'Walking me home?'

'I'm a serious guy.'

'You don't look it.'

'That's what my mum told me. Said son, you'll never have a serious relationship because you're never serious.'

Colin moved off the wall, walking alongside her:

'Anyway, I didn't say I'd walk you home, I said I'd buy you a drink.'

'But if I miss the last train, I'll have to wait until morning.'

'We'll get one on the way.'

Colin spotted a can dispensing machine up ahead, jogged up to it and gestured with his hand:

'What will it be madam? Green Tea? Asahi Beer?'

'A true romantic - beer.'

Colin put money in the slot, took out two cans of cold Asahi, gave one to the hostess. They held up their cans to each other, said "campi", the Japanese for "cheers", and knocked back a hit. The hostess lowered her can:

'I'm Linda by the way.'

'Colin, nice to meet you.'

Linda laughed:

'That's my surname – Linda Collins.'

'Or Colin's Linda.'

She laughed again:

'What about you, what's your surname?'

'Crosswell.'

'Like the teacakes?'

That's what everyone said. Colin tried not to roll his eyes. Crosswell, the famous English bloody teacakes. Usually he said "yea, same name but no relation". But he shrugged, told Linda the truth:

'Yea, it was my Grandfather's company. It was supposed to be passed down but my dad spent all the inheritance. What was it George Best said – he spent nearly all his money on drink and women, the rest was wasted. That's how my dad saw it too.'

Colin paused. Was he going to tell this girl he'd only just met his whole life story? Next he'd be recalling the day his grandfather was taken to hospital with a heart attack. Thirteen years old, he'd been holed up in his room, headphones on so he didn't have to listen to his dad have sex with the local barmaid while his mum was day shopping in London, spending money they didn't have.

They didn't know he was in the house as he'd secretly skipped school and sneaked back in. From his window Colin saw the barmaid leave, but he stayed motionless in his room until the phone rang, making him jump. He let it ring, but his dad didn't answer it. When the phone started up again, Colin cautiously went into the hallway. He peered into his parents' bedroom and saw his dad passed out so he picked up the phone.

Colin nodded silently to the voice from the hospital, the person unsure if Colin had understood the situation. But he was just trying to work out what to do. If he woke his dad up it would be obvious he wasn't in school. But if he didn't, they might not see his grandfather before he died. He called a taxi and shook his dad awake. Half-plastered, his dad didn't question why Colin was there or helping him stagger out to the taxi.

Time they got to the hospital his grandfather was dead, so Colin's decision had been in vain. But it didn't matter as neither of his parents ever asked what he'd been doing at home.

Colin shrugged off the memory and said:

'The company was sold off years ago. They kept the name but it's nothing to do with the family anymore. So if it's money you're thinking of marrying me for, forget it.'

'Must be something else I'm after then, because you've made me miss my train.'

Linda's mouth turned into a wide smile. Colin wanted to kiss that mouth.

A second later he did.

Colin and Linda didn't finish their cans of beer. Nor did they make it to her place. It was late and all public transport had stopped, only extortionately priced taxis remaining, so they went down to the Love Hotels - a bizarre arrangement of architecture, fake gothic structures at odds with the surrounding modern business district.

Most of the places were already full, but one still had vacancies. In the reception area there were screens displaying video stills of all the rooms. For the romantics, there was a Roman style room with 4-poster bed and paintings of voluptuous women, naked and reclining. You wanted something more funky, there was a seventies disco room, complete with ceiling mirrors and glitter ball. Or if you preferred it more hardcore, there was an S&M style room, the bed caged by red metal bars.

The only room still lit up and available was the traditional Japanese room, so that's what they had.

Any room would have done.

They hardly got each others clothes off, straight down onto the low bed, Linda unzipping his jeans, Colin pulling her knickers down - neither noticing the "tatami" straw matt flooring or mirror that went along all four walls at just above bed height.

Second time, Linda rolled Colin to the side and straddled him. Taking her time now, she pulled her dress over her head, revealing small but pert breasts, with bright pink nipples. As she started to ride him, Colin grinned and cupped them with pleasure:

'Cup cakes I could eat.'

Linda though stopped riding, taking offence:

'Are you saying they're small?'

Before Colin could reply, Linda grabbed a pillow and pressed it down over his face. He slapped the mattress in submission and she relented. Colin got his breath back:

'I'm saying I could eat them with tea – a Crosswell speciality.'

Linda's half-turned mouth reverted to a smile as she

forgave him, her tongue darting inside his mouth as she started moving her hips again.

The third time, both sitting, they saw their reflections in the mirror and couldn't stop looking, stars in their own show. They looked good together, matched each other.

He didn't pretend to be the world's most handsome, but he had gleaming blue eyes and a chiselled jaw. Losing his
hair a bit on top, but at six foot one, most people didn't see that, especially in Japan.

She did pretend to be one of the world's prettiest and with her green eyes and high cheeks she pretty much pulled it off. Her pubic hair was dark, showing that she was a fake blonde, but not many would see that. He hoped so anyway, presuming Linda didn't go with just any guy and that her passion was mutual. She'd made a lot of noise and left scratch marks on his back. He was pretty sure it was genuine.

Ten in the morning, the hotel reception phoned the room, telling Colin and Linda it was time for them to leave. Shiny eyed from too much sex and too little sleep, they went to a café for breakfast. Colin looked at the menu:

'Problem with Tokyo is you can't get a decent cup of tea. I mean tea should be brown, dark brown, not green.' Linda joined in:

'And if you ask for toast, they'll probably put bean paste on it and roll it up.'

They laughingly agreed that Tokyo was great for noodle bars but not so hot for cafes.

Over "American coffees" and "French croissants", the nearest they could get to what they wanted, Colin asked:

'Where are you from originally?'

She looked at him quizzically. Wasn't all night sex enough for this guy? What else did he want to know, her favourite colour? She decided to amuse him:

'I grew up in Man-ches-ter,' laying on the accent, 'left when I was eighteen.'

'I grew up with that whole Manchester scene – used to love the Stone Roses, Happy Mondays – showing my age.'

'Twenty eight, twenty nine?'

'Twenty nine.'

'Me too.'

'And look, after the same number of years, we've ended up in the same place in life. How did you end up here?'

'I came out as an English teacher just to get the visa, then I left immediately to get a job as a hostess. Loads of money for simply smiling and letting Japanese men ogle you. And hey, seeing as I get that on the train everyday anyway, I might as well get paid for it.'

'Makes sense to me.'

'What about you, what are you doing here?'

'I don't know really. I started out on the cruise ships as a photographer, got trained on the job. For a while it was great, travelled all over the world, had a great time, had a really good mate called Vinnie - he sorted my visa out for here…'

Colin looked at Linda. She'd told him without hesitation about how she'd got a job on false pretences, so he guessed it was okay to explain:

'…you probably know, you've got to have a degree to get a work permit for Japan and I never finished university, so Vinnie printed me out a fake degree - but the reason I'm here, I got bored of being on the boat, so when we docked in Tokyo, I stopped here, got a job as a fashion photographer.'

'Bet you get lots of girls after you.'

Colin smiled in fake modesty. Linda continued:

'When I first arrived, I saw all these ugly male English teachers, all with beautiful Japanese girlfriends.'

Colin frowned, taken aback:

'You saying I'm ugly?'

'You're an exception.'

'Everyone always wants what they haven't got. The Japanese girl wants the Western man, and vice versa. Don't see too many Japanese men and Western women together though.'

'It's a strictly look but don't touch policy, thank God.'

'Don't know if it's true, but they do have this whole inferiority complex, that Western men, you know…are bigger.'

'I wouldn't know…so do you have a girlfriend?'

'Yea, and yes she's a model I photographed, but she doesn't have a mouth like yours.'

'I'll take that as a compliment.'

'What about you?'

'Uh huh, he's a pilot. I call him when I'm in the mood and he flies on in.'

Colin looked down, went silent. Linda pouted at him:

'Hey, don't be sad. He's okay, but he hasn't got a mouth like yours.'

Colin looked up at her, tried to be cool:

'I'll ditch mine, if you ditch yours.'

'It's a deal.'

With wide smiles, they shook on it.

They saw each other every day, before and after work, the rest of the day just an interlude between sex. Alternating between each other's flats, they would wake up to make love. He would go to his job, wait for her to finish hers, then they would rush back home for more.

On the escalators to the platform in Tokyo central, Colin always stood one step below Linda so that they were the same height to kiss.

In the last train out of central Tokyo, Colin's height and Linda's blondeness stuck out, drawing unblinking stares from Japanese business men over the top of their manga porn. Or a gaggle of teenage girls in long white socks, high-step shoes and shirt skirts would giggle and whisper "gaijin, gaijin," the Japanese for "foreigner".

Oblivious, Colin would tell Linda how he'd been thinking of her all day. Linda would raise her eyebrows – yea, she knew what he'd been thinking about. He'd start to protest it wasn't just that and she'd cut him off with a kiss, her hand surreptitiously rubbing against his groin.

Both their flats were on the outskirts of Tokyo, towards Funabashi. Colin's place was old style Japanese with tatami floor, sliding paper doors and a square bath. For the first month, every morning when he'd risen from the thin futon, he'd cracked his head on the low doorframe. And when he had a bath, he had to sit with his knees at head level. Apart from his camera equipment he kept the flat minimalist, or miserablist as Linda called it. Tokyo was a haven for techno gadgets and Colin had often frequented Akihabra, or Electric City as it was known.

Linda's place was in a modern block, still with tatami flooring, but containing a shower and mod cons. The walls were adorned with photos of Linda striking poses on various beaches. On the floor were beach flip-flops from Ibiza where she'd worked as a tour operator, over the chair was a sarong from Bali where she'd recently been on holiday.

In her flat one morning, as Linda came out of the shower, Colin held up a blonde wig:

'What's this?'

'It was an eighties night, I went as Madonna. When I was little I used to listen to her all the time, especially "Material Girl". Linda put on the wig, started gyrating in her bra and knickers as she sung:

'I am a material girl, living in a material world.'

She took a stance, made a pout. With his hands, Colin made as if to take her photo.

'Must have played that song every day for about a year. Used to drive my dad mad – he was this big time socialist, probably still is, don't talk to him much. He couldn't believe it. He wanted a socialist world and his little girl just wanted to have fun and make money… which is pretty much what I've been doing ever since.'

Linda took off the wig, and said:

'What about you, bet you'd look good in it.'

Colin let Linda put the wig on him, Linda ordering:

'Don't move.'

Naked apart from the blonde wig, Colin stood still while Linda held up the Samsung Smartphone he'd bought for her in Akihabra, Linda clicking a photo. Linda smiled:

'If you ever become famous one day, I'll sell it to the papers…you know who you look like? Jack Lemmon at the end of Some Like it Hot. I love that film.'

Colin wasn't sure what he thought about looking like Jack Lemmon in drag, but he was also trying to think who Linda looked like with the wig on. It wasn't Madonna, but some American actress, he just couldn't think of her name.

That night, they couldn't wait until they got into Linda's flat, doing it fast up against the railing outside, hands all over each other. Suddenly, Linda started slapping Colin on the shoulder. Colin turned to see a teenage boy watching them, his hands down his pants, masturbating furiously with a lewd grin.

Linda and Colin quickly disentangled themselves. But before Colin could turn on the boy, he ran away. Linda was already in the flat, furiously stepping out of her skirt, turning on the portable air con. Even at night it was too hot to wear anything inside. Colin came in, shutting the door behind him:

'That was embarrassing.'

'God, I can't stand this place any more. We're surrounded by perverts. Everywhere I go, looked at for being a gaijin and a blonde.'

Colin was surprised by her anger, but shrugged:

'Then why don't we go somewhere else?'

Linda smiled:

'You know where I've always wanted to go? Cancun. You know, in Mexico. Have you seen True Romance? It's my favourite film. At the end, that's the beach where they run away to.'

'Okay, why not.'

Linda kissed him:

'And you know what else, if we go to Mexico from here, the plane more or less goes past Las Vegas. What do you think, should we stop over, try our luck in the casinos?'

Colin hesitated, taking a breather from her sudden enthusiasm. She smiled a little, letting him take his time. Was he ready to run with her? Did he have the balls? Colin's flickering doubt was that it was all her ideas rather than his. He batted it away. Wasn't that just male pride? He smiled back:

'Sure, let's do it.'

He should have seen what was coming next.

Read the complete book – available from iponymous